RENEGADES

The United States Air Force F-111, one of the most innovative and cutting edge aircraft designs of the 20th century, participated in three major world conflicts. However, there was a flight; one daring and undocumented mission that was profoundly inimitable in its objective and execution. The exact details of the flight were quietly suppressed and never revealed ...until now.

This is the story of the "Spirit of San Jon", an early experimental prototype of the F-111 and two brothers.

Roger McConnell is an Air Force test pilot and Alan "Stormy" McConnell is the lead designer and project engineer for a major aircraft company contracted to build the F-111.

However, nothing in the F-111 flight testing program could have foreseen the delivery of a messianic message with a request for the brothers commitment to fly an unauthorized mission halfway round the world guided and executed by faith alone.

The brothers careers and interests track in close harmony but their faith and belief in God are miles apart. The message presents a personal challenge...and a second chance for all mankind. The message reads...

6/6/19

Jim Hodl

The Miracles Trilogy

Book 1
A Time for War - A Time for Peace
Renegades

Book 2
A Time for Miracles
Breakaway

Book 3
A Time to Explore
Destiny
(2018 Release)

Inspired by true events

_____A TIME FOR WAR...A TIME FOR PEACE_____

RENEGADES

"There is a time for everything...and a season for every activity under heaven."

\- Ecclesiastes 3:1 (NIV)

Tim Hedin

NPA Reunion
2017
Congrad,
Thank you for all
your Aviation notes!

Tim

ISBN: 978-0-615-62964-3

There is a time for everything,
And a season for every activity under the heavens:
A time to be born and a time to die,
A time to plant and a time to uproot,
A time to kill and a time to heal,
A time to tear down and a time to build,
A time to weep and a time to laugh,
A time to mourn and a time to dance,
A time to scatter stones and a time to gather them,
A time to embrace and a time to refrain from embracing,
A time to search and a time to give up,
A time to keep and a time to throw away,
A time to tear and a time to mend,
A time to be silent and a time to speak,
A time to love and a time to hate,
A time for war and a time for peace
-Ecclesiastes 3:1   (NIV)

"These Are Not Just Sunday School Angels!"

"Angels are messengers, guardians and they minister to us personally. Many accounts in Scripture confirm that we are the subjects of their individual concern...We may not always be aware of the presence of guardians with ministering spirits that are sent to help each of us...We can't always predict how they will appear. Often they may be our companions without our being aware of their presence.

But let me tell you, these are not just Sunday School Angels; they are also avengers who use God's great power to fulfill His will and judgment. Angels intervene in the affairs of nations. God often uses them to execute judgment on nations in accordance with His principles of righteousness. Millions of angels are at God's command. Angels keep in close and vital contact with all the events taking place on Earth. Their earthly knowledge exceeds that of men."

- Billy Graham from *Angels: God's Secret Agents, c.1975*

CONTENTS

For Eric and Katie
With all our love
10.24. 2015

A TIME FOR WAR...A TIME FOR PEACE

RENEGADES

Prologue

Of Guardian Angels

A True Story

Pleiku Air Base, RVN, 1966

Air Force Captain Jerry Cook returning from a combat mission needed to land his F-4 Phantom fighter at Pleiku Air Base to refuel before continuing his flight and returning to his home base at Cam Ranh Bay. – By Brig. Gen. Jerry W. Cook, USAFR, Ret.

"The inspired pages of the Holy Bible tell about 'ministering spirits.' Many people believe this means each of us has a heavenly being assigned to us to watch over us or assist us in times of extreme trial or stress.

...It was late afternoon as we climbed out of our cockpits and watched the refueling trucks hook up for our internal fuel loads. After a short briefing, we began preparing our fighters for engine start and departure. Pleiku had no ground-start units, so we were going to have to make cartridge starts. A ground-start unit is a small jet engine mounted on wheels. It connects to an aircraft's jet engine starter and directs air to the aircraft to spin the engine fast enough to start.

A starter cartridge accomplished the same feat by the slow, controlled burning of a special kind of gunpowder. It was like a huge shotgun shell. There was a starter breech under each engine in the F-4 Phantom where the cartridge was installed when needed. No Problem. I set the cartridge for the left engine under the starter breech and went to the right side. You guessed it, no starter cartridge. I informed my flight leader of my problem, and we began asking the flight line personnel if another F-4 cartridge was on base...you guessed again: No!...The command post told me they couldn't get a cartridge to me until tomorrow.

My back seater and I were really hungry. As we began chomping on a couple of burgers at the small officer's mess, I heard my name being paged. Picking up the phone, I heard the

*From "Once a Fighter Pilot" by Jerry E. Cook, c.2002 McGraw-Hill

1

duty controller's voice from the Cam Ranh Bay command post. 'Captain Cook, we've just been informed that Pleiku may be over run tonight by the Viet Cong sappers. The Commander wants you to get your F-4 out of Pleiku now.'

'But I can't,' I protested. 'Does he know that I only have one starter cartridge?' I asked. 'He knows,'came the reply. 'The Colonel said just tell him to get it out of there.' As I hung up the phone in disbelief, after asking for and getting an authentication, the first trip-flare went off in the evening sky. Trip-flares are devices strategically placed around an area to assist in security. When a trip wire is touched by the enemy, a small rocket propels a flare into the sky...Next came the sound of small-arms fire. I hurried back to my table and broke the news to my back seater. His mouth dropped open; and he said 'You've got to be kidding!' Another trip flare lit up the front of the room. He said 'Let's go!'

The sun had just set behind the hills. My plan was to hold the brakes with full afterburner power on the left engine and begin the roll out with the flaps up to get all the thrust I could. I would activate the air start ignition on the right engine with its throttle pushed up to military position. I hoped that the air passing through the engine as we rolled down the runway would be enough to allow an engine start and give us some thrust.

As I rotated I would hit the 'panic' button that was designed to jettison all external stores and bomb racks. I hoped that it would reduce the weight to let me fly. More and more trip flares were going off in the dusk...their smoke was drifting across the approach end of the runway as I prepared to start the left engine.

Suddenly, out of the near darkness, came a camouflaged C-47 with absolutely no markings of any kind. It was banking sharply and in a very steep descent. In fact, it looked as if it were about to crash. At the last possible instant, the bank rolled out, the nose came up, and it made a beautiful landing.

The C-47 then turned off the runway and headed straight for us. As it passed in front of our F-4 and made a sharp left turn, the rear door opened. A figure wearing green camouflage fatigues with black Master Sergeant stripes jumped to the ground, looked at me, then turned back to the open door. He grabbed a cardboard box and walked up to the side of my aircraft. 'Could you use this?' he asked and smiled, He then set the box down, walked back to the C-47, and disappeared inside. The engines revved up, and the C-47 vanished back into the smoky sky as suddenly as it had come.

My back seater hopped down on the right wing and drop tank and hurriedly installed the starter cartridge. With both engines running, I called the tower for taxi clearance. The tower cleared me, and as I began to move, I asked, 'Where did that C-47 come from?'

'We don't know,' said the tower operator. 'It made no radio calls and didn't get clearance to land or takeoff. We didn't even know it was around until it appeared over the runway. Did you see any marking or identification numbers?'

'Nothing' I replied. 'What did they give you?' the tower continued. 'Probably my life,' I thought, but answered, 'A starter cartridge.'

After I landed, I couldn't wait to get to the command post and thank those on duty. They were surprised to see me and assured me they had nothing to do with my 'gift.' I then queried all the other flight members and they had made no calls. In fact, they had assumed that the command post would handle it and had not given it another thought.

As I related my story to them, one of them laughed and said, 'Maybe it was a ghost!' My mind went back to the biblical references about ministering spirits."

Renegades

*"**Belief is a wise wager.** Granted that faith cannot be proved, what harm will come to you if you gamble on its truth and it proves false? If you gain, you gain all; if you lose, you lose nothing. Wager, then, without hesitation, that He exists."*

Blaise Pascal - French Mathematician, Physicist, Inventor, Writer, Christian Philosopher – 1650

Chapter 1
The Sting of a Hornet
April 18, 1942

The USS Hornet – An Early Morning Takeoff

"A Navy man stood at the bow of the ship, and off to the left, with a checkered flag in his hand. He gave Doolittle, who was at the controls, the signal to begin racing his engines again. He did it by swinging the flag in a circle and making it go faster and faster. Doolittle gave his engines more and more throttle until I was afraid that he'd burn them up. A wave crashed heavily at the bow and sprayed the deck."
– Lt. Ted Lawson, B-25 Pilot, Author, *Thirty Seconds Over Tokyo*

It's just after dawn but there's no sun...at least it seems that way. The sky barely reveals its first light from behind a heavy gray veil suspended a thousand feet above the South China Sea. A naval task force of fifteen ships plods through windswept, white capped waters keeping close watch on one particular vessel.

Identified by the Navy as Hull #385; the newly commissioned aircraft carrier *USS Hornet* is the eighth carrier of the American Navy. Most of her 2,200 crewmen onboard are young recruits with an average age of 18. Fresh out of boot camp...few have any shipboard experience...some have never seen an ocean before. Yet, during the next hour, the carrier and crew will become a part of recorded history executing a legendary mission setting into motion the United States entry into World War II.

The *Hornet* turns into the wind and picks up speed. A gale force 30 knot wind spiked with salt water spray showers the carrier's flight deck adding an additional challenge and discomfort for launch crews preparing the bombers for takeoff.

The mission is *top secret*. A squadron of 16 B-25B Mitchell bombers and their 80 crew members prepare for war...a retaliation attack against the Japanese Empire for its Pearl Harbor strike just four months earlier on December 7th.

The carrier's huge bow lurches upward as it rides atop a wave crest...pauses for a moment before sinking downward and into a deep trough of turbulent waters sending a resounding spray high into the air. The bow is held in the trough's deep grip for only seconds before breaking free and rising again.

Archangel *Gabriel* is aboard the *Hornet* and remains invisible; unaffected by the surrounding elements. His spiritual state offers no signs of a physical presence.

Gabriel is recognized to be the principal *Messenger* in God's administration of the universe. But this morning his assignment is to remain unseen and silent...to listen and observe.

As he approaches *Road Runner,* one of the first five aircraft preparing for takeoff, Gabriel watches the arrival of a large number of *guardian* angels. The *guardians* have been specially assigned to members of each flight crew. Their orders dictate the strict maintenance of an invisible spiritual presence and complete silence.

Gabriel stands beneath the nose of *Road Runner*. The engine on the right side comes alive, roaring defiantly against the surrounding maelstrom of wind and sea spray. It sends a trail of grayish, black exhaust smoke swirling back over the wing. The propeller on the left engine begins to rotate slowly...but instantly transmits a high pitched searing and painful cry from the starter mechanism. The mixture of fuel and air injected into its 14 cylinders refuses to ignite. The propeller's motion stops and freezes in place with a sense of rebellious finality.

Gabriel observes the development more closely with a heightened sense of curiosity; fascinated but confused with the

Chapter 1 – *The Sting of a Hornet*

technology that surrounds him. He knows *Michael* would probably have a better understanding of this entire experience.

Michael is *Prime Minister* in the administration of God's universe. He assigned Gabriel to travel back in time and visit the crew of *Road Runner*. However, the purpose of his assignment was never discussed. Gabriel has mentally searched his past travels for an answer;

"I've never flown in an airplane before...and certainly not from the deck of a floating barge in the middle of this vast ocean! My journeys have been in 'simpler' biblical times...The 20th century machines are intriguing as they are devastating! Perhaps this is the reason Michael ordered me here. The term; 'technology' associated with all these devices carries an infinite number of both positive and negative consequences."

Gabriel's consciousness returns to the moment. His transparent spirit allows him to effortlessly pass through the aluminum fuselage of *Road Runner*. He finds the interior of the bomber small, confining and heavily loaded...filled with explosive devices and many small metal containers.

Less than an hour ago, a Japanese patrol boat spotted the *Hornet* and radioed a warning to Japan. The unexpected encounter requires the bombers to depart ahead of schedule; 800 miles from the Japanese coast...400 miles further than originally planned. Extra fuel in five gallon containers are aboard each aircraft.

Gabriel moves forward through the aircraft and enters the cockpit where the pilot, Captain David A. McConnell and co-pilot, Lt. Ronald Graves are at the controls.

McConnell, born and raised in San Jon, New Mexico, is 25 years old and of medium build. His short, red curly hair compliments a generous collection of freckles; giving him a more youthful appearance. In another place and time he could be the "all American boy next door"; an iconic character for a Norman Rockwell painting. But today, his eyes and manner are serious and focused. His voice is calm and orders are given with a delivered tone of thoughtful confidence.

Systematically, McConnell and Graves repeat the preflight

checklist before a second attempt to start the troublesome port engine.

Gabriel listens carefully. McConnell scans the instrument readings while engaging in casual conversation with his co-pilot;

"You know Ron...this is only the start of the war. The Brits are in deep trouble with the naval losses they took in Singapore. Hell...and what's going to happen to them in Europe? I'm afraid there's some real combat mileage ahead of us...but when it's all said and done the only reason I'm here is so we can end this war sooner and I can get back to New Mexico, the ranch and family again! "

Ron nods in agreement;

"You got it right captain...but this could be a long war with Japan...and Europe is on deck too! The world's a different place...especially this morning."

Gabriel notices Captain McConnell has a small photograph of his wife and two sons fastened on the instrument panel just to the right side of the landing gear control lever.

McConnell completes the last item and stows the checklist saying;

"Okay Ron, one more time...Let's get that port engine onboard with the program!"

He reaches for and advances the port engine throttle control. A B-25 is a two-pilot airplane. Hands begin to fly all over the panel in synchronized harmony as the engine startup procedure begins... McConnell calls out;

> "BOOST PUMPS ON..."
> "Hold down the ENERGIZER..."
>   "STARTER engaged..."
> "Counting six blades..."
> "Okay, both MAGS ON..."
> "PRIMER to ON..."
> "Mesh the IGNITION VIBRATORS..."
> "Okay, holding PRIMER till start."

The prop continues to rotate under the power of the starter but no ignition occurs. The rotation is halted.

McConnell pauses for a moment, then quietly whispers under

his breath;

"Come on girl…It's time to go. Don't let us down now!"

He repeats the entire startup procedure again…holds down the energizer control…waits five seconds and presses the engaging switch that meshes the spinning starter mechanism with the engine. The propeller begins to rotate and continues turning for 5…6…and 7 revolutions.

Finally, the engine is awakened and speaks with several loud reports; backfiring twice…then three times in quick succession. Dark smoke and fire bellow outward from the engine nacelles. Seconds later, the engine thunders triumphantly to life seemingly finding its mark and running smoothly without any hesitation.

McConnell smiles to himself…slides open the side window and looks out towards the engine with increasing confidence. He pauses for a moment and listens with a practiced ear to its signature beat. He knows the sound of each engine like a member of the crew and could easily identify if even one cylinder was misfiring.

A fine sea spray filters through the open window. Satisfied with the engine performance, he slides the window shut and switches the mixture control to "FULL RICH" McConnell turns to Ron and with his accustomed casual and infectious grin says;

"A little noisy on that startup…our port engine doesn't appreciate damp ocean air. I think it's telling us something…it's time we go! We sure got the attention of some of those navy boys though! I saw more than a couple seamen 'hit the deck!' "

Then returning to a more serious attitude McConnell turns to Graves and reads the pre-takeoff checklist;

"Turn off the booster pumps and go through the final system check."

Graves scans the panel and is pleased with the indicated numbers;

"Alright so far, we're looking mighty fine here Captain! Fuel and oil pressure are all right on…engines are steady and warming up nicely at 1200 rpm…and we've got1100 psi on the hydraulics…they're right on. We're ready to fly captain!"

McConnell glances at the hydraulic pressure gauges. The B-25 appreciates solid and reliable hydraulic pressure maintained in its

Renegades

system. Everything from flaps, landing gear, brakes, bomb-bay doors, cowl flaps and even the small carburetor air filter doors are all powered by hydraulic pressure.

McConnell comments to Graves on one of the instrument readings;

"Have you looked at the vertical speed indicator?...this boat is rockin up and down so damn much *Road Runner* is showing a 100 foot climb and descent rate! We're on a floating roller coaster."

McConnell removes his headset;

"Take the controls Ron...two planes are still ahead of us...I want to make a final check on the crew before we go."

The compact confines of a B-25 require some physical dexterity and precise movements. McConnell eases himself out of the left seat and maneuvers through the narrow aisle towards the center of the aircraft where the navigator, Lt. Robert Daniels is stationed. Gabriel follows close behind.

"How's it going Daniels? I hope you know where we're headed on this historic morning?"

Daniels, a young lieutenant and math major recently graduated from college, leans over his navigation chart and points to the present location of the Hornet. With his finger, he traces a thin, precisely drawn 270 degree course line that touches the shores of Japan and continues on a straight line bearing directly to Tokyo. He taps the target city with his finger and looks up at McConnell and confidently reports;

"This is our target today sir, non-stop all the way to Tokyo!"

McConnell offers a slight grin and a reassuring hand on Daniels shoulder adding;

"When we finish our target run and you see those empty bomb racks Daniels...I want you on the intercom calling out loud and clear the new course heading. I want the fastest way '*Outa Dodge*'...you got that?"

"Yes sir, we'll be on the express route all the way...you can count on me captain!"

McConnell looks across the aisle and eyes the flight engineer and gunner Sgt. Clayton Williams and offers a "thumbs up." Williams nods and returns the sign.

Meanwhile, the aircraft taxies slowly...moving forward

Chapter 1 – *The Sting of a Hornet*

towards the takeoff position. Graves looks back towards
McConnell and shouts over the engine noise;

"We're moving into the takeoff slot captain!"

McConnell returns to the cockpit, lowers himself into the seat
and calls to the bombardier on the intercom.

MSgt. Robert Pellam is checking the calibration of the
aircraft's Norton precision bombsight.

"How's *Mr. Norton* doing this fine morning Sergeant?"
McConnell asks;

"Captain, Mr. Norton, as always is feeling precise, accurate
and right on target! We're ready to go sir."

"Very good sergeant...you two stay sharp!"

McConnell takes the controls and positions Road Runner into
the takeoff slot. He applies the parking brake, slides open the
side window and looks down at the navy deck officer who's in
charge of the launch. The officer hollers loudly above the idling
engines and wind;

"You're next Captain...just look at me and follow my flag
commands."

Gabriel is equipped with a complement of very unique powers
of *time management* granted to him before his departure from
Heaven. Gabriel is able to freeze and transfer the current
moment to a *time envelope* then jump ahead in a *time stream* and
instantly experience a clear mental picture and message
revealing future events. The first message Gabriel receives is
short and positive:

All five crew members will survive the mission.

A second, more detailed narrative is communicated to
Gabriel's consciousness. He winces upon its receipt;

*In three months, Captain McConnell will lead a combat mission
over Europe...His B-17 will be downed by enemy fire...The crew
bails out over enemy lines...but McConnell will remain with the
aircraft when it crashes.*

The message ends abruptly. Gabriel's consciousness returns to
the events taking place in the cockpit. He hears the launch officer

loudly call out the final instructions to McConnell:

"Go to full power but don't release the brakes till I give you the final '*go*' signal when I lower my flags!"

McConnell acknowledges the order with a customary departing military salute. He closes and locks the side window then checks and confirms that the parking brake is engaged. The throttles are eased forward…slowly at first…advancing them till they reach their full power *takeoff* position. He returns his attention to the deck officer who is now circling his flags furiously while listening to the throbbing roar of the engines.

The flags are waved faster and faster. McConnell leans the fuel mixture slightly on each engine…a few more RPMs are added. The entire aircraft shakes violently…the sound inside the cockpit is deafening.

Gabriel monitors the thoughts from each crew member. He "hears" McConnell's thoughts;

"Oh God, please protect my crew…don't let me fail."

The launch officer monitors the changing pitch of the carrier and as it drops down into a wave trough…he stops circling and lowers both flags.

McConnell releases the brakes and announces over the intercom;

"Here we go!"

The plane moves forward…slowly at first. McConnell feels the full weight of the fuel and bomb load. He looks directly ahead through the forward windscreen. A foreboding gray, violent and unsettled ocean lies just over the edge of the flight deck. Whitecaps are clearly visible.

The carrier deck begins to pitch up. The aircraft is moving faster now. McConnell slowly eases back on the control yoke lifting the nose wheel off the deck. The carrier deck drops away. Suddenly, *Road Runner* is airborne!

The familiar feel of flight is welcome. McConnell reaches for the landing gear control handle, pushes the lever forward, retracting the gear…then moves his hand slightly to the right with a practiced motion...lightly touching the photograph of his wife and two sons.

Gabriel realizes it's time for him to depart...but a painful sense of loss accompanies him; sadness and regret are deeply felt. He ponders the thought;

These extraordinary men are led by a most honorable and God fearing captain. Why does the captain lose his life?

Angels have emotional feelings like humans. It's difficult for Gabriel to accept the final outcome of Captain McConnell. His sons will lose a father. A wife will be without a husband.

Gabriel knows from experience, having lived from the beginning of time, *Wars* always result in the catastrophic elimination of human life. In addition to the immediate toll of armed conflict; *Wars* create a painful aftermath with long-term consequences for its survivors and culture...lasting years beyond the time of actual conflict.

Gabriel wonders if humans will ever *"breakaway"* from the spiraling, continuing cycle of armed conflict that spreads like a deadly plague from one generation to the next.

He stares at McConnell one more time...and offers a silent departing prayer. Gabriel lowers his head and is gone.

The Final Outcome of the Tokyo Raid

- A total of 80 pilots and crew took off from the carrier Hornet. 71 survived the mission.
- Because of a shortage of fuel 11 of the 16 crews bailed out over China; 4 crash landed near the Chinese coast.
  The only surviving bomber No. 40-2242 made a wheels down landing in Siberia about 40 miles north of Vladivostok;
  The crew was interned by Russians and finally released.

The B-25 bomber, 40-2242 was never returned by the Soviets and despite several search attempts has never been located.

Renegades

Sidebar: Chronology–The 1940's & 1950's

1941-1945
Pearl Harbor - U.S. enters World   War II.
Doolittle Raid targets Tokyo.
War Production - Civilian auto production halted.
Holocaust: 6 million Jews annihilated.
Normandy Landings
President Franklin D. Roosevelt dies.
Harry S. Truman assumes Presidency.
U.S. drops atomic bombs on Hiroshima and Nagasaki.
World War II Ends - Japan Surrenders.

1948
The Cold War
The Berlin Blockade
The modern–day state of Israel is established.

1950 -1953
Korean War
Dwight D. Eisenhower elected President.

1955
American advisors sent to Vietnam.

1957
The *Space Age* begins - Russia launches Sputnik I
First commercial nuclear power plant begins service.

1958
Explorer I, first U.S. satellite launched into orbit .
The integrated circuit invented.

1959
Soviet Premier Nikita Khrushchev tours United States.
Alaska and Hawaii admitted to the Union.

Chapter 1 – *The Sting of a Hornet*

Thirteen Years Later

The 1950's were "Happy Days"

The end of the Second World War marked the beginning of a new era and better times for most of the world. The end of the war in the United States was greeted with celebration, hope ...but with some uncertainty for the future. The country emerged after the war with higher world recognition and increased responsibility as the victorious superpower. Prosperity defined the postwar era but tempered with a new worry...the chill of a prolonged "Cold War" with the Soviet Union

Renegades

Chapter 2
Airborne!
San Jon, New Mexico
July 4, 1955 - 11:00 a.m.

The Bluffs of Llano Estacado are part of the High Plains stretching nearly 250 miles along the West Texas and Eastern New Mexico borders. Known as the Caprock by the locals in the town of San Jon, New Mexico, a nearby bluff rises over 300 feet above the canyon like floor.

A small one-man glider positioned at the edge of a high bluff is being prepared for flight. Similar in appearance to the Wright brothers' early designs; the glider is smaller and offers a simple more streamlined mono wing construction. Two brothers, Alan and Roger McConnell design, build and fly gliders. Alan is 19 years old and the aircraft designer for the project. His given middle name is "Stormy"…in remembrance of his birth date when a tornado touched down and destroyed the family's barn less than a hundred feet from the ranch house where he was born.

Roger, 18 years old is the pilot. They both love airplanes. They both love flying. Standing together however, it's not readily apparent they are brothers. Alan's thin and slightly stooped figure offers a rather "bookish" and scholarly appearance to those who meet him for the first time. His movements appear somewhat disconnected and awkward offering an impression of someone whose mind is occupied on other matters. Alan's dark brown hair is trimmed to a closely cropped crew cut.

In contrast, Roger is tall with an athletic build. His physique mirrors four years participation and notable performance on San Jon's High School football, basketball and track teams. Like his father he has a generous amount of red curly hair but only a light spattering of freckles. His personality radiates confidence coupled with a friendly openness and appealing vulnerability.

Their father, Captain David McConnell, a WWII hero and decorated "Doolittle Tokyo Raider", lost his life flying a bombing mission over Germany just months after the Tokyo flight.

Mrs. Janet McConnell is near the launch site and watches the pre-flight activity surrounding the glider. Asked by many others in the town if she ever worries about the safety of her two sons and their adventurous flights from the Caprock cliffs;

"Like their father, my sons have always shown a special talent and love of flying from an early age…and they don't take any foolish chances. Alan built an electric powered wind tunnel in our basement to test his model plane designs when he was only 12 years old. The whole house used to shake when he turned it on!

During their high school years they both worked on weekends down at the Clovis Airport and earned their pilot's licenses. I still tell them to be careful though…like a mother should!"

The weather conditions along the Estacado are sometimes treacherous. High winds and sand storms appear in minutes without warning. But for the two teenage boys, the high cliffs and thermal updrafts have always provided good flights and an ideal launching point for their custom designed glider.

Today the weather is fair and mild with only a light surface wind from the west. The morning is warming up and new thermals are being generated from the canyon below. It's a good day for a launch.

All of the past glider flights attracted a strong local following from the town's people. Today's *July Fourth Celebration* at San Jon has generated a sizeable increase in spectator attendance. The increased holiday atmosphere is readily seen by the number of lawn chairs randomly spaced along the edge of the canyon. It's a well-attended, relaxed family event with everyone enjoying the day. Children are running and playing together…waving small American flags. There are many more tourists in attendance as well. A major east-west highway, *Route 66* becomes Main Street and runs through the center of town. Restaurants, motels, service stations and other service businesses are all doing well. San Jon is also a transportation center served by the railroad. The future looks bright for San Jon.

The town's long time mayor, Jed Thurber is in attendance. He has known the McConnells for many years;

"They are a fine family. The boys have been a little rowdy at

Renegades

times but Mrs. McConnell is one strong lady! She did a fine job keeping the family together and raising those boys after David was killed in the war. Alan and Roger are both going off to college this fall. Roger leaves in a couple days. He's got an appointment to the first class of the new Air Force Academy out in Colorado. Alan is enrolled at Purdue with a full engineering scholarship. Today is probably going to be their last flight together. They will always be remembered. These are San Jon's finest!"

At the launch site Alan finishes tightening the last of six wing support cables attached to the center framework. He rechecks the tension on each before turning to Roger; who's adjusting the elevator and rudder movement at the rear of the glider.

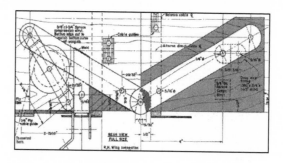

Alan reports;

"The airfoil controls are more accurately aligned compared to the last flight Rog...you'll like the new settings...but remember... take your time in testing the *swing wing* controls...see how it handles at 10 degrees before you go to the 30 degree setting."

The purpose of the glider flight is to test the effects of changing the angle of two 5 foot sections on each end of the main wing. Both sections are able to change their configuration from a conventional straight wing to a modified swept design. The mechanism that controls the swing wing movement is a single lever connected to an orchestrated collection of pulleys, springs, control cables and two specially built rotating hinges.

Roger walks to the forward section of the glider and inspects

Chapter 2 – *Airborne!*

the harness and emergency parachute connections under the main wing. He positions himself beneath the wing that's resting on a wooden support frame and "straps on" the glider. After tightening the harness and rechecking the flight controls; he moves the lever of the swing wing through two complete cycles of extensions and retractions. With all checks completed he slowly stands up... lifting the glider off the support frame. He grimaces slightly;

"Okay, seems a little bit heavier for some reason...feels okay though...just about ready to go Alan!"

For a brief moment Roger stands motionless...staring at the sky saying nothing."

A minute passes by. Alan becomes impatient and finally breaks the silence;

"Something wrong Rog?...you see something?"

Roger turns and answers;
"No, no problem Alan...all set to go...just offering a short prayer...you know...for a good flight!"

Alan smiles slightly and responds immediately;

"There's nothing to worry about brother...you know that...it's a solid plane, perfect to the specs...you'll have a good flight."

Roger smiles back with an understanding grin reaffirming his strong confidence in his brother's design but adding;

"I know! You designed a fine aircraft...but remember...God controls the winds! I've got to check in with Him too!"

Alan reflects on the thought for a moment, shakes his head and answers;

"Now you're getting too philosophic for me Rog!
...You need to get airborne and clear your head!"

Alan laughs to himself but is unexpectedly interrupted by a tap on his shoulder from behind. He slowly turns and is taken aback.

An aged looking man, short in stature stands only inches away. His complexion appears unnaturally weathered; accented with deep lines randomly etched into his facial architecture. He squints dispassionately with deep set eyes that are dark and disturbingly penetrative in their intensity.

Alan feels a sudden chill shoot through his body...a feeling never experienced before. He takes a step back.

Renegades

The left side of the stranger's upper lip rises slowly …communicating a sense of hidden arrogance…as he speaks his voice is uncomfortably forced and high in pitch;

"You're gonna try to fly this thing today are ya?"…he pauses before continuing. His stare continues with unrelenting intensity.

"I was on the road driving south in my ole Chevy pickup when I saw the crowd gathering here. I stopped and asked someone; 'What's going on here neighbor? Was there an accident?'"

The stranger laughs quietly to himself as if enjoying a hidden joke…then after a short, deep breath continues;

"My name is Devlin, Mr. Devlin Windstedt."

He verbally repeats his name again and emphasizes "Mister Devlin" with a slow, almost caring intonation before changing his introduction to a louder, fast paced staccato of charged accusations;

"I ask you; what's going on here neighbor?"

He pauses for only a second;

"… I don't hear any answers son! Is there a problem?"

His jaw drops and his stare becomes aggressively mature.

"What's wrong…You can't talk boy!…is that the problem?"

"Maybe you don't like the way 'ole Devlin' looks at ya? …Well you better get used to me son…cause we're gonna be friends for a long time now…both of ya…you and that young brother of yours over there!"

Then the stranger suddenly grasps the main control cable near the swept wing. He holds it firmly while looking at Alan…then with a rapid head movement turns his attention to Roger. He smiles broadly at him as he tightens his hold on the cable…a dim, yellow and red glow of light emanates beneath his hand.

Without notice, he releases his grip…then, instantly with a sudden burst of unnatural speed appears at the edge of the cliff… He slowly turns and directly faces both brothers. His face now displays a blank, disconnected expression…worn like a featureless mask.

He folds his arms, leans backward and with complete control purposely falls off the edge to the canyon below.

Alan, initially stunned, unable to move, discards his emotions and runs to the cliff's edge. Looking down to the floor of the canyon…he sees nothing but scattered rocks and sand below!

Chapter 2 – *Airborne!*

Alan turns and shouts to a man, a nearby onlooker;

"Did you see the old man who was talking to us?...He just fell off the edge!"

The man appears somewhat puzzled and shakes his head. Shrugging his shoulders, he answers almost apologetically; "No, I just saw you two boys working on the glider...there was nobody else I could see!"

He pauses for a moment...then casually asks:

"Are you boys going to be taking off soon?"

Meanwhile Roger places the glider back onto the support frame and releases himself from the harness. He approaches Alan;

"What the hell is going on? That was weird...really weird! Who was that old guy?"

Alan, still shaken and confused, shakes his head;

"I have no idea what's happening Rog."

He lowers his head for a moment to gather his thoughts...then looks up.

"Roger, let's recheck the glider again...really close. Maybe we should cancel the flight?"

A half hour is spent inspecting the framework for its integrity and strength...especially the cable that the stranger was holding so tightly. They complete their inspection with Alan reporting;

"Everything looks okay Rog...I can't find any part that's damaged!"

Roger nods...adding;

"Okay...let's do it! ...Let's fly!"

Roger straps himself back into the glider harness with a renewed sense of confidence and says;

"Hey...where's our "*good luck cow bell!*" We definitely need the cow bell today!"

There is a "ringing of the cowbell" tradition which began on the glider's first flight a year ago when several cow bells were secretly attached beneath the forward section of the glider by Joe Mitloff – one of Roger's high school friends. Joe Mitloff earned a well-documented reputation as the class prankster. He attached two cow bells inside a closed panel of the glider's framework just before the flight.

Renegades

22

When the glider maneuvered above the town and was tossed about in the air currents...the cow bells could be heard ringing for quite a distance. The continuous ringing drew the attention of many residents of San Jon who looked to the sky in search of flying cows. It's still a topic of amusement among the town's people. Now, before all launches...a cowbell is rung for good luck and to announce the flight.

The town folks, accustomed to the routine of the launches, have already sensed an imminent takeoff and formed a single line stretching along the edge of the bluff.

Alan is about to ring the bell and looks towards his brother who is standing about 50 feet from the edge of the bluff looking straight ahead prepared to begin his takeoff run. He offers his brother a final departing message;

"Hey Rog...I was just thinking ...with college and all...this is our last flight for a while!"

Roger doesn't reply immediately. He shrugs his shoulders and repositions the weight of the glider on his back...then reflectively answers;

"I don't like the way you said 'last flight' brother!" ...then continues;

"Let's do it!...This wing is getting heavy! I'm ready to fly!"

Alan rings the cowbell and like the report of a starter's gun at a track meet...Roger reacts like an Olympic champion exploding from the starting blocks.

Though lacking the speed of a true sprinter...his running ability is admirable considering the cumbersome size and weight of the glider. Without any hesitation, Roger approaches the edge of the bluff. The spectators become silent. At about five feet from the edge...a thermal updraft from the canyon below catches the main wing and like a giant invisible hand lifts Roger and the small glider into the air.

Roger is airborne and immediately moves his legs rearward to a more comfortable flying position with his feet positioned in a set of specially designed stirrups. The harness now supports his whole body in a horizontal position. Looking straight ahead with his hands firmly gripping the flight controls; Roger holds the glider in level flight. He hears the distant cheers from the onlookers below as he soars upward riding the strong thermal.

Chapter 2 – *Airborne!*

Several minutes pass. The sounds of the earthly activity below begin to fade. Roger's attention turns to a widening and unbelievable panoramic view of the New Mexico horizon. The open and expansive canyon landscape on this perfectly clear morning is accented with painted ribbons of thin white cirrus clouds against a light blue sky that stretches to infinity.

The landscape is unique; exploding with a singular and visually austere beauty...yet speaks to the soul in a soft whisper. Roger often thought he could hear a faraway voice calling in the wind.

Roger turns away from the view and glances at his watch...The flight has already lasted seven minutes and the temperature is starting to drop as the glider continues to climb. It's time to break away from the powerful thermal. He makes several steep banking turns, flying in a widening circle searching for the outer boundary of the updraft.

Roger knows he must stop the ascent. He lowers the nose and pulls the lever on the swing wing mechanism moving the outer 5 foot sections of each wing to a 10 degree swept back angle. Both wings snap solidly into place and lock into the new configuration. He remembers Alan's advice to take time and analyze the effect on the flight controls.

The glider remains in straight and level flight. He begins a shallow bank to the right...then left with no adverse response. He notices the glider seems to have lost some of its lift...it's no longer climbing...but still not descending. Roger continues to fly an expanding circle but is unable to leave the thermal's forceful grip.

Roger grasps the wing's control lever, hesitates for a brief second then pulls the lever back to its full rearward position. The wing angle increases and locks into place at 30 degrees. The response is immediate and unexpected...

The glider begins to descend at high rate of speed. Roger pulls back on the stick in an effort to regain control. There's no response. The glider loses all maneuvering control and enters a spiraling spin.

The uncontrolled dive and increasing speed will cause structural damage to the main wing. Roger pushes the wing lever control forward in an attempt to return the swept wings back to their original position. He can't move the lever. He pushes harder.

Two connecting cable wires snap…flailing backwards and slashing a cut into Roger's right shoulder. The ground is rapidly approaching. There's no other option.

It's time to bail out!

The emergency parachute is attached to McConnell's back harness…but first, he must pull an emergency disconnect cord that releases him from the glider. Roger removes his feet from the stirrups and pulls the release cord. He falls away from the out of control glider.

All is lost.

He waits a few seconds and pulls the ripcord…opening the parachute package on his back. The war surplus parachute unfurls and all its panels open with no tears. Roger, relieved to see a full canopy above him, begins to relax until he realizes a new danger.

The unmanned glider has leveled off and established its own flight path. Without his weight… it's flying again at an altitude slightly above him but descending in a steady, ever tightening turn. Each circling pass seems to get closer to the parachute canopy. Even after trying to maneuver the chute by pulling the shroud lines…Roger is unable to maneuver away from the glider and its approaching path.

Roger calculates the glider will probably make contact with his chute on the next pass. He's at an altitude about 1000 feet above the canyon floor. He looks up.

The renegade glider is approaching. It's lower now…almost at eye level. Roger can see the cables and control surfaces in stark detail. He grips the chute's shroud lines as tight as he can and waits for the inevitable. He mutters to himself;

"Oh shit…Sorry Lord…I messed up!"

Then it happens!

Then. Suddenly…he couldn't believe what he's seeing. The

control lever spring mechanism on the swept wing engages… both outer wings snap smartly back to their original glide position. He hears the mechanism solidly lock into place. The glider reacts and instantly soars skyward…missing the chute.

Roger continues to monitor the glider's flight…it's climbing again but at too steep of an angle. It begins to slow. The free flying glider stalls, loses all forward airspeed, and falls nose down back to earth. As it falls, the glider gradually gains more airspeed again…levels off…and executes a perfect landing in the canyon below.

Roger can't believe what he's just seen…but turns his attention back to the moment. The ground is coming up fast now…he'll land about a quarter mile from the glider.

Roger's spirits are running high…It's turning out to be a lucky day. The world is good again! He looks below. His landing area is clear of large boulders and rocks.

Roger touches the earth…standing upright on both legs! His shoulder stings with the cut from the cable but otherwise he's fine…and elated.

Releasing himself from the parachute harness, he struggles to pull in and gather the billowing parachute that's filled with the steady wind blowing through the canyon.

In the distance, he sees Alan racing down the canyon road in the pickup. There's a trail of dust following his dogged course through the canyon's rock scattered surface.

Finally, reaching the landing site, Alan leaps from the pickup and rushes toward Roger…throwing his arms around him and shouting;

"I thought I lost you…I thought I lost you for sure Rog!"

Then, for reasons unknown they both look at each other and begin to laugh…slowly at first but then reaching an almost hysterical level. Alan stops laughing for a moment…just long enough to proclaim;

"Damn…you are one hell of a hot pilot brother…Did you talk the glider into that landing…I've heard of horse whispers…you are the *plane whisperer* brother! I drove past the glider. It isn't damaged at all! Unbelievable!

Roger and Alan pause and wave in response to the loud and resonant cheers of onlookers from the ridge above.

Renegades

Unnoticed and standing alone at a more distant location far from the spectators is *Gabriel*...looking down from the ridge at the glider and two brothers.

Gabriel is pleased with his protective and unnoticed interaction with the brother's flight. He smiles, bows his head and is gone.

The Next Morning- McConnell Ranch

The glider, retrieved from the canyon, transported on the back of the pickup to the family ranch, is unloaded in the barn that has served as a hangar and workshop for their flying projects.

Alan, with a flashlight in hand, is beneath the main wing examining the hinge mechanism.

Roger enters the barn with a coffee mug in hand, pauses for a moment and looks at the glider and says;

"The 10 degree setting...was no problem...when I went to the 30 degree mark...I lost it...there was no flight control at all."

Alan pulls himself out from underneath the wing...steps back from the glider while drawing some sketches and calculating some numbers on a notepad.

"I made a mistake Rog...the center of gravity shifted a lot farther than I first calculated...the glider was out of balance when you went to the 30 degree setting. Then the cable...the one the stranger was holding before the flight...failed and added to the problem. But what I really don't understand is what *happened* to the metal hinges on the wings. They're in a different but perfect alignment and trim...and physically reshaped into a much improved design! That's the reason for the gliders perfect landing."

Just then a familiar voice echoes from the entrance of the barn. A man of medium height and slender build is silhouetted against the morning sunlight of the open barn door.

"That was some flight yesterday...everybody in town is talking about it this morning."

A young priest, Father Juan Martinez, from the local parish in San Jon shares a mutual interest in aviation and always supports and encourages the McConnell's and their flying exploits. He approaches the two boys with a welcoming handshake and an enthusiastic pat on the back.

"I thanked the good Lord many times yesterday…and this morning as well that you weren't injured Roger. Have you figured out what happened up there?"

Alan hesitates and regretfully admits;

"I have some more work to do Father…the swing wing changed the center of balance on the glider a lot more than my calculations predicted…the controls and everything changed. It was like a completely different aircraft when the wings swung back. My brother was very lucky yesterday. My mistake is inexcusable. If anything happened to……"

Roger interrupts;

"Alan, tell Father about the stranger…the old man… the *Devlin* character…and how he was handling the glider cable just before I took off."

Father Martinez's attention is immediately heightened with a strong undertone of concern;

"'Devlin' you say…Oh my goodness…that's the name given to all unholy demons!

It is said that all of Satan's agents when in human form use 'Devlin' as their first name but change their last. I was never able to understand why…but that's the way it has been passed on through many centuries. 'Devlins' are not visible all the time…but angels can see them.

If it was actually a 'Devlin', it probably received spiritual instructions of some importance. It may have been on a special assignment from the evil one…there's a reason for concern here."

Alan responds, shrugging his shoulders;

"I'm sorry Father…I don't believe in spiritual things…like demons, ghosts…or angels. There's always a logical reason for everything. I appreciate your biblical knowledge Father but I don't carry the same amount of religious faith as my brother. I have 'faith' in numbers, equations, the laws of physics…these are real to me."

There's an uneasy silence before Father Martinez continues;

"Let me just add this thought for both of you…the physical

world we experience everyday needs no explanation…I call it the *"City of Man"*. Our five senses provide needed information for us to live and work day to day.

The spiritual world; the *"City of God"* is unseen to us…so we tend to ignore it…but it exists and is in a constant state of warfare. There's a continuing spiritual battle between good and evil being fought that overflows into our physical world

I understand your feelings Alan but don't let your heart become hardened to the existence of a spiritual world because it may be labeled by others as 'religious fantasy'.

You both have a long life's journey ahead…there will be challenges and wonderful surprises. I know your father would be most proud of the course you've each chosen.

I will always keep both of you in a special place in my heart…and my morning devotions…especially now! Let me know immediately if you have any more encounters with that *Devlin* spirit.

Well, I must be going. I heard you're both leaving in the next couple days so I'll depart with just one more final thought. Please forgive me if you think I'm preaching too much;

This is important for you to know…The Lord assigns a destiny to each of us which we must reach in our lifetime. He also provides us with the special talents needed to reach that destiny. It's up to us to discover those talents and use them for His glory. Listen to the Holy Spirit that is written on your heart. The Spirit will guide you to your destiny. Pray about this daily. Prayer through the Holy Spirit is our direct communication with God.

I believe both of you have discovered your calling…and talents. Keep them close to your heart! Many people I know have let others decide their path in life. Stay in control, have faith…again I say; stay close in the shadow of the Lord with your prayers and He will always guide and protect you.

We'll, that's the end of sermon boys!

Alan, I know you'll be busy with your studies at Purdue and Roger…good luck at the new Air Force Academy in Denver. God bless you both. I will stay in touch…and as we discussed;

Chapter 2 – *Airborne!*

I'll check on your mother as well."

Roger considers the young priest a close friend and knows he will miss the many informal conversations over coffee they shared together in recent years.

Father Martinez "bear hugs" each of the boys, turns and walks away in his characteristic brisk and confident stride. He approaches the barn door...slowly turns and offers a final sweeping wave and message before leaving the barn.

"God be with you!"

A silence falls over the barn. A gust of wind slams the outside door shut adding a sound of finality to the moment.

Alan looks to Roger and with some hesitation asks;

"So tell me brother about you and the Air Force Academy.

I don't get it!...you want to be a fighter pilot? What's that about? You've always been the religious one in the family ...talking good works...doing good deeds. Mom told me she's not sure how she feels about someone in the family serving in the military again. Are you sure you know what you're getting into?"

Roger, still holding his coffee, looks straight at his brother who appears to be waiting for an instant answer. He lowers his eyes and takes a short sip of coffee. The coffee is still too warm and he savors only a small taste.

He looks up...and begins to speak in an understanding voice that carries a tenor of cutting edge honesty that has always bonded the brothers close relationship;

"Those are tough questions Alan...and I've thought about those exact same things. I've been struggling for some answers.

The appointment to the Academy up front offers me an academic degree with no tuition and a pipeline to an aviation career... that's hard to beat! What I really like is after graduation...if I pass the physical; I have an almost guaranteed entry into the pilot training program. The Air Force's flight training is the best in the world.

*On being a fighter pilot...*God is about acting in peace and love...but I know God doesn't want us to allow evil and injustice to run unchecked. I haven't worked out all the answers yet Alan ...but that's where I'm at now.

As far as how I stack my priorities; *God* comes first, *Family*

Renegades

30

is second and then the *Job*…if it's a fighter pilot or running a ranch…the job priority is always third. That lower priority doesn't mean a diluted interest or loss of excellence. What I'm saying is…If you keep God, faith and prayers working together as number one…the right path will always be taken and you will always have the best outcomes for the priorities of *Family* and *Job*.

Faith is more than a Sunday only experience…it has to be worked on every day. Taking on God and Faith as a guide is dangerous…It's not like your formulas and math Alan…you don't know exactly where it's going to take you…you have to run on trust…but I guess that's what a journey of faith is all about."

Roger pauses and then turns to his brother and asks;

"But Alan!…hey, what about you? Purdue University and an engineering scholarship…not too shabby! Where do you think you're headed?"

Alan pulls a nearby chair next to the glider and sits down, folds his hands together in a relaxed manner and looks at Roger and simply replies;

"I'm not on any special journey Rog…

You know, for a little brother…you've got some big time serious thoughts. Me…I just want to design airplanes. I see the airplanes flying today and I see a hundred changes I could add to make it fly better, higher and faster! If you put me near a wind tunnel…you'll never hear from me again brother!"

Roger, smiling gives him a "thumbs up";

"Say, sounds like you've got a great plan Alan and just don't realize it!…I'm with you all the way."

There's a pause in the conversation. Alan continues;

"You know...both of us have never been too far from San Jon and New Mexico…and Mom is going to be alone."

Roger nods and adds;

"I know what you're saying…there's going to be a lot of changes in our lives…and in hers. San Jon has been a safe harbor while we've been growing up. We've got to stay in touch with each other brother…and with Mom.

You know…more than ever; I sure wish Dad was here. I still remember him."

Chapter 2 – *Airborne!*

Sidebar: *All About Demons*

Selected Text From:
"Do Demons Exist and What Are They Like?"
By Dr. Erwin W. Lutzer *

Within in the church, and throughout broader society, a great deal of mysticism and superstition surrounds the reality, the ability, and work of demons. Because of this haze of opinions, we must root our understanding in scripture.

Satan is the origin of evil, the father of lies (John 8:44).

Demons disguise themselves (2 Corinthians 11:14). For this reason, we must cautiously discern the validity of any professed vision or prophecy originating from angelic beings. In essence, "do not believe every spirit" (1 John 4:1).

They can operate in groups (Luke 8:2; Matthew 12:45; Mark 5:9).

Satan and his servants blind the minds of men (2 Corinthians 4:4). They ever desire to steal away the Word of God to promote unbelief (Matthew 13:19).

Satan resides upon the Earth and rules it (Ephesians 2:1-2; Revelation 2:12-13; Job 1:7; Revelation 12:12). He is also described as the "god" of this world (2 Corinthians 4:3-4). While it is argued that some powerful fallen angels supervise large areas (Daniel 10:12-13), the demonic realm primarily influences us in a personal manner. Through contact with leaders and select individuals, they can warp, manipulate, control, and corrupt societies, cultures, and groups.

---

*Erwin W. Lutzer is an evangelical Christian pastor, teacher, author and the senior pastor of Moody Church, Chicago, Illinois.

Renegades

Chapter 3
A Time to Plant
1955 - 1959

July 9, 1955

Dear Mom,

Arrived in West Lafayette and met other freshmen at the downtown bus station. The university had a station wagon to pick us up. I'll be looking for an apartment next week and be staying in the university dorm temporarily until I find a place.

The land is very green, lots of trees but it seems awfully crowded here...not a lot of open space. I feel somewhat lost.

Need to register for my classes tomorrow. I'll be taking all basic engineering courses, calculus and science. Also, yesterday I talked to my advisor; Dr. Jerome Beckman. He's also the director at the University Aero Lab. They needed an additional lab assistant to work on an aircraft research project for a Texas aircraft company...so I signed on.

I also bought a new slide rule the other day. All the engineering students here wear them on their belts...like side arms.

How are you doing Mom?

Love,
Alan

Day One – Purdue University
"Registration Day"

Alan arrives at the auditorium ahead of schedule. The other sophomore students in his dorm warned him of the challenge ahead...the unrewarding process of registering for fall classes.

Securing the scheduled academic classes that faculty advisors so optimistically present to each freshman student is no guarantee...it is a document requiring tenacious activity balanced with an overdose of patience and waiting in long lines to validate its existence.

Alan McConnell turns the corner and opens the double door to the auditorium. He's unprepared for the mob of students massed before him and the many singular lines stretching the entire length of the building.

Overhead speakers come alive; making an announcement that's distorted with intermittent static;

"Introduction to Calculus 101 and 102 are now closed."

The message is bland and unemotional...a distant and monotone voice emanating from an unknown location in the auditorium.

McConnell looks at his class schedule. His first Monday, Wednesday, Friday morning class is..."Calculus 101" which has just closed!

He looks at the next course on the schedule; Tuesday and Thursday afternoon; Mechanical Drafting 101. McConnell walks over to a large bulletin board where the latest "open" and "closed" class status updates are posted.

While searching the list a student taps Alan on the shoulder;

"You're McConnell right?...I'm Bill Smithers. Your counselor sent me over here this morning to help you. We have a student registration service at Purdue to help all the freshman students. For twenty bucks I'll take your class

Renegades

schedule and have you registered by Noon today! You don't have to waste your whole day waiting in line."

Before Alan has a chance to answer, someone suddenly appears directly behind Smithers...a towering figure that grabs his shoulder and easily turns him around so they are facing each other. The tall and physically dominant stranger looks down on Smithers and speaks softly but with a commanding voice;

"Hello Devlin!...Mr. McConnell has no need for your kind of help. You know what I'm saying?...Why don't you move on now?"

Smithers answers with noted disdain...his earlier friendly nature no longer present;

"My name is Smithers...Who in the Hell are you?"

"Devlin, I know who you are...and I think you know who I am!"

Devlin's eyes take on a fiery appearance.

"Never call me Devlin...remove your hand ...release me!"

He breaks away from the tall stranger's grip and disappears into the surrounding crowd of students.

The tall stranger smiles calmly and seemingly unaffected by the verbal encounter hands Alan a large manila envelope.

"Your classes are all here...you're registered Alan...and no charge. God be with you."

Alan is about to ask his name but is again tapped on the shoulder from behind, he looks away for only an instant, but when he turns back...the stranger is gone.

"I'm sorry I startled you Alan, My name is Gretchen, Gretchen Summers. I'm from Santa Fe...a fellow New Mexican transplanted to this place they call the Midwest! I saw your picture in the student directory and that you're from San Jon and an engineering major. I'm an engineering major also!"

Alan's attention is split from greeting the attractive looking student from New Mexico and looking about the auditorium for the tall stranger that seemed to disappear.

Alan asks; "Did you see that tall fellow standing next to me Gretchen? He must have been at least seven feet...looked like he was on the basketball team."

Chapter 3 – *A Time to Plant*

Gretchen smiles saying; "You were standing here all alone Alan…that's why I wanted to meet you. Did you register yet?"

"That's another story Gretchen…How about a coffee over at the Union?"

Coffee Break at the Union

Alan finds a corner table and signals to Gretchen who is carrying two cups of coffee from the service line on the far side of the Union.

She makes her way through several narrow, mazelike pathways separating the tables. Balancing two cups of coffee on a small tray; she gracefully avoids the barrage of moving students with precise fluid movements demonstrating a form of exceptional grace and coordination.

Gretchen reaches the table, smiles and sits down after carefully placing the cups on the table and remarking;

"This place is really busy and noisy. Careful Alan…the coffee is quite hot."

Alan glances at Gretchen for only a second. Her light blond hair is trimmed short with small hints of curls on the side. She is slender, very fair skinned with eyes of the lightest shade of blue. Alan is quick to begin a conversation but searches and fumbles with his opening words;

"Yes…ahhh…thanks Gretchen!...You know, I wonder if the Union is always this crowded or is it because of the registration. I really don't like crowds very much."

There is no response and Alan immediately changes the subject and tries again;

"You told me earlier that you're from New Mexico?" Gretchen nods and replies;

"Yes, Santa Fe. My parents have a home there…just outside the city. My father is a scientist at Los Alamos. He spends most of the week there and weekends in Santa Fe. My mother works at one of the artisan shops."

"Okay, I've got to ask...You have to tell me Gretchen…What's with you and engineering? Why do you want to be an engineer? This is not exactly the first field of choice for women today. In fact, you may be the very first in Purdue's history!

Gretchen replies without any hesitation;

"I'm actually interested in aeronautical engineering. Flying and airplanes are my true loves. I've had my private pilot's license for several years...since I was 16. My father is a pilot and has his own plane.

Gretchen adds a most infectious if not mischievous smile to emphasize her strong conviction.

Alan is unaware that while listening to Gretchen he has been gradually leaning farther back in his chair at a slow but steady rate. The chair is balancing on two legs. Alan loses his balance for a split second. The chairs falls backward but Alan grabs the side of the table and is able to make an awkward looking but successful recovery...returning himself and the chair to a full upright position. Alan attempts to maintain a controlled look of composure as if nothing happened.

"Well that's terrific...really good Gretchen...you're a pilot too! Now don't tell me...you're on Dr. Beckman's project team?"

Gretchen hesitates then slowly nods in the affirmative. "Yes, I also saw you signed up on the project Alan." Gretchen continues;

"You asked why I'm interested in engineering as my major. I'll share my thoughts with you. My focus in aviation is different from most engineers. It's actually more philosophical than scientific or mathematical.

I envision myself flying and designing advanced aircraft of the future with all sorts of new technology that can make the world a 'gentler' place to live...a way to know our distant neighbors better. I see small aircraft serving in foreign lands carrying people, food and medical supplies to hospitals and small villages that would take days to reach by walking but hours by airplanes.

Someday there will be super large...*jumbo* jets large enough to carry 500 passengers anywhere in the world and at a price most everyone can afford. The world will be a much smaller place and it's our generation that will do it."

Alan listens intently but shakes his head with an added

expression foretelling a negative response. With a half-smile he begins;

"You know Gretchen...I like your personal philosophy and take on the future...it sounds nice and all...but maybe a little too idealistic?...It sounds like you want to *'save the world'* with aviation....you'd do much better in a different field...maybe Political Science or become a missionary!

Look at the direction aircraft design and development is going today...it's all geared to the military...faster fighters, heavier bombers and larger government contracts. The *Cold War* is blossoming!"

Alan sees the reaction on Gretchen's face and suddenly realizes his words have been cutting and way too harsh and realizes...What was he thinking? His response was too immediate, unthinking, impersonal and hurting...a real put down!

Gretchen lowers her head and becomes very quiet. She looks down at the cup of coffee in front of her and holds it thoughtfully between both hands. Alan instantly wishes he was somewhere else.

Gretchen looks up again. Her eyes remain clear, focused...and understanding. Alan feels relieved...he had expected tears and an emotional goodby...he really likes Gretchen and would like to remain friends. Gretchen seems to sense Alan's true feelings;

"Oh Alan...please listen, I understand your thoughts and exactly what you're saying...but engineering is more than just formulas, numbers and government contracts...it's how you direct your knowledge.

A personal decision has to be made; either stay on the main road everyone else is traveling or choose a never explored path that makes a real difference in your life and for others."

A controlled, polite smile slowly reappears but her eye contact is unusually direct. It's as if she's reading Alan's thoughts...making sure he understood her message.

Gretchen takes a short, final sip of coffee and says; "Alan, I've got to get back to the dorm. Let's stay in touch!"

Alan is still thinking about what Gretchen said and replies

with only half-hearted conviction in his voice;

"Yes, for sure…by all means Gretchen…we'll stay in touch. I really enjoyed meeting you."

Alan immediately feels his words too trite and understated. He has never met a girl with such strong convictions and a deep sense of direction for her life. Alan recognizes something very special and different about Gretchen.

Chapter 3 – *A Time to Plant*

USAF Academy
Lowry AFB
Denver, Colorado

July 11, 1955

Hello Mom,

I reported to Lowry at 6:00a.m. or should say 0600 yesterday and began training. There are 300 students in my class. We're the Class of 1959. The Academy commander told us that more than 6000 applicants applied to join this first class.

There are students here from every state. My roommate is from Mississippi. Our pay is $111.15 a month. The food is okay.

I just returned from getting a haircut. I've really been scalped! I also found out that I'm a "Doolie." The freshman, first year cadets are all called "Doolies" by our Air Training Officers …everyone calls them ATOs.

We already had some basic drill instruction so we could march in the dedication ceremony on the flightline tomorrow. Walter Cronkite is supposed to be on base to report on the ceremony…be sure to watch the news.

I think I'm going to like it here. Have to go…getting ready for our first inspection. Hope all is well with you. Miss you.

Love, Roger

Renegades

Day One - The USAF Academy
The First Inspection
July 12, 1955

A new permanent site for the Air Force Academy is under construction in Colorado Springs. The temporary site is Lowry Air Force Base...near the city of Denver.

The first months of cadet training at Lowry is purposely designed to sever the strings of attachment to civilian life and introduce the new cadets to the discipline of military training. The first year Academy cadets, called "Doolies" are assigned rooms in the stark looking barracks used during World War II. Two cadets are assigned to each room.

The first "official" inspection requires each Doolie to display all "arrival" civilian clothes and personal articles on top of their assigned bed.

Roger's roommate, Bill Delaney, is from Mississippi and not pleased with his first day at the Academy;

"I don't understand why we're being treated like inmates at some kind of POW camp...this is not what I thought the Academy was about!"

Roger tries to console his new roommate; offering advice on how to cope with the situation;

"Hey Bill, remember this is only the first day...you have to cool it! When we get through a couple more weeks...things will get better. This is a game their playing...that's all. Just do what they tell you and we won't have any problems."

Roger's conversation is interrupted by the sound of cleated footsteps walking down the barracks hallway. The steady approaching and cadenced sound carries a quality of unquestionable authority. The footsteps suddenly become silent and a single commanding voice echoes throughout the room.

"Attention!...Stand at the head of your bed Doolies!"

Two Air Training Officers (ATOs) wearing "Smokey Bear" style hats enter the room. Their tan uniforms are immaculately pressed with sharp crease lines in all the right places and black leather military boots shining with an unreal reflective luster.

They both are wearing white gloves. Not a speck of dust is permitted in the cadet quarters. One of the ATOs inspects the upright clothes lockers. The other walks towards Delaney and positions himself "nose to nose" and opens an up close and personal conversation;

"*Doolie Delaney*...I like the sound of that! Let's see what you have on display for me this morning."

The ATO makes a quick scan of the items placed on the bed. There is the usual shaving kit, a pair of canvas shoes, jeans, a couple t-shirts, underwear, a small radio...and then he notices several hardcover books. He picks up each book examining the titles with a look of astonished curiosity.

"What do we have here? What kind of books are you reading Doolie?" He holds one book directly in front of him and reads the title with an exaggerated satirical tone of voice;

"*The Thoughts of Plato*"...he looks at the next book;

"*Getting To Know The Socratic Way*"...and then examines the final book...and painfully announces;

"*The Philosophy of Aristotle!*"

Delaney remains at a strict attention looking straight ahead showing no emotion. There is an uneasy silence.

The ATO stares cooly at Delaney and then looks dispassionately at the entire collection of books.

"Shit!...Delaney, what are you bringing into my house!

Plato!...Socrates!...Aristotle! Are you trying to impress me? Maybe you're some kind of professor?"

The ATO has discovered a golden nugget of personalized harassment for Delaney. He tosses the books back on the bed.

"You know Doolie...I think I've got a special name for you while you're visiting here...

"*I'm going to call you the 'fuckin professor'!*"

Roger, standing near his roommate, is unable to contain his emotions any longer...releases a suppressed, short burst of muted laughter. The ATO instantly turns his attention to Roger.

"Well, well...sounds like you're enjoying your stay here Mr. McConnell...You know I'm not here for your personal entertainment Doolie!

Get down and give me fifty!...I want fifty pushups and I want to see and hear them now!"

Renegades

McConnell drops to the floor and vigorously begins pumping out the assigned pushups counting them out loudly while the ATO inspects the articles on his bed.

As McConnell completes the final pushup; he leaps back to his feet, stands at attention and looks straight ahead.

The ATO looks at McConnell and almost apologetically says;

"Everything looks in order McConnell." But then adds a warning;

"I'm going to be watching you. Tell me…why are you here McConnell?"

McConnell maintains his stiff posture…looks straight ahead and answers with a loud confident voice;

"Sir, I want to be a fighter pilot sir."

The ATO shows no emotion; and manages to hold back a smile before returning his attention to Delaney.

"Professor Delaney…I suppose you want to be a fighter pilot too!"

Delaney responds instantly:

"Sir, yes sir!"

The ATO nods, steps back and looking at both cadets says;

"You each have five demerits….five more and you'll be qualified for special duty and a reservation at the dining hall steam room where there's a stack of dishes waiting for you. You should be glad that I'm in a kind, generous and understanding mood today!"

Both ATO's make a final visual check of the room and exit the barracks.

As they walk outside one ATO turns and says to the other;

"You know cadet McConnell who you were talking to?…his old man was one of the original 'Doolittle Raiders' that bombed Tokyo…then was killed on a mission over Germany."

The other ATO answers;

"Yea, I know…I read McConnell's personnel file last night. He's a good kid.

He's going to make it through the Academy alright.

He's all Air Force."

Chapter 3 – *A Time to Plant*

Four years later - 1959

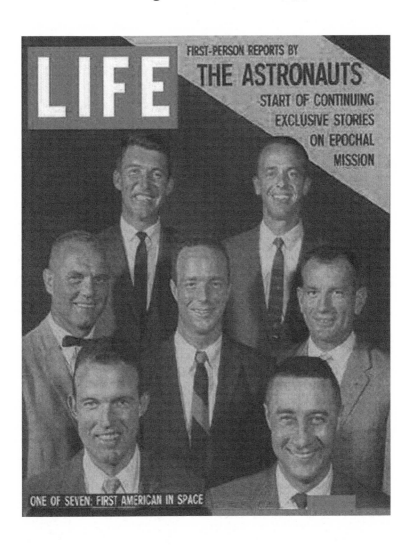

Renegades

Purdue University
February 1, 1959

"Stormy's Renegades"

Dr. Jerome Beckman's Engineering Office is adjacent to the University Aero Lab. He's on the phone talking to *General Dynamics* Project Director, Richard Greenberg;

"How are things at the airplane factory in Fort Worth this morning Richard?"
There's a slight pause...

"It's looking good here Jerry, real good...The *Convair* acquisition with the B-58 *Hustler* bomber project has been very profitable for the company.

The reason I called though is to let you know I really liked the results on the B-58 study you did for us. Your report was thorough and more relevant than expected. You collected some very valuable and useful data for us. Your study resulted in design changes on the MB-1C external fuel pod making it significantly more efficient. The modifications provide the B-58 *Hustler* with the added speed and range we were looking for and brings it up to specs. Please pass along to your team our congratulations and a 'thank you' for a job well done.

We were in a real competitive situation for winning this contract. The Strategic Air Command was looking for a replacement for Boeing's B-47 bomber. Boeing had the inside track but we were awarded the contract because of the cutting edge design technology and the *Hustler*'s high Mach flight model. This was a big win.

Jerry interrupts;

"Richard I'm really pleased to hear that; this is good news. I share your enthusiasm but I'd like to tell you more about the team that worked on the project. It's kind of a side story but they were the ones that made the real difference. Have you got time?"

"You bet...go ahead" Richard urges;

"Four years ago a freshman student, Alan McConnell, an engineering major in our program, was assigned to me as his academic advisor.

Chapter 3 – *A Time to Plant*

My initial impression of him was of a 'typical freshman engineering type'...quiet, laid back and looking somewhat lost in the student population here...he came from a small town somewhere in New Mexico.

Well, it turned out... I was wrong...*really wrong!*

I needed an extra lab assistant for your project and invited him to join the team. Alan accepted and within a year he totally surprised me by developing what must have been some hidden or undeveloped leadership skills. Alan's enthusiasm for the project was contagious. He developed a loyal, dynamic team that did more than follow the book...the team consistently pushed the design envelope...each member challenged the other in a healthy competitive spirit. It was exciting to see.

He reorganized the entire team and showed me a couple areas gleaned from their independent study leading to a substantial and significant increase in the amount and accuracy of data collected. The supporting data clearly indicated the advantages of the redesign of MB-1 pod. The team under his supervision even built a miniature supersonic wind tunnel!...unbelievable!

They even came up with a name for their team; they call themselves '*Stormy's Renegades*'! From what I understand Alan was given the middle name 'Stormy' when he was born... something to do with a tornado that was in the area.

Anyway...Alan and all his *Renegades* will be graduating soon. Richard interrupts;

"Jerry, I'd like to meet your "Stormy" McConnell and learn more about this *Renegade* group. We are experiencing a difficult and protracted flight test program involving thirty B-58 aircraft. We could use some extra help here. I'll fly you both out here to Fort Worth for a weekend. Could you set up a time?

Jerry's reply is immediate; "Yes, yes...will do...sounds great! I'll talk to Alan this afternoon and get back to you!"

"The Renegades" Of the Round Table
An after class meeting at the Purdue Memorial Union
Three Weeks Later

Alan walks into the dining area at the Union. It's packed with
students inundated with the sound of Chuck Berry and *Johnny B.
Goode* piped through an inadequate and highly treble sounding
PA system. Alan has some important news to share with the
team after returning from his meeting in Fort Worth and General
Dynamics. He searches the area and spots the four members of
the *Renegade* team sitting at far end of the Union at one of the
tables. As he walks toward them he can't help but recall some of
the individual traits that define their talents and personalities;

There's **Tom Robinson***; he's wearing a faded blue, highly
wrinkled Purdue Crested sweat shirt, jeans and smoking a
sophisticated looking estate pipe; a marble stone bowl with a
rosewood stem...a pipe which Sherlock Holmes himself would
have enjoyed. Tom, one of the older members of the team,
served four years in the Air Force and finished a year's study at
Cal-Tech before transferring to Purdue. Electronics and
advanced avionics are his specialty. He's also the only member
of the Renegades who has hands on experience maintaining and
repairing jet aircraft. His added prior life experience may be the
reason he sometimes becomes arrogant in his relationship with
the other team members...but the team and I manage to keep him
humble when necessary.*

Sitting next to Tom is **Paul Lancer***. Paul is short in stature but
big on powerful engines. He's interested in what powers
airplanes...and won't even talk to you about piston propeller
aircraft. It's jet engines all the way!...he's obsessed with
them...no other discussion needed! He worked a couple
summers at Pratt & Whitney testing turbine blades before
they're added to the production line engines. That lit the fire that
led him to engineering and Purdue. He keeps reminding us how
inefficient jet engines are today...and how he could redesign
them. Paul isn't just talking...he's got some real innovations
that keep spinning around in his head and are constantly
delivered to the team.*

Chapter 3 – *A Time to Plant*

*Then there's **Donald Gibbs**. He's the one with the crew cut and the large dark rim glasses...like me...he's a fledging aerodynamicist. Donald has a solid grasp on computing formulas that are the defining numbers of a flight envelope... numbers that enable an airplane to fly with just the right characteristics of airspeed, lift, balance and control. His quiet nature hides a brilliant and problem solving mind. He's an engineer's engineer.*

*Finally, there's **Gretchen Summers**...the only female student enrolled in the engineering department at Purdue. What makes Gretchen even more unique is she's friendly, very smart and physically attractive...consistently rated a "10" by most students that know her. Her appearance and manner are complimented if not overwhelmed with a highly disciplined approach to solving engineering problems and presenting them in an organized fashion.*

Gretchen's father is a scientist and engineer at Los Alamos Laboratory in New Mexico. She seems to be following in his footsteps. Gretchen has kept the team on course and focused during our project for General Dynamics. I also confess a continuing personal interest in this team member since our first meeting and coffee during my freshman year.

Alan approaches the table and speaks loudly so he can be heard over the pop *Frankie Avalon* music being blasted throughout the Union.

"How's it going guys?" Alan purposely pauses for a second while glancing to the side at Gretchen... who is about to add a corrective comment.

Alan continues and directs a subtle wink to Gretchen adding; "...and of course Gretchen!"

The question is rhetorical. The group remains silent. Alan pulls an additional chair from a nearby table and sits down.

For some unknown reason the sound of *Frankie Avalon's; Venus"* suddenly ends and the student union becomes strangely quiet.

Alan looks around the Union and turns to everyone at the table and asks;
"Okay, who turned that off?"

Tom Robinson is puffing faster and more aggressively on his

Renegades

estate pipe as he slowly removes his finger from a black box device with a short antennae and a single toggle switch.
Robinson looks at Alan and says;
"I really can't take *Frankie Avalon* anymore Alan."

There is a brief round of slow clapping and approval shared by everyone at the table.

The adulation ends when Robinson speaks up and pointedly asks;

"Okay '*Stormy*', so tell us! What happened at your meeting with General Dynamics? Were they interested? Did you get a great job offer?"

Alan looks at the entire group…and is noncommittal in appearance and verbal response…he finally replies in a casual and subtle voice;

"Oh yea…They were interested alright."
But then Alan follows with a persuasive inflection of "a battle victorious" to his voice announcing;
"I made a deal…a really great deal for the whole team!"

Alan reaches for a remaining single bottle of Pepsi that's on the table and asks;
"Anyone have an opener?"
Donald slides his Swiss Army knife across the table.
Alan fumbles in technique while opening and examining the many varied blades of the knife as he searches for the opener. Everyone remains quiet.
Alan notices the silence but continues:

"Graduation is approaching…I don't know exactly what everyone's planning after Purdue. Some of you mentioned interest in continuing on with graduate studies.

However, if you're interested…there's an offer I believe to be a once in a lifetime opportunity for all of us…and I mean 'all of us'… the whole team."

The team's level of interest heightens.
Alan opens the Pepsi bottle…the cap falls on the table and the carbonated sound of the newly opened drink seems amplified in the still silence. Alan remains quiet and takes a short sip of Pepsi before continuing;

"So here it is…the bottom line…Each one of you; all of us so called *Renegades* have been offered a job… an engineering position…an opportunity to join the General Dynamics B-58 Project Team in Fort Worth. The B-58 is a cutting edge aircraft that's the fastest, most aerodynamically advanced airplane ever built!

On its last test flight it was clocked at Mach 2, that's 1,320 miles per hour! They're forwarding a contract to each of us for review and are including a flight to Fort Worth to visit the plant and meet with the project engineers there."

Donald Gibbs reaches across the table and retrieves his Swiss knife. He is first to speak.

"Do they plan on paying us adequately in proportion to our *aerospace disciplines and abilities*?"

Paul Lancer shakes his head showing immediate disgust with Donald's question;

"Donald…What's with the '*aerospace disciplines*' linguistics? Who are you trying to impress? That's a dumb question! Of course we're going to get paid fairly. You're missing the entire significance of this development. It sounds like Alan has the whole team vectored into an unbelievably outstanding first job opportunity…I'm in Stormy!...and thank you.

Donald responds;

"I have to see the contract…but count me in …I'll go with the team."

Paul is quick to answer;

"I'm with you Alan…I'm for keeping the whole team together and going to Fort Worth.

Tom Robinson agrees;

"Count me in Stormy…I like Texas."

Gretchen finally adds;

"I've been reading about General Dynamics. They're growing fast. They bought out Convair a couple years back. They're working on building airliners too; the Convair 990 *Coronado* is the fastest commercial airliner ever built.

Tom interjects;

"You're absolutely right Gretchen…General Dynamics is big and growing both in military and commercial business.

Gretchen continues;

"I agree, this is a real opportunity Alan…but you know;   I have one concern….and it's just a first reaction. The B-58

Renegades

carries a variety of external pods underneath the fuselage. We worked on the fuel pod…but there's also a nuclear weapons pod which our design is also applicable. Does that bother anyone else? How do the rest of you weigh in on that issue?"

Tom leans back in his chair, casually smoking his pipe and asks;

"Tell me…you're not a *'peacenik'* are you Gretchen?"

Gretchen shakes her head convincingly;

"No, no…of course not. I'm with the team and am going to Fort Worth but I keep reading how the Soviets and the United States continue to add to the stockpile of nuclear weapons and systems to deliver them. It's an out of control arms race…and we'd be supporting it!"

Tom finishes another short puff on his pipe and adds;

"That's exactly what the *Cold War* is all about Gretchen…

It's making sure you keep up with building an equal amount of nukes that the other side is making so as to insure mutual self-destruction many times over…an unimaginable result that no one wants…it's a shared unwritten doctrine that there can be no winners… only losers in a full blown nuclear exchange. That's how we keep the peace!

As for the airplane project…yes, it's part of the arms race you mentioned. You wait and see; the Soviets will have to develop their own version of the B-58 to keep up…at least it will provide more jobs for the Ruskies too!" Tom offers a half smile and short laugh before returning to his pipe and releasing two quick puffs of smoke.

Gretchen turns to Alan and asks; "What do you think Alan?"

Alan is uncharacteristically apologetic but honest in his answer;

"You know…I never really thought about the bigger picture…the consequences of what we'd be doing… or even the *Cold War*. I've always just concentrated on the engineering aspect.

My brother is in the Air Force training to fly fighter planes. He takes religion more seriously than most…more serious than I do. He once said 'God' is about acting in peace and love…but God doesn't want us to allow evil and injustice to run unchecked. I guess you could call my brother a *'Christian fighter pilot!'*

Donald seems to find a sense of intellectual humor in the

comment and replies with a half-smile;

"A *'Christian fighter pilot!'*…sounds more like an oxymoron to me!"

Gretchen interjects and looks directly at Alan;

"Your brother makes an interesting observation that I would agree with. In the future; beyond the days of our *Cold War* there will be a time when all of us…the entire world will be vulnerable to unimaginable acts of evil and terror that will require several strong military responses."

Alan appears somewhat perplexed at Gretchen's prediction and is about to reply when music on the PA system suddenly bellows into the room again at nearly twice the volume. Sheb Wooley's *'The Purple People Eater'* echoes loudly throughout the Union. The Renegade team hears the music, look at each other and know the meeting is over and time to leave.

The USAF Academy
Colorado Springs
A Question of Honor
March 6, 1959

A sealed letter from the Academy Superintendent, Major General James Briggs is hand delivered by special messenger to Cadet McConnell during his English class.

The instructor accepts the letter during his lecture. He notices the sender and casually hands it to McConnell without missing a point in his presentation. Roger holds the envelope, studies it for a minute then holds it to the light of an outside window hoping for a quick preview as to the nature of its contents.

The instructor looks at McConnell and interrupts his class presentation;

"Mr. McConnell, I can understand your interest in the communication you just received but could you postpone the opening of the Superintendent's letter till after class?"

McConnell pushes the letter aside; placing it in the corner of his desk;

"Yes sir, very good sir."

The entire class directs their attention towards McConnell.

Renegades

Every cadet's expression in the room reflects a look of foreboding doom. A special letter from the Academy's top General is not the most anticipated or welcomed communication to any cadet. They know McConnell is in the midst of an Honor Code hearing and awaiting a final decision.

The class lecture continues…McConnell can almost feel subtle vibrations coming from the corner of his desk. Finally, the lecture ends and the cadets leave for their next class. They pause for a moment as they file past McConnell's desk and offer encouragement;

"I'm with you McConnell…I'll vouch for you!"
"Good luck man…"
"Let me know if I can help."
"Hey…my dad's a lawyer in Denver…just let me know."
"My prayers are with you."
"God speed Roger McConnell!"

McConnell's four years at the Academy were not without incident. He earned high recognition for his demonstrated athletic abilities and leadership skills as captain of both the new Falcon track and basketball teams. Academically, he consistently remained in the top ten percent of his class.

However, his high visibility and popularity were countered by a small group of training officers who didn't like McConnell's strong religious attitude and the biblical mores he emulated. They sought to have him dishonorably discharged and dismissed from the Academy by creating an elaborate Honor Code scheme falsely implicating McConnell.

The Honor Code is a centerpiece of Academy life. It simply states;
"We will not lie, steal, or cheat, nor tolerate among us anyone who does."

Cadets are expected to report themselves for any Code violation. Furthermore, they must confront any other cadet they believe may have violated the code and report the incident if the situation is not resolved.

The scenario accused McConnell of cheating on a final examination, a serious violation of the Honor Code.

Chapter 3 – *A Time to Plant*

A hearing was held and McConnell awaits the decision that will decide his future at the Academy and the Air Force.

McConnell places the letter in between the cover pages of his literature book...leaves the classroom in Fairchild Hall and walks across the expansive academy Terrazzo to the Cadet Chapel.

He enters the aluminum spired chapel. The late afternoon light filters through the long strips of stained glass that reach skyward between the tall spires of the chapel. The entire chapel interior is painted in a rainbow of colors.

His roommate Bill Delaney, "The Professor", sits alone in one of the pews towards the front of the chapel.

"I knew you'd come here Rog. You got the word today didn't you?"

Roger reluctantly answers with a sense of frustration;

"Yea, I've got the letter here...I really don't want to open it. I still don't understand how this whole incident started."

Bill is hesitant to answer but wants to support his roommate and friend for four years.

"You may find it hard to understand Rog but some of the officers here think you separate yourself too much from the rest of the military...you're not conforming to the military lifestyle and traditions...They say you have a 'holier than thou' perception; that you're a 'Holy Joe.'"

Roger listens...his head bowed down, then looks at the letter but says nothing.

Bill continues;

So, look at the damn letter okay, Let's see what's happening? Are we still roomies?"

Roger tears off one end of the envelope, removes the letter, opens it and scans its contents...his eyes skip ahead to the midsection of the page where the decision is highlighted. He smiles...announcing;

"I'm still here Bill! I'm still in the Academy! It says there were three officers who covertly planned and executed the whole scheme..."

McConnell pauses for a moment.

"I thought there were only two! Listen to this;

Renegades

'*A fabricated and unsustainable allegation of an Honor Code violation was directed against the character of Cadet Roger McConnell. The fabrication of an alleged test score alteration by Cadet McConnell was planned and executed by Lt. Gordon Cowling, Lt. James Brewster and Capt. Devlin Sardoz. This activity mandates the immediate dismissal of these three officers from the Academy and recommends further investigation through Air Force Judiciary action. Cadet McConnell is cleared of all charges and eligible for graduation with the class of 1959.*'"

He continues to hold the letter. His hands are shaking. His expression becomes more serious as he repeats the name of the third officer who filed the violation against him;

"I can't believe it…who is Devlin Sardoz! How can this be happening?"

Bill is confused and asks;

"What's wrong Rog…hey, you won! They nailed those bastards!"

McConnell replaces the letter into the envelope.

"My brother and I had an earlier life threatening experience, an encounter with another 'Devlin'…I believe there's a demonic connection here."

Bill slowly leans back in the pew, placing his hands behind his head in a more relaxed position and offers a half smile and replies with a touch of sarcasm;

"That's really good news Rog…I feel much better now. For a moment I thought you were really in trouble!"

Roger replies;

"Back home, before I left for the Academy, the priest from my parish warned me to be alert for any person with the forename 'Devlin'. This is for real. There's a historical precedent for this type of demonic identification. You'd better stay on guard too Bill.

Bill leans toward Roger and is direct in his response;

"Hey, we're two fighter pilots right! I'm your wingman Rog… Remember that…I've got you covered and I'll be looking out for you….and us. You can count on it."

Bill pauses for a moment…then continues;

"For a moment forget about the 'Devlin connection'…I've got

some good news; 'flying airplane' kind of news!

Our orders were posted today. After graduation next month were both headed to beautiful San Antonio, Texas and Lackland Air Force Base for *Preflight Training School*...that's for just a couple months...then were off, to *Primary Flight Training* at Bainbridge, Alabama. Finally, we'll get to *Basic Flight Training* next June and fly jets at Vance Air Force Base in Oklahoma."

Roger's mood begins to change. He looks up and says; "That really is good news. I'm ready to leave this place and go flying!...What do you say we head off to Mitch's." *(Mitchell Hall is the cadet dining hall)*

Roger asks;

"Bill...I have a question."

"Yea, go ahead Rog..."

"You don't think I'm a *Holy Joe* do you?"

"No way Rog! No way!"...Bill exclaims.

Unnoticed and sitting in the upper balcony of the chapel is Captain Devlin Sardoz. He watches silently as the two cadets walk down the center aisle and leave the chapel sanctuary.

May 10, 1959

Hi Mom,

Graduation Day is near. Lots of Good news: I was offered
and accepted a position with General Dynamics in Fort Worth,
Texas. General Dynamics is pursuing some very interesting
research in advanced aerodynamics. They hired all the members
from our Purdue "Renegade" team I told you about.

Brother Rog and I have kept in close communication and are
sending you airline tickets so that you'll be able to attend each of
our graduations! I'll call you this weekend.

Love, Alan

USAF Academy
Colorado Springs, Colorado

May 15, 1959

Hello Mom,

Graduation is only weeks away now. You'll have a chance to see the new academy site in Colorado Springs. Only a handful of buildings were completed when we moved here last year from Lowry...but it's looking better now.

President Eisenhower visited and inspected the Cadet Wing and addressed our class at Mitchell Hall today. I shook hands and had a chance to talk with him...he's much more personable than he appears on television.

It looks like both Alan and I are headed for Texas. After graduation on June 3...I have some leave time before I report for pre-flight training at Lackland Air Force Base near San Antonio. I'm assigned to Class 61D. To tell you the truth...I sure want to get out of the classroom and into a cockpit!

See you soon Mom,
Love, Roger

Chapter 4
A Time to Mourn
June 1, 1959

The entire 207 member cadet Class of 1959 stands at attention on the Academy's outside Terrazzo in preparation for the graduation ceremony in two days.

Roger McConnell's eyes look skyward and to the horizon. In the distance a flight of four T-33 jet trainers are seen approaching the Academy. Thirty seconds later they perform a high speed, low altitude fly-over. Flying in a tight formation, wingtip to wingtip, they roar overhead with the commanding sound of their thunderous engines echoing against the surrounding buildings.

For a brief moment, McConnell imagines himself piloting one of those T-33s. Suddenly, the spell is broken;

"Cadet McConnell...Could you please step out of line and follow me."

McConnell recognizes Colonel Don Samuels; the Academy Chaplain. He's always friendly, open and casual in character but now his formal greeting instantly communicates something serious is going on.

"Roger, let's take a walk to my office...I have some news." Samuels continues to talk as they walk towards the Chapel;

"I'm afraid I have some bad news Roger. Administration just called me. They received a phone call fifteen minutes ago. Your mother was killed early this morning in an automobile accident outside of Clovis, New Mexico. She was hit by another vehicle that lost control and crossed over the center line. It was a head on collision. Your local minister from San Jon, Father Juan Martinez is waiting for your call...he has more details. I have his number here.

McConnell's strident walk suddenly slows to a complete stop. He looks at the Chaplain in disbelief and says;

"My mother was driving to Clovis and planned to meet a friend who was going to take her to Lubbock for the flight to Colorado and the graduation here. I just talked to her yesterday afternoon! We planned on having dinner together this evening. I can't believe this happened."

As they enter the Chapel...the cadet choir is rehearsing the assuring and familiar lyrics of *Amazing Grace.* The hymn releases an onslaught of emotion as McConnell picks up the phone in the Chaplain's office and calls Father Martinez.

The phone rings for an extended time...there's no answer. McConnell is about to hang up when a familiar voice is suddenly heard;

"Hello, this is Father Martinez..."

McConnell immediately answers;

"Father...it's so good to hear your voice. This is Roger ...I'm calling from the Academy. I heard the news. This is not right. I can't believe it! Tell me what happened."

"Roger, I'm so sorry...my prayers are with you and Alan. I must say when I visited your mother just this morning...all was well...I shared a prayer with her and asked for a safe journey...she was in such good spirits...very excited and looking forward to seeing you again and attending the graduation.

An hour later, Captain Sanchez from the New Mexico State Patrol, you know Richard...he's from San Jon. Well, he called me and reported your mother was in an accident. He said it appeared to be a head-on collision with another vehicle that apparently lost control. Your mother was air lifted by helicopter from the accident site and was enroute to Lubbock and the hospital there. She passed away while inflight. She was only about 10 minutes from the hospital but had sustained a substantial number of serious internal injuries. I was told the medical attention she would have received at the hospital may not have made a difference...I have already spoken to Alan and he's on the way back to San Jon."

Roger asks;

"What about the driver in the other vehicle?"

Father Martinez doesn't immediately reply;

"This...I do not understand Roger...the State Patrol investigators were unable to find the driver. The vehicle had no plates...it was a 1948 pickup truck...a Chevrolet. "

Roger is quick to respond;

"I wish you hadn't said that Father...I'm afraid I know

Renegades

what's happened...you warned me earlier about a'Devlin'? I'll talk to you soon. I'm taking emergency leave and will return to San Jon tomorrow morning. Thank you for your help Father."

Roger completes the call and slowly replaces the phone on the cradle. His hand remains on the phone. Chaplain Samuels interrupts;

"I know you have a lot on your mind now but I need to tell you something before you leave. As you know, I was asked to serve on the Honor Code Committee that reviewed your case a couple months ago. Captain Devlin Sardoz; was the officer who created and was responsible for the whole honor code scenario against you. He was able to convince two other officers to participate in his plan to have you dismissed from the Academy.

I had the most uneasy feeling the moment Captain Sardoz entered the hearing room. He never made eye contact with me even when I was questioning him during the investigation. There was a feeling...a very strong sense of something...an emotion I had never experienced before. It can only be described as being cold, unforgiving...and evil. Several other members of the board shared a similar uneasiness. Be careful Roger and remain vigilant of those around you.

You have left a very positive and powerful record of achievement with the first graduating class from the Academy. Stay the course.

Chaplain Samuels concludes;

"Roger, before you leave I'd like to offer a prayer;

Father in Heaven travel with Roger on his journey home. Guide and protect him from all danger. Let the fruits of the Spirit; love, joy, peace, patience, kindness, faithfulness, gentleness and self-control continue to rule his heart and guide his career. Amen. "

Roger whispers an "Amen" and remains quiet; taking an added moment of reflection before picking up the phone and calling the administration office.

The admin office answers; his request is short and direct;

"This is Cadet Roger McConnell...There has been a death in the family...my mother passed away this morning. I need orders

Chapter 4 – *A Time to Mourn*

processed for emergency leave as soon as possible…I'll be returning home and will be unable to attend the graduation ceremony tomorrow."

62

Academy Graduation Day
June 3, 1959

*The United States Air Force Academy Class of 1959
Graduation Benediction, written almost 800 years ago by Saint
Francis of Assisi was read by Col. C. E. Zielinski, the Catholic
Chaplain at the conclusion of the graduation ceremony.*

Lord, make me a channel of thy peace,
That where there is hatred I may bring love,
That where there is wrong I may bring the spirit of forgiveness,
That where there is discord I may bring harmony,
That where there is error I may bring truth,
That where there is doubt I may bring faith,
That where there is despair I may bring hope,
That where there are shadows I may bring Thy light,
That where there is sadness I may bring joy,
Lord, grant that I may seek rather to comfort than to be
comforted,
To understand than to be understood,
To love than to be loved,
    For
It is by giving that one receives,
It is by self-forgetting that one finds,
It is by forgiving that one is forgiven,
It is by dying that one awakens to eternal life.

Chapter 5
A Time to Heal
Wheatland Cemetery
San Jon, New Mexico
June 11, 1959

It's a *"Shining New Mexico Day";*
a sun shining bright, warm and comforting...complimenting a
resolution perfect blue sky broken with only random traces of
thin high cirrus clouds.
The two brothers; Alan and Roger McConnell are together
again for a final visit at the gravesite where their mother was
laid to rest a week ago. Father Martinez is present and offers
consoling words before the brothers depart;
"There's a verse in the favorite 19th century hymn, *Amazing*
Grace that speaks of Heaven and those that enter there. It was
your mother's favorite hymn. I have always remembered and
repeated the last verse to those who lost a loved one. As I
recall...it reads;

> *'When we've been there ten thousand years,*
> *Bright shining as the sun,*
> *We've no less days to sing God's praise then when*
> *We'd first begun'"*

Father Martinez continues;
"Alan and Roger...know without any doubt and have complete
certainty that your mother resides in Heaven and will be
sustained in God's loving care for all eternity. It is an
undeserved gift of grace and love given to her and offered to all
of us... if we believe."
The three leave the grave site walking slowly with no words
spoken. They reach the shade of a willow tree and stop for a
moment. Roger looks back at the gravesite;
"Dad's body was never found after the crash in Germany...he
should have been buried here...next to mom."
Alan nods in agreement...There's a prolonged silence before
he says;
"...and why haven't the police found the other driver that

63

killed mom?...the person who caused the accident. There has been absolutely no evidence or leads as to the identity of the driver. I don't understand! How can the state police investigation reveal nothing?"

Roger replies;

"Remember our last glider flight...the old guy who bothered us...Devlin was his name? He drove an "old Chevy pickup"...that thought keeps coming back at me. I had another *'Devlin'* encounter at the Academy that almost did me in...and you told me your experience at Purdue...during your freshman year. We're being targeted for something and I don't think it's going to end. I'd like to know... why *us*?

Father, what's happening? Is there something we should know?"

Father Martinez is careful in his response;

"Roger and Alan... you told me about your encounters. Be extremely careful now...but I believe you will be receiving help. These fallen angels or demons you have encountered are aware of a plan God has enacted and of your direct participation. Somehow, you have become part of a battle plan taking place in the spiritual world... and part of that battle is taking place here and now on earth. This is fierce, unrelenting warfare between *good* and *evil*.

Have faith... continue to pray for guidance. Your question will be answered and I believe it will be soon and in a way least expected."

It's only a short distance to the parking area. When they reach their cars and are ready to depart separate ways; Alan turns to Roger;

"I have to tell you what's happening at the aircraft factory. There's a new project at General Dynamics being talked about called TFX. It's a *variable sweep-wing* aircraft... sound familiar?

When the time comes for flight testing the government requires military pilots be integrated into the development program. Keep that in mind brother. Let's stay in touch.

Chapter 5 – *A Time to Heal*

Sidebar: *The Doctrine of Angels*
*Synopsis of Bible Doctrine by Charles C. Ryrie**

I. The Existence Of Angels
   A. **The Teaching of Scripture.** Existence taught in at least thirty –four books of the Bible. The word *Angel* occurs about 275 times.
   B. **The Teaching of Christ.** Christ knew of and taught the existence of angels. (Matt.18:10; 26:53).

II. The Creation Of Angels
   A. **Fact** of their creation is shown in Colossians 1:16.
   B. **Time.** Before the creation of the world (Job 38: 6-7).
   C. **State** of their creation was in holiness (Jude 6).

III. The Personality Of Angels
   A. **Intellect** (1 Peter 1:12)
   B. **Emotion** (Luke 2:13)
   C. **Will** (Jude 6)

IV. The Nature Of Angels
   A. **They Are Spirit Beings** (Heb.1:14)
   B. **They Are Without Power to Reproduce after their kind** (Mark 12:25). Angels are designated by masculine gender in Scripture (Gen18:1-2; cf. Sech.5:9 for possible exception).
   C. **They Do Not Die** (Luke 20:36)
   D. **They Are Distinct from Human Beings** (Ps.8:4-5)
   E. **They Have Great Power** {2Peter 2:11).

V. **Number Of The Angels**
   Innumerable (Heb.12:22).

VI. Organization Of The Angels
   A. **One Archangel Is Named, Michael** (Jude 9).
   B. **Chief Princes** (Dan. 10:13
   C. **Ruling Angels** (Eph. 3:10).
   D. **Guardian Angels** (for all, Heb.1:14; for children, Matt. 18:10).
   E. **Seraphim** (Isa. 6:1-3). Have to do with the worship of God.
   F. **Cherubim** (Gen. 3:22-24) Guarding the holiness of God.
   G. **Elect Angels** (1Tim. 5:21).

VII. The Ministries Of Angels
   A. **To Christ.**
      1. Predicted His birth (Luke 1:26-33).
      2. Announced His Birth (Luke2:13).
      3. Protected the Baby (Matt.2:13).

    4. Strengthened Christ after temptation (Matt. 4:11).

    5. Prepared to defend Him (Matt. 26:53).

    6. Strengthened Him in Gethsemane (Luke 22:43).

    7. Rolled away stone from tomb (Matt. 28:2).

    8. Announced the Resurrection (Matt. 28:6).

B.   **To Believers**.

    1. General ministry of aiding (Heb. 1:14).

    2. Involved in answering prayer (Acts 12:7).

    3. Observe Christians' experiences (1Cor. 4:9; Tim. 5:21).

    4. Encourage in time of danger (Acts 27: 23-24).

    5. Interested in evangelistic effort of Christians (Luke 1510; Acts 8:26).

    6. Care for righteous at death (Luke 16:22; Jude 9).

C.   **To the Nations.**

    1. Michael seems to have a special relationship to Israel Dan. 12:1).

    2. Angels are God's agents in the execution of His providence (Dan 10:21).

    3. Angels will be involved in the Judgements of the Tribulation (Rev. 8, 9, 16).

D.   **To Unbelievers.**

    1.   Announce impending judgements (Gen. 19:13; Rev. 14: 6-7).

    2.   Inflict punishment (Acts 12:23).

    3.   Act as reapers in the separation at end of the age (Matt. 13:39)

Ryrie Study Bible, New American Standard
Charles Caldwell Ryrie, Th.D., Ph.D.
Moody Publishers, Chicago - c.1986, 1995.

Chapter 5 – *A Time to Heal*

Chapter 6
A Time to Build
Cathedral of St. Francis of Assisi
October 17, 1959

Michael and Gabriel are the two highest ranking angels in God's administration of the universe since the beginning of time. Michael has chosen to meet Gabriel at the Cathedral of St. Francis of Assisi in Santa Fe, New Mexico.

The city of Santa Fe was founded in 1610. An adobe church was built but destroyed seventy years later during a revolt by the Pueblo Indian tribe in 1680. A new church was not rebuilt till 1714 and was named in honor of Saint Francis of Assisi, the Patron Saint of Santa Fe.

Gabriel sits alone on a wooden park bench located in the courtyard of the *Cathedral of St. Francis* in Santa Fe, New Mexico. He waits patiently for Michael to arrive with an important communique. Michael has an important message from the Lord that needs to be delivered.

It's early October and an afternoon wind with an early winter chill blows gently across the downtown Plaza and into the courtyard. There's a scent of pinion in the air.

Every year…usually in mid-October, when the evening temperatures start to dip; "Santa feans" begin to light their fireplaces. The wood of choice is piñon. The distinct piñon scent is already in the air and will last all winter long.

The tourist season has ended. Only a small volume of auto traffic navigates through Santa Fe's narrow streets. Gabriel has shed his invisible spiritual cloak and chosen to appear as an elderly gentleman in his late 60's. He wears a dark gray woolen jacket, brown trousers that reveal a slight sheen from apparent wear. A contrasting dark green fedora is jauntily positioned atop his head; slanted slightly to the side. A small cropping of white hair from beneath his hat falls over a portion of his forehead. Gabriel opens a chessboard he has carried with him, positions it on the bench and begins placing the pieces in the positions he remembers from the last time he met Michael. Michael is a chess player; a challenging opponent who thoroughly enjoys the game when in human form.

Gabriel looks towards the nearby central Plaza hoping to see Michael. As he returns his attention to the chessboard a youthful looking mother, wearing a white, light-weight quilted parka and jeans sits down on the far end of the bench with her young daughter. The daughter is also wearing a parka, a light blue one. She's carrying a book; *Island Of The Blue Dolphins* and opens it immediately upon sitting down next to her mother.

"That's a well written and most exciting story you're reading young lady." Gabriel observes.

She answers without any hint of shyness;

"It's about a little girl that's left all alone on an island!"

Gabriel's friendly looking caricature readily opens an immediate response and an easy conversation with the mother;

"Our family just moved here from Dayton...Dayton, Ohio. My 8 year old daughter, Sandra misses her friends...I think she feels somewhat like the girl in the story who is all alone, trying to survive on the island." She smiles, pauses for a moment before continuing;

"We are all starting over here...a fresh start. My husband is a carpenter. He had some very serious health problems...but he's much better now and wanted to take a new direction in his life. My father lives here in Santa Fe and invited us to stay with him till we find a place."

Gabriel nods his head; confirming an understanding of their situation and adding;

"New Mexico has always been a special and welcoming place for those seeking a new beginning...you will do well settling here. I will ask for God's blessing for you and your family."

"Thank you, my name is Cheryl...You are most kind."

Her attention is momentarily interrupted and directed to the Plaza's circular drive.

"Oh, I see my husband's car!"

She turns and says to her daughter;

"Sandra...You must finish your book...we've got to go; your father is here."

She turns to Gabriel;

"Thank you again Mr...?"

She pauses momentarily...

Chapter 6 – *A Time to Build*

"May I ask…what is your name?"

Gabriel replies with an immediate smile and adds a touch of private humor to the encounter;

"Yes, I'm Mr. Gabriel…Mr. George Gabriel."

Cheryl replies;

"It's been nice meeting you…Mr. Gabriel!"

The mother and daughter leave the courtyard walking hand in hand together. They break into a short run as they greet the waiting father.

Gabriel savors the enjoyable human experience just as Michael arrives. Angels have a great affection and interest in humans.

Michael arrives and is most enthusiastic;

"I love this Cathedral Gabriel…this is one of my favorite meeting places!"

Michael is brimming over with what seems to be an extra amount of energy. His visible appearance is of a middle aged Hispanic gentleman with dark hair neatly trimmed to a short length and parted to one side. His medium athletic frame is well defined with dark tan trousers, a red turtleneck sweater and tan leather jacket looking very stylish in its slightly worn but fashionable condition.

"Gabriel, I see you're trying to tempt me again with that chess board of yours!"

Gabriel is equally excited and pleased to see Michael again.

Michael sits down on the bench opposite the chessboard. He studies the various pieces and their placement…then looks up at Gabriel;

"I really like that green fedora you're wearing Gabriel…it gives you the appearance of an earthly, friendly and…very distinguished gentleman."

Michael pauses, then becomes more serious and asks;

"Gabriel, tell me about your time aboard the *Hornet*?"

Gabriel removes his hat and places it on his lap and lowers his head.

"It was a very enlightening but difficult experience. I have great respect for the Americans but there 20th century mission was still just another added link of a never ending chain of wars. As I travel through the centuries; *the times of war and violence* are increasing at a greater rate than *the times of peace*.

Renegades

Wars are more violent and sustained in their execution. There are so many new weapons employing highly destructive forces that are unimaginable. The human casualties of war are indiscriminate. Innocent citizens; those who are not participants in a conflict have become targeted victims. There is another more troubling side effect; the perceived value and respect of human life is slowly being lost.

Lucifer and his agent demons seem to be gaining an advantage; their disruptive tactics in everyday affairs have intensified.

I have taken special interest in watching over Captain McConnell's family. His two sons, Alan and Roger have had direct contact with a *Devlin*...I found it necessary to intervene and protect them.

Michael at this point interrupts;

"Agreed, yes Gabriel, the demonic activity you speak of is more than troubling. These events are increasing and are very disruptive and directly conflict with our mission.

Love dominates God's universe. It is the framework and most powerful force in *Heaven* and the entire Universe...*Evil* will always lose against *Love*.

Yet, *'Love'*...its very name is trivialized to near meaningless value in the earthly world.

I directed you to visit the *Hornet* to gain first-hand experience of an earthly military battle against *Evil*. There are many prayers sent from Earth with questions asking about the relationship between God and war.

Let me say this; Remember, God does not desire war and its patterns of destruction. He favors acts of love and peace as much as possible but when the opposition fails to accept these; evil and injustice must not be allowed to prevail.

I have come from a meeting with our Lord...He has a very special mission for us requiring our assistance on this very issue. The Lord in His infinite mercy wants to help Earth. I can best summarize His intention with His words;

"Two thousand years have passed...and now the human race will be given another chance."

"This assignment begs for an increase of activity on Earth to

Chapter 6 – *A Time to Build*

defeat evil and enhance the power of love. The Lord speaks of a spiritual awakening worldwide…a miracle to ignite and show the way for a renewed and rewarding spiritual pattern of life on a "good" Earth.

The current world has fallen deeply into difficult and troubling times… it will be put to rest."

Michael continues;

"Gabriel, as God's messenger, you are to deliver the Lord's message and offer a dialogue of guidance and ongoing protection to several specially chosen individuals who will participate in the fulfilment of God's plan.

I must warn you again; the 'fallen ones', the many demons on earth are committed to destroying God's mission and those that support it. You must watch over and protect these individuals;"

Alan David "Stormy" McConnell –*You already have a relationship with Alan by your protective action that was needed at San Jon several years ago…even though he was unaware of your presence. Alan is a young aircraft design engineer who will be working in Fort Worth, Texas. His exceptional technical skills, unconventional solutions, original thinking and leadership of a special talented group of other young engineers is a part of God's plan. Unfortunately, he has a continuing history of strong resistance to the existence of all spiritual matters; including, the Holy Spirit and faith in our Lord. Alan needs your intervention so he may know the Spirit, reach his destiny and fulfill God's plan.*

Roger Franklin McConnell – *Roger is a very dedicated, strong and faithful servant to our Lord…he has experienced your life saving encounter at San Jon but is unaware of your direct intervention. Roger is on course with God's plan. The Holy Spirit dwells deeply in his heart. He needs additional protection because of his strong faith that attracts demonic intervention.*

Dr. Amelia Anoza – *An earthbound Angel and physician. She completed her assignment in the city of Chicago and has received notice of a new mission assignment to Africa. Amelia is most capable and can provide you with additional and invaluable assistance. In the past, I've entrusted Amelia with supporting the Lord's most important assignments.*

Jean Paul Boyer – *A young university student, missionary's son and servant of the Lord in Africa. He will have a significant future role in the final outcome of God's plan. The Holy Spirit is with him. His life must be protected at all costs.*

David Richardsen - *the young son of foreign Envoy Donald Richardsen Sr. He ls destined to become President of the United States at the time of the Lord's miracle. His protection is a top priority. He is a strong believer of the faith and follows the guiding pathway of the Holy Spirit.*

Michael concludes by saying;

"Gabriel, The Lords word, His protection and personal message is to be delivered to each of these individuals. This powerful tapestry I present you offers protection to all its holders. It holds the Holy messages you are to deliver."

Michael hands Gabriel what appears to be a single small piece of cloth. Gabriel opens it to its full and much larger size. The cloth is a thin tightly woven fabric; black in color but highlighted with a multitude of interwoven golden threads. The threads appear to move slowly and with great precision across the cloth forming a continuous parade of changing geometric patterns. A soft and thinly transparent golden luminance seems to float inches above the patterns providing a continuous light source. Gabriel studies the patterns for a moment…smiles at the messages which only he can decipher. He refolds the cloth, dutifully inserting it into a small, specially made leather courier's case that remains permanently attached to his belt.

It's late afternoon and the early shadows of evening begin to appear on the Cathedral's garden walls.

Michael laments;

"As I have said too many times before Gabriel; I'm afraid we must postpone our chess game for a later time.

We will continue to work together and complete the Lord's mission…and perhaps then we will find a moment for a chess game good friend!"

Gabriel gathers the chess pieces and board, places them in the wooden storage box.

The hourly bells of the Cathedral begin to toll as the two leave the courtyard and walk towards the Plaza. As they walk, their figures fade into formless gray shadows…gradually at first, then finally melting into the gathering shadows of the evening. As the Cathedral bells sound their final toll…they are gone.

Chapter 6 – *A Time to Build*

Chapter 7
Midway
November 3, 1959

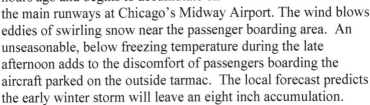

A light snow began falling several
hours ago and begins to accumulate on
the main runways at Chicago's Midway Airport. The wind blows
eddies of swirling snow near the passenger boarding area. An
unseasonable, below freezing temperature during the late
afternoon adds to the discomfort of passengers boarding the
aircraft parked on the outside tarmac. The local forecast predicts
the early winter storm will leave an eight inch accumulation.

Doctor Amelia Anoza arrives early at the airport for the start of
a "marathon" flight to the African continent. She has a
scheduled flight departure to New York in three hours on *United
Airlines* and a connecting trans-Atlantic flight with *Pan Am* to
Dakar… from Dakar it's another flight on *Air Mali* to Timbuktu.

Amelia is a physician, a practicing surgeon…*and an
earthbound angel.* Her mission in Chicago, supporting a
medical clinic on the city's west side, has been completed. She
awaits a final mission briefing at the airport before leaving for
Africa.

Michael has only hinted as to person she will meet with; saying
only that it will be '*an old friend*'. Reservations are for dinner at
Marshall Field's airport restaurant, *The Cloud Room.* Amelia
smiles to herself reflecting on how Michael always seems to
enjoy "keeping her guessing with surprises."

Amelia enters the main airport lobby. It's quite busy with
passengers hoping to leave before the storm intensifies and
closes the airport. She waits in line for several minutes and
listens to complaints of Chicagoans as they experience the start
of an early winter. Amelia checks her baggage and confirms the
flight times; then walks up a flight of stairs to the second floor
and through the elegant glass door entrance of the *Cloud Room.*

As she arrives, the maître d' cordially greets her;

"Good Afternoon! You must be Dr. Anoza…Mr. Gabriel is
already here and has a table reserved. Please follow me!"

Amelia smiles to herself. So it's Gabriel!…and he wants to
meet in the *Cloud Room! I believe he's developing a real human*

sense of humor!

Amelia walks beneath and admires the free floating Alexander Calder mobile hanging from the ceiling. Her attention is diverted by the panoramic view of airport activity offered through the restaurant's large ceiling to floor windows.

Gabriel sees Amelia and immediately stands up from the table to greet her:

"Hello Amelia...you're wearing a most contagious smile. You are surprised to see me?"

Amelia adds a trifling laugh to compliment her smile;

"It is so good to see you Gabriel...and I most enjoy having dinner here at *The Cloud Room!*"

Gabriel replies;

"I wanted to make sure you had a good dinner before you embark on your journey and next mission. Please sit down Amelia...I was just noticing the weather outside...It's beginning to look a bit challenging."

Amelia nods in agreement but says;

"Well...the flight is still scheduled and the weather in New York looks much better; so hopefully... I will make it out of Chicago on time. Have you ever flown in an airplane Gabriel?"

Gabriel becomes more animated and replies;

"Oh yes, Amelia...Just recently Michael sent me back in time on a most exciting and fascinating mission. I actually flew off the deck of an aircraft carrier in the South China Sea in a B-25 bomber with the Doolittle Raiders! You know, of course, I've sailed on a 15th century Philistine *Man of War* but there's no comparison... those vessels couldn't even sail into the wind!"

Gabriel suddenly realizes he's speaking too loudly. A gentleman sitting at a nearby table stares inquisitively at Gabriel and visually examines the contents in Gabriel's water glass.

"Oh my...I must be more careful in conversation Amelia." Gabriel continues the conversation in more reserved tones... whispering;

"Amelia...Do you see that gentleman sitting over there... in the corner... all by himself?"

Amelia answers; "Yes, I certainly do."Gabriel moves closer to Amelia and whispers;

Chapter 7 - *Midway*

"That's Jimmy Stewart, the movie actor. I had a chance to speak with him...very briefly. We both arrived at the restaurant at the same time. He's on his way back to Hollywood...a fine man. I told him how much I enjoyed *It's A Wonderful Life*...and that it is one of my favorite films! I told him it was a *wonderful* tribute to all working angels! He laughed and was most cordial. Humans are so interesting aren't they Amelia?"

Amelia still smiling replies;

"I do believe you're enjoying the 20th Century Gabriel!"

Gabriel nods and becomes more reflective;

"Yes, you're absolutely right and I especially enjoy and have a great deal of admiration and affection for these Americans. They have an abundance of creativity, energy and such optimism in all they do. They're a very kind, generous and God-fearing people. You know, following the war they gave billions of dollars to rebuild Europe and much needed assistance to Japan as well. I hope they never change."

Gabriel pauses for a moment.

His conversation becomes more serious.

"I must share this with you Amelia; I am afraid there are troubled and challenging times ahead...

The Lord foresees an approaching era of great upheaval; an examination of traditional values, acts of violence and conflict that have no borders. The earth's environment will be active with extreme and destructive natural forces. It's a time when the entire world will be severely challenged. The Lord wants to give the good earth and all its inhabitants another chance ....a chance for peace. There will be no repeat of a biblical flood and it is not the right time for His second coming.

Instead, God will guide the earth through the perilous times. He will perform a miracle, a powerful event for all on earth to see and experience...this will be a "breakaway" event to reset the world on a new secure and anticipative future.

The Lord has given us an assignment...an assigned task to support His mission and make the necessary preparations for that special and miraculous time."

On first hearing this; Amelia does not know how to respond.

"Gabriel, I was not prepared for a message of such magnitude.

Renegades

I thought my new assignment to Africa involved medical and clinical work. I was told of a great need along the Sahel region. Please continue, tell me what does the Lord wants me to do?" Gabriel continues;

"Remember the Lord's plans are not coordinated to earthly time references and schedules. A hundred years may only be less than a second on the Lord's scale of time. However, His preparation for the event begins now. God's army of angels await His orders. Special guardian angels have already come to earth in human form to provide protection and assistance to several important individuals in God's plan.

Angel Jophiel is a guardian assigned to **Roger McConnell**, a pilot and Air Force officer. The angel's earthly identity is *William Delaney*.

Roger's brother, **Alan "Stormy" McConnell** is an aircraft design engineer. *Angel Uriel; the Archangel of Wisdom* is Alan's guardian and has been given the name and identity of a college student, *Gretchen Summers*.

The Lord calls upon all angels to watch and protect **Jean Paul Boyer;** a missionary's son and future agricultural scientist of great distinction. He is a faithful servant of the Lord in Africa and has a significant future role in the final outcome of God's plan. **David Richardsen**, the son of Envoy Donald Richardsen Sr. will be President of the United States. These lives must be protected at all costs. "

Gabriel pauses for a moment and reaches into the leather couriers case attached to his belt and opens the cloth tapestry given to him by Michael. He opens it and begins to read. Amelia listens attentively as Gabriel describes a maelstrom of events that will occur while she is in Africa:

"There are anti-colonial riots against France taking place now in the capital city, Leopoldville...this and other acts lead to the Congo's independence in August. However, you should be aware this event will only foster several other periods of continued unrest. European doctors will flee the country overnight, leaving the Congo's medical system in the hands of the remaining missionary doctors. You will need to leave Mali and provide assistance to the Congo hospital in Stanleyville.

Chapter 7 - *Midway*

Know that these events preclude and set the stage for the miracle of the Lord."

Amelia assures Gabriel of her commitment;

"As always Gabriel, I will continue to do the Lord's work with all my strength and ability as instructed."

Gabriel returns the message cloth to its case and replies;

"Amelia, may the blessings of the Lord follow and guide you to a successful completion of your mission."

Gabriel and Amelia remain silent as both realize the significance of the moment as God's plan is set into motion.

The silence and moment of prayer is interrupted…

"Are you ready to order maam?" The waiter politely asks.

Amelia answers;

"Yes we are…most definitely. I have a flight to catch."

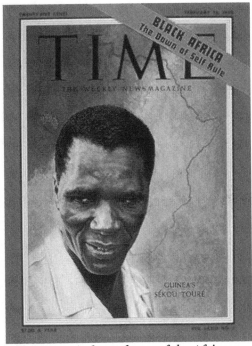

The future independence of the African continent in 1960 - Storm Clouds Ahead

Sidebar: The Revolutionary 1960's

1960 -1961
Africa: Between January and December of 1960, 17 sub-Saharan African nations, including 14 former French colonies, gained independence from their former European colonists.

President John Kennedy proposes *Apollo* program with the goal of "landing a man on the moon and returning him safely to the earth" by end of the decade.

Vietnam War: President Kennedy deploys an additional 400 military advisors. (900 total)

Alan Shepard pilots the *Freedom 7* capsule to become the first American in space. - Early design-development of the **TFX** - *F-111* by General Dynamics.

1962
The Cuban missile crisis: U.S. and Soviet confrontation.
John Glenn becomes first American to orbit the Earth.

1963
The Atomic Test Ban Treaty signed.
Dr. Martin Luther King Jr., delivers historic *"I have a dream"* speech.
President John F. Kennedy assassinated by a sniper in Dallas, Texas.
Lyndon B. Johnson is sworn in as President.

1964
Operation Rolling Thunder begins in the Vietnam War.
Protest March against Vietnam War in Washington D.C. – Over 25,000 protestors.
1965
Vietnam War continues to escalate – Troops total 184,000.
 Palestinian terrorists attempted to bomb the National Water Purification Plant - the first attack carried out by the PLO.

"The Times They Are A-Changin"

A decade of hope, innocence and cynicism

It was a decade of revolutionary change and conflicting contrasts: flower children and assassins, idealism and alienation, rebellion and backlash, the Vietnam War and the first manned spacecraft to orbit the moon. It was the best of times and the worst of times.

At the start of the decade; a young senator from Massachusetts; John F. Kennedy announced his candidacy for president. He won the nation's highest office the following November.

At the end of the decade, President Kennedy was assassinated. His brother Robert and the Rev. Martin Luther King were murdered. America's cities became embattled as African-Americans, despite historic gains toward legal equality took to the streets. A "generation gap" developed between parents and the younger generation caused by differing perceptions of patriotism, drug use, sexuality, and the work ethic.

Renegades

Chapter 8
On the Road Again
June 11, 1960

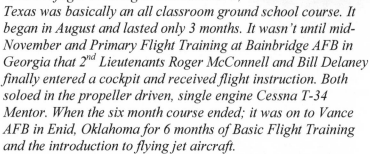

*The Preflight Training at Lackland AFB,
Texas was basically an all classroom ground school course. It
began in August and lasted only 3 months. It wasn't until mid-
November and Primary Flight Training at Bainbridge AFB in
Georgia that 2nd Lieutenants Roger McConnell and Bill Delaney
finally entered a cockpit and received flight instruction. Both
soloed in the propeller driven, single engine Cessna T-34
Mentor. When the six month course ended; it was on to Vance
AFB in Enid, Oklahoma for 6 months of Basic Flight Training
and the introduction to flying jet aircraft.*

Roger McConnell and Bill Delaney, in civilian clothes and
onboard a city bus, are headed to downtown Bainbridge and the
Greyhound bus station there. They have a week before reporting
to their next assignment at Vance Air Force Base in Oklahoma.

McConnell is staring out the window and sees a nearby
farmhouse. Without warning, he shouts to the front of the bus;
"Hey Driver, Stop…Stop now! I've got to get off here!"

The bus slows down, pulls over to the side of the road. The
driver looks back at McConnell who is walking down the center
aisle towards him. Delaney follows close behind.

Several passengers onboard are disturbed at the unannounced
interruption and direct despairing looks at the two as they make
their way forward.

"What the hell's the problem?" the driver asks.
"I'm not supposed to make any stops like this…it's against
company rules!"

McConnell is quick to reply;

"Sorry for the inconvenience but we've just got to get off
here…We have to meet someone. You can drive on."

The driver shakes his head in a disgruntled fashion and opens
the door.

McConnell and Delaney exit the bus and watch it speed away
trailing a cloud of dust.

Bill looks at Roger and asks;

"Okay Rog…you got me…what's happening here? Who are we going to meet?"

Roger offers a widening smile enjoying the unexpected moment he has created;

"Bill, you see that sign over there…it caught my eye from the bus; *'Car for Sale…$1000.'* I think it's time we get some real wheels. We've been throttled for four years in the academy. It's time for some freedom my friend!"

They walk up a winding dirt road for about a quarter mile to a farmhouse and barn that's in close proximity to each other. The barn door is open and inside the shadowed outline of a covered vehicle is clearly seen…covered by a worn and tattered canvas tarp.

The farm house and barn are in need of paint and serious repair. The barn; except for the car is completely empty. There are no livestock, hay or farm equipment visible.

McConnell is rapidly becoming less enthusiastic of his decision to leave the bus;

"It looks like the farm has come on hard times Bill. I bet there's an old Ford…a really old Ford under that tarp!

Bill who is circling the vehicle and is about to lift the tarp remarks;

"You're not being very optimistic Rog…I bet it's a *Studebaker*! I do believe we should have stayed on the bus. Your professor says it's one very long walk to town."

McConnell hears the squeaking sound of a farm house screen door opening…then slamming shut. He turns toward the house and sees a man approaching with a welcoming smile;

"Good Morning boys…Jeb Stewart is the name…How can I help yah?"

McConnell guesses the man probably is in his early 70's. He's wearing a pair of well-worn blue coveralls and a faded red baseball cap embossed with a *Farmall Tractors* logo in white letters.

McConnell replies;

"We saw your sign from out on the road…and would like to see the car. You're asking a thousand bucks eh?"

Jeb replies;

Renegades

82

"Yep, it's a good runin machine for a thousand dollars. She's a beauty! ...but I can't drive her any more...she gets away from me...it's got too much 'git up and go'!"

He carefully removes the tarp from the front end revealing a glistening pure white body. Its recognizable lines easily identify the vehicle.

Roger's eyes widen. He can't believe it;

"Holy Shit...It's a Corvette!"

Bill's responds with equal surprise;

"Holy Cow...It's a 'Vette' Rog...a convertible."

Jeb remains unemotional to the two responses and finishes removing the tarp and retrieves the owner's manual laying on the driver's seat.

"This is a 1957' Chevrolet Corvette and the manual says it's painted in *Polo White*, has a four speed transmission, 250 horsepower and something called *Rochester fuel injection*. I know for a fact that it makes this baby really go! Never been there before but those folks living in Rochchester must lead a fast movin life....yes siree...I bet they do!"

Roger laughs and asks almost sarcastically;

"How did you ever get this car Jeb?"

Jeb doesn't seem to hear the question and continues his dialogue;

"You can see there's not a lot mileage on her...the red interior is all leather. I've been taking her out of the barn and for a drive about once every month. Millie and I go to town and back to pick up our groceries."

Jeb continues;

"This is my son's car."

His voice changes and resonates with a father's strong conviction as he begins a story;

Chapter 8 – *On the Road Again*

"He went to the University, earned a degree and then was drafted into the Army and became an officer. They sent him overseas as some kind of an *Advisor*...and was killed six months later by terrorists in a place I never heard of...*Saigon.*

They said he served his country well and died with honor. Millie and I went to Washington and were presented with his Congressional Medal for heroic leadership in battle...I know he believed in what he was doing...we talked about that before he left. He's buried at Arlington with all the other heroes.

I have to admit though...hell if I understand why we're sending more young Americans over there to Vietnam. That's halfway round the world!"

Jeb pulls out a handkerchief from his back pocket reaches into the car and lightly wipes off the top of the steering wheel.

"Had a little bit of dust on top here boys."

Jeb continues to wipe down the entire wheel and the driver's side of the dashboard.

"Maybe I shouldn't have told you that story," remarks Jeb.

Bill interrupts, speaking softly with a relaxed calm in his voice;

"Your son John was taken to Heaven by an angel... and he's doing well. Those of us who remain on Earth after losing a loved one always suffer the most. You'll be together again... the Lord has promised you that."

Jeb is instantly affected by the unexpected directness and accompanying healing spirit of the message that seemed to fill his heart. There was a sense of peace he hadn't felt for a long time.

Roger continues to stand quietly nearby watching Jeb as he carefully folds and returns the handkerchief to his back pocket.

Roger is equally affected by Bill's message and purposely shifts his attention to re-examining the condition of the car and engine compartment. He wonders how Bill knew the name of Jeb's son.

As Roger closes the hood of the Corvette he tells Jeb;

"My father was killed in World War II. I understand your feeling of loss Jeb. It never leaves you.

Bill and I are both military...Air Force. We're on our way to

Vance air base in Oklahoma."

Jeb nods and says;

"If you want the car...it's yours. My son would be pleased that it went to someone serving their country."

Roger replies;

"Okay, it's a deal Jeb. Your Corvette just joined the Air Force!"

Jeb smiles politely and just as his eyes begin to swell up with emotion he immediately changes the subject.

"You boys have to meet my wife Millie...we were having coffee and some of her homemade blueberry pie when you came up the road. Let's head over to the house...join us for a bit. You'll like Millie. She'll be happy to know where the car's going.

A "Vette" On the Road

Roger, Bill and the newly purchased Corvette have been on the road for several hours heading west on Route 62 to Oklahoma City. The convertible top is down and the radio is belting out Nelson Riddle's Route 66 Theme above the wind and engine noise. It's a great day to be riding in the open air. They slow down as they approach the small town of Meeker, Oklahoma.

"There's a gas station just ahead...we need to fuel up."

Roger downshifts and pulls into the station; stopping at an open pump. Roger quips;

"The engine's been running really smooth after we blew out some of the carbon. This is one sweet lady!"

The station attendant walks out of the office;

"What can I do for you men today?"

Roger answers;

"Filler up...premium...and could you check the tire pressures."

Bill has been looking at the car manual and says;

"I'll check on the engine oil for you Rog...How about unlocking the hood for me."

They both climb out of the car and huddle over the engine

compartment. Bill looks for and then reaches for the dipstick.

Roger asks;

"Bill, I have a question…Back at the barn when we were talking to Jeb…How did you know the name of his son?…he never mentioned the name *John* anytime in conversation.

Bill removes the dipstick and closely examines it;

"The oil is right up there; looks good Rog" and then continues to answer the question;

"Hey, did you forget Rog…I'm the *Professor* who knows all!"

Bill pauses a moment sensing Roger is not satisfied with his easy answer, and continues;

"I guess you could call it a lucky guess…that's all…It seemed right at that moment…'John' just seemed to slip off my tongue."

Bill closes the hood and looks at Roger. We better get movin. We've got some jets waiting for us.

Chapter 9
The Demons Den

A meeting is underway in a dark, uncharted and demonic place in the lower universe chosen for its total isolation from all earthly and Heavenly activity. Four demons are present; Wilbourne, Sunhell, Sardoz and Makarovich

Devlin Wilbourne paces the floor and turns to demons **Sunhell, Sardoz and Dudorov**. As he prepares to speak his arms reach upward in a wide expanse adding physical and emotional emphasis to the opening of the meeting;

"The heavens and firmament above are filled with talk of a major miracle to take place on earth!"

He pauses for a moment as if to gather more strength before continuing. He takes a deep audible breath and announces in a deeper tone of voice;

"The Lord Himself is directing this action!"

Then, with much quieter and slower whisper like tones he adds;

"But the nature of this major miracle is known only to the highest order of angels."

Suddenly his voice heightens to a louder higher pitch summation;

"This means those two damn 'do-gooders'; Michael and Gabriel are involved!"

There is a stunned silence generated from the gathering before the meeting returns to a more normal tone;

"Yes, my friends, the spiritual battle continues on earth with more ferocity...and we will respond with no hesitation ...What shall our next step be? What action shall we take?"

A long silence follows as Wilbourne waits for a response. ...There is none.

Devlin Sunhell did not want to attend today's meeting and sarcastically voices his displeasure;

"Once again Wilbourne you speak to us in your grandiose godlike theatrical tones!"

With an imitative, sarcastic voice and dramatically exaggerated body gyrations, Sunhell mocks Wilbourne's presentation;

*"A major miracle from Heaven is planned by the Lord!
Michael and Gabriel are actively involved!...Oh My! Oh My!
What shall we do!?"*

Sunhell continues with a condescending voice and says;
"You offer no details or possible solutions. It's always...*What
shall we do!*
You contribute nothing!
You need to return to Hell's Fires Wilbourne! Maybe someone
there will appreciate your theatrics!"

Devlin Sardoz is severely irritated and interrupts with a loud and
commanding voice replying;
"Demon Sunhell, remain still! Your constant sniveling and
cheap performances annoy me and test my patience.
My friend Wilbourne means well...besides, I have already
identified two key human participants whose destinies are
directed by the *Heavenly Orders* in support of the so called
"miracle event."
The two humans are brothers... Roger and Alan McConnell.
They call Alan *Stormy*! I'll show him some real storms!"
The group breaks out into loud laughter. When they become
quiet Sardoz continues;
"I have taken the preliminary steps of creating a series of
challenging scenarios to play in their everyday lives and in such
a way as to completely obliterate their participation and support
of the so called *Heavenly Orders* from the Lord.
Oh, a special applause to Brother Windstedt; who, driving an
old pickup truck, disguised himself as an old and vial looking
man and visited the brothers in San Jon. Shall I say he
'introduced' himself with his unique and personal style of
cordiality.
I had an encounter with one of the McConnells at the Air Force
Academy. It was not completely successful...but in the very near
future when conditions are right; I will retaliate with another,
catastrophic and I must confess... "a devilishly macabre event."
It even employs an historical icon; my favorite foreboding

Renegades

symbol; the *Black Raven.*

It will be a very "good and demonic" day.

So, I am glad to report all is well good friend, brother… and my leader DemonWilbourne!"

Devlin Wilbourne is elated;

"Excellent work …very good indeed…I can always depend on you Sardoz!...continue with your work.

Wilbourne continues with the meeting and calls out to Devlin Dudorov:

Demon Dudorov…what political activities do you have to report?

Dudorov reports;

"I also have only good news to report . The Paris Summit Conference was cancelled by the Russian leader; Premier Nikita Khrushchev…cancelled because of an American spy pilot.

I knew of spy pilot Powers and his regular U-2 missions over the Soviet Union for quite some time. I was able to provide the exact coordinates of the U-2's secret flight plan from fellow demons working undercover in the United States and forwarded the information to Soviet missile crews. The U-2 was an easy target. These *Cold War* activities are fueled even more by lies and mistrust…my two specialty items! It gets even better.

The Americans made fools of themselves; claiming Powers was on a weather research mission and wandered off course! Lies work so well and do so much with very little effort. There will be no Paris Summit.

I am also pleased to report; my active participation in the KGB is been rewarded. I've been assigned a key position and post in Africa. Brother Sardoz identified the McConnells in God's plan…I have identified another player in Africa...**Jean Paul Boyer.** He is the young son of an American missionary and some kind of student scientist, do-gooder who is gaining massive local popularity along the Sahel because of his knowledge in agriculture. His intervention has provided more food and hope to the natives there. I believe he is a key person in God's miracle plan…so, I have an alternate plan offering a final resolution and end to this individual and his work. It involves *Gulags.*

I love the Russian Gulags. Gulags and lies always work

together so well...don't you agree brother Wilbourne?"
Wilbourne replies;

"Oh yes most definitely Dudorov...Just proceed with your
plan. I will not question or need to know all the details or tactics
of your plan. Just do it! The Master will be very pleased with
your progress and continuing efforts.

Concluding our meeting, I received a brief report from brother
Devlin-Dinh Ton, a Colonel and pilot in the North Vietnamese
Air Force. He reports shooting down two American naval
aircraft! He says he is enjoying his new assignment!

Our meeting must end now. There is much work to be done.
Let us depart and continue our Master's bidding.

Oh, and **Sunhell**...Come here. I would like to talk to you. I
have a very special assignment in mind.

I am sending you to Moscow and a mission to Siberia as a
Russian soldier. You will assume the name and character of
Master Sergeant Devlin Poplavski. You will be given a
'special assignment' when you arrive in Moscow."

Chapter 10
"The Dollar Ride"
July 18, 1960
Vance AFB - Enid, Oklahoma

    A month has passed since 2nd Lieutenants Roger McConnell and Bill Delaney pass through the main gate of Vance AFB for Undergraduate Pilot Training. They are assigned to the "B Flight" student squadron and to the base dormitory quarters.

    Thirty students compose the class. The majority are Air Force with two Navy ensigns and a Marine officer. The first month of training is a long course of academics; an information rush of all things related to flying from meteorology to parachute landing to high altitude chamber testing.

    Gradually building is a new and swelling sense of individual competition. Every student has one goal in mind; to be the best. Earning a high academic and performance score means selection to the coveted career track of a fighter pilot...not an air transport or helicopter driver...but a pilot at the controls of a single seat, supersonic fighter aircraft.

    Finally, the day of the first jet flight arrives. It's called "The One Dollar Ride". The instructor pilot (IP) is more or less a tour guide on the student's familiarization ride in a jet aircraft. The IP does the majority of the flying. The student is a passenger. It is a tradition for the student to give his instructor a tip; a one dollar bill at the end of the flight. The dollar is usually creatively enhanced by the student with added graphics or sayings that may or may not reflect the highest standard of Air Force protocol.

The Day Begins - 5:00 AM

    The Flight Room has its own character. The walls, covered with pictures of aircraft, awards and memorabilia given to the instructors also display several posters with various quotations that have earned a place of recognition by past pilots;

"May your landings always equal your take offs!" or

"What's the difference between God and a fighter pilot? God doesn't think he's a fighter pilot."

The instructors desks are positioned along the side walls. The 30 students of *B Flight* are sitting in chairs positioned in a circle in the center of the room. McConnell and the others wait in silence for the class to begin.

On recommendation from students of earlier flights most students of *B Flight* decided against the usual morning breakfast as aerobatics may be part of the flight.

The silence of the room is suddenly interrupted; "Good Morning Gentleman...Welcome members of *Bravo Flight* and congratulations on your selection to five months of intensive study and Air Force pilot training that is the best in the world. I'm Colonel Peter Warren, head of Flight Training here at Vance. We'll get right to business this morning as we have a tight flying schedule ahead of us.

However, before you leave for the flight line and your familiarization flight; we have a game to play gentlemen! It's called *"Stand-Up"*; a game especially enjoyed and played by all past generations of Vance aviation cadets. Your participation is required. For the next three weeks you'll have to qualify for the privilege of your daily flight training. Each student will come forward and stand in front of the class and provide answers to questions derived from the *Notes, Warnings, and Cautions* section in the T-37 pilot's technical order you have all been studying; affectionately known as '*Dash 1*'.

If your answer is incorrect...you are to sit down. The next student will be given the opportunity to provide the correct answer for the item that was previously missed.

If you are unfortunate enough to sit down three times; you will be removed from the flying schedule for the day and remain here to study your *Dash 1* manual.

Your IP...who will continue the briefing this morning is Captain William Ramos.

Captain...let's get the ball rolling this morning so we can go flying!"

Captain Ramos walks briskly from the back of the room

and turns to the class. He smiles and begins;

"Thank you Colonel Warren…Gentlemen, the T-37 jet aircraft you will be flying today is a 'forgiving aircraft'. It is 'forgiving' when and only when you speak to it properly…you speak to the aircraft by your correct inputs to the flight controls and following all the procedures and notes you have studied in *Dash1*.

Okay! I will begin and ask for volunteers. Who wants to lead the formation and be the first to play *Stand-Up* and go flying?"

McConnell is surprised at his uncontrolled action. Before Ramos even finishes the sentence; his hand is fully extended, raised high in the air. Ramos looks pleased and nods to McConnell to come forward;

"Very good…Lt. McConnell displays an aggressive attitude that we like to see in a fighter pilot."

His friend, Bill Delaney is sitting nearby and whispers to McConnell as he stands up;
"Good luck man…bold move!"

As McConnell walks forward he wonders why his arm volunteered so eagerly. He reaches the center of the class and turns facing them.
"Let's begin with this situation Lieutenant!" Ramos speaks in an optimistic tone of undiluted confidence as if knowing he'll hear the correct answer.

"You are flying straight and level at cruising altitude. A *Fire Detect* warning light on the panel illuminates. What would you do?"
McConnell recalls the exact procedure and answers;

"Sir, first, the fuel shutoff T-Handle is pulled to the **Off** position …and Second, the throttle is pulled full back to **Cut-off**. After the **fuel shutoff** T-handle is pulled, an immediate drop in fuel flow to 100 PPH, which is the minimum reading, is an indication the fuel shot-off valve has operated. Failure to get indication that the fuel shutoff valve has closed could indicate a continuing source of fuel to feed a fire even after the engine is shut-down with the throttle."

Ramos continues the scenario;
"Okay, these corrective actions did not extinguish the fire, smoke is in the cockpit…what would you do now?

Chapter 10 – *The Dollar Ride*

McConnell pauses for less than a second;
"Sir, I would have to eject from the aircraft."

Ramos nods with approval;
"Okay, okay...very good McConnell. I'll accept all your answers. Grab your gear and report to the flight line."

Ramos pauses till McConnell leaves the room.

"Let's move on...this is the final call for volunteers, otherwise, you'll have to wait till I provide a personal invitation! Who's next?"

On The Flight Line

The Training Aircraft
Cessna T-37A
Crew: 2
Length: 29 ft. 3 in
Wingspan: 33 ft. 9⅓ in
Height: 9 ft. 2 in
Empty weight: 4,056 lb.
Max.takeoff weight: 6,569 lb.
Powerplant: 2 × Continental-Teledyne J69-T-25 turbojets
Maximum speed: 425 mph / 369 knots
Range: 810 nautical miles / 932 miles
Service ceiling: 35,000 ft.

The Cessna built T-37 is a new training aircraft for the Air Force. It's given the unofficial nickname "Tweet" or "Tweety Bird" from the high pitched whistle made by its small twin turbojet engines. Some pilots hearing the engines for the first time call it a "6000 pound dog whistle".

The T-37 sits low to the ground. The crew can step into the cockpit while standing on the tarmac...no large step-up ladders needed. The cockpit is designed for the student and instructor to sit side by side. This allows the instructor to provide constant monitoring and direction during the flight. The close proximity also allows immediate and remedial correction by the instructor which is usually a simple hand slap if the student reaches for the wrong switch or a more severe recourse given by a solid yank on the connecting hose of the student's oxygen mask.

Renegades

McConnell steps outside the hangar and onto the tarmac. He sees two long lines of T-37s parked and being preflighted by ground crews. He hears one of the "Tweets" starting its engine. His fascination with the flight line activity is interrupted;

"Lieutenant McConnell...I'm Captain Russ Meradith. I'm your IP today. Are you ready to go flying? It looks like a good day for your first flight!"

McConnell instantly likes his instructor's informal attitude and offering a kind looking smile with his greeting. A "kind smile" is a rare commodity not often seen by student pilots.

As they walk to the aircraft Meradith reveals a bit of personal history as a former "Hun Driver", a fighter pilot of an F-100 Super Sabre who recently returned from Korea.

Nearly an hour is spent preflighting the T-37 exterior and interior following the long checklist covering every system from flight controls to the location and procedure for removing the safety pins on the ejection seats and canopy systems.

As they climb into the cockpit Meradith asks;
"By the way McConnell, are you the guy with the white Vette I've seen parked on base?"
"Yes sir...but I've not had any time to take it for any rides lately." McConnell replies.
"That's one fine machine. I think you'll appreciate the *Tweet's* precise handling as well even though it doesn't have the 0-60 acceleration of your vette."

As the clear plexiglass canopy of the T-37 is lowered, Meradith and McConnell fasten and tighten their shoulder harnesses, flight helmets and adjust the oxygen masks.

Meradith switches on the intercom:
"Have you had any civilian flight time in addition to your Primary training in the T-34?"

McConnell is somewhat startled at the loud and clear sound of the first communication through his helmet. He answers;
"Yes sir, I have my private license with about 300 hours."
Meradith casually replies;
"Very good...I'll go through the checklist, demonstrate the procedures for engine startup and handle all radio communication today...Our radio call sign is *23 Bravo*. I'll let you taxi out to the runway and handle the takeoff. How does

Chapter 10 – *The Dollar Ride*

that sound?"

McConnell's broad smile is completely hidden by the oxygen mask covering his face. He calmly replies trying to control his excitement and maintain a professional attitude;

"Sounds like an excellent plan, thank you sir!"

Takeoff

McConnell is on the taxiway guiding the T-37 to Runway 35C. After initially over controlling with the brakes and steering and wandering slightly left and right of the centerline he begins to get the "ground feel" of the aircraft. He arrives at runway 35C. The tower controller is following the progress of aircraft *23 Bravo*;

"Delta Flight 23Bravo hold short of runway 35 till further instructed."

McConnell presses both toe brakes on the upper portion of the T-37's rudder pedals. The aircraft comes to a complete stop behind the white line marking the end of the taxi way and the entry point to the active runway. Another T-37 is landing and passes overhead and touches down on the runway. Two puffs of white smoke are seen as the main wheels touch the pavement.

Meradith gives some final instructions;

"Okay Lieutenant, when tower gives us clearance, I want you to turn onto the runway…line up with the centerline and come to a complete stop. Then, apply full brakes…slowly advance engines to full throttle and finally release the brakes. At 65 knots begin to gently pull back on the stick and raise the nose. The aircraft will lift itself off the runway at about 90 knots. Maintain your runway heading with the centerline and always be looking outside and clearing the area for other aircraft. Don't bury your head in the instruments."

The tower frequency comes alive;

"Delta Flight 23 Bravo; you're cleared for immediate takeoff."

Meradith replies; "23 Bravo" and then opens the intercom.

"Okay Lieutenant…the aircraft is all yours."

McConnell presses the rudder pedal toe brakes as hard as he can and eases the throttle steadily forward till reaching full military power. He immediately notices the engine's lack of spontaneity compared to prop aircraft. The RPMs gradually build till finally reaching 90 percent. McConnell releases the brakes. The T-37 responds with gentle acceleration. He had hoped for more performance but he can now validate the rumor circulated by many pilots who thought the new *Tweet* was underpowered. McConnell is somewhat disappointed in the performance. He remembers the *Vette* offering much more acceleration than this!

The airspeed increases but at a slow pace. At 65 knots he pulls back on the stick and lifts the nose wheel off the runway. Then seconds later, almost politely, the Tweet becomes airborne without any fuss. He reaches over and raises the gear handle to the full up position. The gear cycles and three green lights are displayed on the panel.

McConnell is gaining respect, confidence and excitement in the "tweet" as the airspeed increases. He's flying over 200 knots now and still increasing.

Meradith seems satisfied with the takeoff;

"Okay...good, reduce your airspeed to 170 and turn to a heading of 200 degrees and delay your initial climb out for about a minute...maintain 1200 feet. There's some traffic just above us.

We'll be heading to the practice area this morning as soon as the traffic situation looks a little better...

Okay, turn to a heading of 270 degrees."

Suddenly, without warning Meradith grabs the control stick and banks sharply to the right. McConnell is slammed to the side of the cockpit.

The entire cockpit explodes. A small flock of birds slam into and break through the right side of the windscreen. McConnell's visor is down and offers some protection. He looks down at his flight suit covered with blood, flesh and bone. Blood is deposited everywhere in the cockpit.

The wind noise is deafening. All loose items; the charts and checklists are sucked out of the cockpit by the swirling suction of the damaged windscreen.

He looks to his right. Meradith is motionless. He's slumped forward, face down...held in place by his restraining shoulder straps. His visor is down but cracked and broken in several pieces. His face is partially visible; covered in blood streaming from the left side of his face. The bird strike was a direct hit on the right windscreen panel.

McConnell suddenly realizes he has lost his instructor and is now the pilot in command. He firmly grasps the stick and returns the aircraft from a descending and severe right banking turn to straight and level flight. With his hand he wipes debris off the airspeed indicator and altimeter with his glove.
He calls Vance tower and declares an emergency.

"Vance tower this is Delta Flight 23Bravo. I have an emergency.
We've had a bird strike. The right windscreen is gone…the left side in front of me is still intact."
McConnell looks to his right at Captain Meradith.
"My instructor is injured and unconscious. I'm 20 miles north of the field at 2000 feet. Tower, I need your assistance."
The tower responds immediately;

"23 Bravo understand your situation…emergency vehicles and medical support are dispatched…we have you on radar and will vector you for a straight in approach to Runway 35 Charlie.
How many hours do you have logged in the T-37?"
McConnell looks at the panel clock;
"About 20 minutes tower…"
There is a long silence with no response.
McConnell reopens the communication;

"Tower, I can handle this…I have primary flight time and a couple hundred hours on my private license. This Cessna "37" reminds me of the Cessna "172" I used to fly…It's from the same family with a couple added steroids! Vector me in. I've got to get my instructor back on the ground …he's in really bad shape."
The tower responds with added confidence;
"Roger on that…Come to heading of 3-5-0. We've cleared the area of all traffic. Remember the checklist; landing gear down and locked…add full flaps with slight increase on the throttle…You need to maintain an airspeed of 95 knots till touchdown. After landing come to a complete stop and shutdown your engines. Emergency vehicles are standing by to assist."
McConnell glances to his right at Meradith;
There's still no movement. He returns to the immediate situation

of lining up with the runway and landing..

The landing gear extends and locks in place. McConnell sets the wing flaps to the landing position and inches up the throttles. The aircraft continues to perform admirably... but the runway is coming up too fast.

McConnell adjusts his descent; pulls back slightly on the stick. At about 10 feet above the runway he throttles back the engines to idle.

The T-37 settles down, gently touching the runway. He immediately brakes and retracts the flaps. The aircraft comes to a complete stop. McConnell shuts down the twin engines.

Emergency vehicles arrive and form a circle around the aircraft. Ground crews rush forward. McConnell is helped out of the aircraft. Meradith is unfastened and lifted out of the ejection seat. McConnell watches as emergency crews secure the aircraft... then walks hurriedly towards the ambulance. He parts his way through the surrounding emergency personnel and sees the flight surgeon attending Meradith.

The entire medical team is working to revive the unconscious pilot. The team steps back while the surgeon continues with a series of electric defibrillations in an effort to restart the pilot's heart.

Finally the flight surgeon succumbs to accepting the final outcome...and steps back. He looks up from the lifeless form and visually acknowledges McConnell who is standing nearby. The surgeon shakes his head and reports to McConnell;

"There's nothing more I can do. He didn't make it son."

As he speaks, tears begin to cloud McConnell's eyes. He struggles to keep them back.

For others standing nearby the tears flowed freely. There was no "manly" shame for the emotions shown at that moment. The life and fledging career of Captain Russell Meradith, a young officer, a decorated combat veteran, who was well-liked by his contemporaries and loved by his family...just suddenly and tragically ended.

McConnell walks to the edge of the runway and sits down on the grass. The morning air feels fresh and clean but he suddenly feels weak and tired. The adrenalin rush is over. He lowers his head and closes his eyes. The events of the last hour begin replaying in his mind.

He senses someone nearby. He looks up. It's his friend Bill Delaney. Delaney is first to speak;

"Are you okay Rog?"

Roger nods but says nothing ...then looks up; his eyes are teared over. He replies;

"It was just a training flight Bill...that's all it was...a damn training flight...I don't understand."

Delaney sits down next to his friend and surveys the surrounding scene of flashing lights from the emergency vehicles and the abandoned T-37. He turns to Roger;

"You did good Rog...sometimes God doesn't seem to be in control...we don't understand why bad things happen to good people. We don't have the overall plan God has in mind. God is still in charge...even today Rog. Keep the faith."

Colonel Warren, the chief flight training officer, arrives on scene and closely inspects the aircraft. He finishes talking to the inspection team and walks toward McConnell and Delaney.

McConnell begins to stand up as he approaches.

"At ease men...as you were." the Colonel kneels down next to McConnell and asks;

"Are you doing okay Lieutenant?...that was an unfortunate accident...this is a new aircraft we've just introduced into training and we're discovering that your experience is not a unique or an isolated incident. Cessna is finding out that the forward windscreen has a design flaw with the Plexiglas material...and under certain conditions, such as your bird strike; it will shatter. The windscreen doesn't meet the original design specs and the manufacturer is working on flight guidelines and an appropriate replacement fix.

Bird strikes are always an ongoing problem in the flying environment...mainly at low altitudes; during takeoff and landings. You have to be alert...*and live with it.*

If everything checks out okay with the flight surgeon; I'd like to get you flying again as soon as possible. You're off tomorrow... then back on a full training schedule again. Does that sound okay Lieutenant?

McConnell answers;

"Yes sir... understood... I need to 'get back in the saddle

again' right?"
"That's right… I have one last item I'd like to discuss."
The Colonel becomes more conciliatory in tone.

"What you did today lieutenant was heroic. I was in the tower and listened to your radio communication. You took immediate command of the situation …and returned the aircraft and your instructor to base. You demonstrated a natural flying ability and remained cool in a very challenging and difficult situation… traits not usually seen in a student pilot.

I want you to know that when your training at Vance is completed…you have a guaranteed slot at Luke Air Force base for jet fighter training."

McConnell looks up and in a quiet voice acknowledges the offer;
"Thank you sir…very much appreciated."

A Discovery

An investigative team continues examining the T-37 before it's moved off the runway and to a hangar. Two officers finish taking photos of the interior cockpit area. One officer spots something unusual and calls out to the other;
"These bird 'remains' are different from anything around here.
"I don't believe it…Will you look and see what I found here?"

An entire body of a bird is discovered…seen wedged beneath the left side of the ejection seat.

"Careful…let me double check to make sure the safety key is in place...Okay, we're good; it's in place … I should be able to reach in and pullout that bird…

Okay here it is!...Let's see what we've got…it's chirping like crazy! Damn... I don't believe it! It's still alive!
The bird remains still for only a matter of seconds then spreads its wings and flies away.

The officer watches the bird disappear into the distance. He remarks;
"I know all the migratory birds in the area around here…but that bird is definitely not one of them…that was a *Black Raven*!

Chapter 10 – *The Dollar Ride*

They hit a whole flock of Black Ravens!
   Damn..I look at what happened here… all these Ravens.
I get a real bad feeling. This was no normal bird strike!"

"*Should my end come while I am in flight,*
Whether brightest day or darkest night;

Spare me your pity and shrug off the pain,
Secure in the knowledge that I'd do it again;

For each of us is created to die,
And within me I know, I was born to fly."

Chapter 11
Envoys in a Foreign Field
January 24, 1961-Timbuktu-Mali, Africa

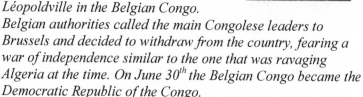

January 1959, under the leadership of Patrice Lumumba, riots broke out in Léopoldville in the Belgian Congo.
Belgian authorities called the main Congolese leaders to Brussels and decided to withdraw from the country, fearing a war of independence similar to the one that was ravaging Algeria at the time. On June 30th the Belgian Congo became the Democratic Republic of the Congo.

Between January and December of 1960, 17 sub-Saharan African nations, including 14 former French colonies, gained independence from their former European colonists. An entire continent was caught up in revolutionary times. United States intervention was needed.

Special Envoys have been used by every administration to address high-stake conflicts The Special Envoy is empowered by the President and Secretary of State, have clear mandates and a degree of latitude beyond normal bureaucratic restrictions.

Special Presidential Envoy Donald Richardsen

Donald Richardsen Sr. is a 42year old Special Envoy from the U.S diplomatic service. Richardsen's background is academic with a doctorate in African Studies and previous ambassadorial experience in four other African countries. The administration recently selected Richardsen as a primary candidate for Assistant Secretary of State for International Organization Affairs.

Postwar Africa has opened the door to a large number of "Cold War" confrontations between the U.S. and the Soviet Union over the dozens of newly independent and non-aligned African nations. Richardsen is dispatched to Africa. The current situation in the former Belgian Congo is very tense as new leadership struggles to establish a government under its newly acquired independence.

Richardsen is meeting with his Soviet counterpart Nikolay

Komarovsky in Mali at an open courtyard of the University of Sankore. The University is located in the remote North East district of Timbuktu and housed within the historic 989 A.D. Sankore Mosque.

There is only modest activity in the courtyard during the midmorning and the setting provides an opportunity for informal and private conversation. Both men walk across the courtyard, meet at a small weathered wooden table under the shade offered by the dense foliage of a 100 year old baobab tree.

Nikolay Komarovsky is a large Russian with a boisterous voice and matching ego. He speaks English and French fluently and greets his American counterpart;

"Ahhh Envoy Richardsen...my good friend from the United States...We meet again!"

Nikolay provides a Russian "bear hug" greeting upon meeting Richardsen.

Nikolay is unshaven and appears tired from lack of sleep. He wipes his moist brow with an over-used handkerchief. The above-normal morning temperature has already reached 90 degrees.

Nikolay asks;

"How is your son David? He is a young man now...am I right?"

"Yes, you're right, in fact he just graduated from college, worked on President Kennedy's campaign last year and now he's part of the administration and the new Peace Corps program. He accompanied me to Africa to lay the groundwork for an agricultural program in Tanzania. I believe he has more political aspirations than I have. He told me that he's planning to run for Congress."

Nikolay continues;

"Your new President Kennedy has some very idealistic goals and seems very dedicated to a revolution of human rights. He speaks to the young the people of a new generation."

Nikolay pauses in brief reflection before continuing;

"I appreciate your making the long flight from Leopodville to my station here in Mali. This is also a very long way from our last meeting at that wonderful air conditioned hotel in Paris!

I am not made for this climate. I ask you...what did we do

that was so deserving for our governments to send us here to this god forsaken out of the world place?"

Richardsen, assigned to the new Democratic Republic of the Congo is stationed in Léopoldville. He has lived and worked in Africa for many years and is familiar with the political environment and culture.

Wearing a white short-sleeve shirt and khaki shorts; he appears relaxed and comfortable in the austere desert surroundings.

He is genuinely pleased to see Nikolay. A working friendship and a mutual respect for each other helped form a long and uncluttered pathway to many successful negotiations that benefited the relationship of both countries. Richardsen smiles and replies:

"Nikolay…You seem unhappy with your assignment here. You forget that we are both pawns and servants to our governments…we have little control over our own destinies but are supposed to guide the future of our governments!"

Nikolay smiles and with a muted laugh…begrudgingly agrees;

"During the war Richardsen, I probably told you this many times, I was a ranking intelligence officer in the Army and coordinated many joint combat operations with your military. It was a good assignment. The United States and Russia…we were allies and together we defeated Germany. I always liked the Americans…we had much in common."

Nikolay pauses for a moment and wipes his brow.

"But now, with Khrushchev in power there is a cold wind of change. Unfortunately, it appears that we are no longer allies Richardsen! How did this happen?"

His voice drops to a lower more somber tone and answers his own question;

"I do not know. I do not understand!...but I do know the Party does not appreciate my work here in Africa…I've been recalled to Moscow and replaced by a KGB officer; Victor Devlin Dudorov. Dudorov is what you Americans call a 'bad ass' troublemaker. He has already been dispatched…

You'll know when he arrives."

Chapter 11 – *Envoys in a Foreign Field*

Nikolay pauses and again wipes his brow.

"I heard of your assignment to the Congo. This is a great challenge for you to be sure. The Congo acquired independence from Belgium but its first elected Prime Minister Patrice Lumumba was just murdered in January. The rebellious *Katangan* secessionists are responsible but there are signs that your CIA may have also been involved.

You listen...I am telling you this Richardsen...both countries are responsible. Lumumba's death and the increased warfare is caused by the intervention and supply of Russian guns and bullets to fight the opposition...this is the work of the war lover and KGB mentality of Dudorov and his political henchman! ...and this is the man who is to replace me!"

Richardsen interrupts;

"I was not aware of any Russian arms support to Lumumba. The United States was unsure of Lumumba's alliance...was it to the East or West?

Personally, I don't think Lumumba liked either of us very much Nikolay!"

Nikolay laughs loudly and adds;

"But Lumumba knew all too well we were both interested in the Congo's vast deposits of copper, gold, diamonds, cobalt, oil ...and uranium.

You have *the bomb*...the one delivered to Japan. Moscow claims you made it with African uranium. Russia also is working on *the bomb* and looking for a source of uranium. The Congo is important to both our countries."

There is an uncomfortable pause in the conversation. Richardsen changes the direction of discussion;

"Nikolay, I am truly sad to hear of your recall from Africa. I had hoped we could have worked together in certain areas to quiet these developing revolutionary forces and begin to build a basic framework for peace and stability."

Nikolay slowly nods his head in agreement...then looks directly at Richardsen and speaks in a stronger tone of voice;

"I share your thoughts...even though they are perhaps much too idealistic for the current state of affairs. I have read a report that UN Secretary-General, Dag Hammarskjold is flying here next month sometime; to lead negotiations for a cease fire agreement. He has a very difficult if not impossible task and is not a welcomed figure by many factions here....

However, we must move on. Before leaving I'd like to share another item of interest with you. Khrushchev is continuing an ongoing policy of closing a large number of prisons...the infamous "gulags" of the Soviet Union. I still regularly receive a monthly report of prisoners remaining in the most northern Siberian gulags. These isolated locations still remain 'open for business' as you say.

In the last report...I noticed one of the prisoner's name. It caught my attention as it stood out from the rest on the list. It seemed very out of place. The name never appeared on any previous reports. In a Soviet bureaucracy you can become lost in the system for many years and then suddenly without reason resurface and be found again!

Your government may be able to identify him. The name is McConnell...Captain David A. McConnell. He's not a new prisoner...I was able to locate and speak to the administrator at Verkhoyansk...the gulag where McConnell is being held. The administrator remembered seeing him on the very first day he arrived at Verkhoyansk...McConnell was a prisoner then...and that was 15 years ago. I could not obtain any other background information regarding his history or details of his present physical condition."

Nikolay hands Richardsen a copy of the report. Richardsen glances at the report and notices additional information on the other prisoners;

"There are nearly 100 other prisoners listed here...Most are from previous occupations in government scientific areas. The list also contains many artists and writers and church leadership..."

Richardsen interrupts;

"Nikolay, this looks like a specially designated gulag exclusively for highly educated individuals that did not go along with the political program!

I'll wire this information to Washington...be assured it will be encrypted and given *Top Secret* priority. Thank you for your attention to this detail...If I can ever be of any assistance.....

We must remain in communication even if conditions are

Chapter 11 – *Envoys in a Foreign Field*

difficult."

Nikolay responds with noticed regret;

"From the list you can see I too may not have the future I had hoped for. Moscow has probably already decided my fate.

There is a long, noticeable silence. Nikolay changes the direction of conversation and hesitantly asks;

"Do you believe in a *God* Richardsen?

Richardsen is somewhat surprised and taken aback by the question;

Yes, yes I do believe Nikolay. Why do you ask?"

Nikolay continues;

"Perhaps I've become more religiously aware in the autumn of my years…Religion has become more important to me…a point of personal focus. I joined the Orthodox Church in recent years…and it was good.

But now an anti-religious campaign is being undertaken by Khrushchev…it began last year. There have been mass closures of our churches, monasteries and seminaries. A campaign has banned the parental right to instruct religion to their children. This action is in addition a law restricting the attendance of children at church services.

I have publicly spoken and submitted written positions against these practices. I have become an old, almost retired revolutionary…a renegade! It is no surprise that the KGB is asking questions in upper government circles regarding my career record and past history."

Richardsen interrupts;

"Oh Nikolay, you've got to be more careful!…surely you know you're wading into very dangerous waters."

Nikolay nods in agreement but reaffirms his position for speaking out;

"Yes, of course, I know this, but when you reach those critical core areas of your belief system that define you…the point where you must take a stand no matter what the consequences…It becomes not a matter of choice anymore but a matter of necessity. I have reached that point."

Richardsen agrees and adds;

"I know exactly what you're saying …I've been there many times before".

Renegades

Richardsen continues;

"We both share many of the same views; the world is changing very rapidly; the political climate is changing between East and West…and the religious climate is becoming more volatile. If you need help Nikolay…let me know…I may be able to do something…would you consider coming to the United States?"

Nikolay lowers his head for a moment and then looks up;

"No…but I thank you for your kind words and the offering of support…but I must leave now. I should go. I have many matters to complete before leaving for Moscow."

There is a strong embedded sense of sorrow cradled with his departure;

"Have a good life my friend. Take care of yourself…and God be with you."

Richardsen continues to detect an ominous sense of finality in his departure…a voice lacking his customary optimism.

Nikolay stands up from the table. Richardsen follows and together they walk from the courtyard. They leave the university, exchanging remembrances and add departing words before continuing on separate paths.

Richardsen begins to walk on an unpaved city street towards the airfield adjacent to the University. A small chartered aircraft and pilot are waiting there for his return flight to Léopoldville. The narrow city street has several market places on each side which were crowded and busy earlier in the morning...but now are all strangely unattended…the street seems unusually quiet.

He continues to walk and is only a short distance from the airfield when without warning a series of rapid fire gunshots ring out. Richardsen turns and in the distance several blocks away sees his friend Nikolay falling to the ground. He's immediately picked up by two men and hurriedly carried to the covered rear cargo area of a large truck. The cargo door slams shut and is secured. The black unmarked truck pulls away and speeds towards Richardsen. A trail of dust and small stones are thrown into the air as it passes by.

The truck is a World War II, Russian upgrade of a *GAZ AA* military vehicle. It turns at the first connecting corner street and disappears from sight. Richardsen can't help but recall

Nikolay's exact words at the meeting when he spoke of his KGB replacement...Victor Devlin Dudorov;

"He has already been dispatched; you'll know when he arrives."

Richardsen struggles to process what he's just witnessed. His mind reels in confusion. His heart suddenly beats faster as he mentally replays and physically reacts to the visual impact of seeing the inhuman, indiscriminate fatal shooting of his friend. His walk becomes hurried and detached from the moment. Richardsen is almost unaware of his arrival at the airfield. He looks for the small unpainted aluminum hangar where the chartered twin engine aircraft was parked just a few hours ago. Now, instead, an unmarked grey auto is parked in its place. Two men sit quietly inside.

Suddenly, a young African boy comes running towards him. He's short of breath and frantically calls out in broken, struggling English;

"The pilot...your pilot...He is a friend of mine and had a big problem. He had to go home. He will fly back tomorrow morning and pick you up. He very, very sorry for any problem...that okay with you?"

Richardsen, irritated by the announcement snaps back in a short reply;

"You tell your friend; no return to Timbuktu...Richardsen gone...he found another pilot. Do you understand?"

The boy nods yes and says;

"I understand what you say. I tell my friend no return to Timbuktu."

The boy turns and runs off.

Richardsen looks at the unmarked grey vehicle still motionless and parked nearby. He knows he's being watched.

Richardsen looks around the airfield and sees a small single engine aircraft belonging to *Mission Aviation Fellowship* at the far end of the field. He can see the pilot and begins to walk with a brisk determined stride towards the aircaft.

The MAF pilot; Captain John Gadden is finishing his walk-around preflight inspection of the Cessna. He looks up and sees Richardsen approaching in the distance. He turns to his passenger, Dr. Amelia Anoza.

"It looks like we may have company Dr. Anoza. I hope it's not government trouble."

Captain Gadden and Dr.Anoza just completed a visitation and medical supply flight in support of several clinics along the Sahel region.

With the refueling accomplished, they are ready to takeoff and a flight to the nearby town of Mopti. The small hospital there is over run with emergency and critical care patients…very much in desperate need of medical assistance.

Because of the rush to African independence nearly all the European medical doctors left the country causing a critical shortage of medical care. There was never a program considered or promoted to establish medical schools or healthcare programs to educate and train native Africans as doctors or healthcare workers.

Dr. Anoza talks with the MAF pilot Gadden as he checks the engine oil and closes the engine cowling.

She asks;

"John, I never had a chance to ask but how long have you been flying with MAF?"

Gadden makes sure the cowling cover is secured…thinks for a moment and replies with a controlled smile;

"Everbody asks me that question doctor…I guess it must be about 30 plus years I've been a bush pilot.

I've got plenty of experience! I've flown in the Pacific, the United States and all over Africa. Most of my flying has been with *Mission Aviation Fellowship.* I have some 16,000 hours of flight time in little planes like this that get into short and rough airstrips of grass or dirt and sometimes runways "in the rough"…cut out of jungle bush.

You're probably also wondering …why I do it? My answer is simple.

It's a calling. I love God but I am no saint. I am at my happiest when I'm in hot pursuit of Him… and even better on the occasions when I actually catch up and spend time with Him…lots of time!

I keep my life simple. There are three aspects of my life that really define me; Family, Flying and God. Africa is an awesome place and I love it.

All of us from the west, especially from the United States assume people generally think like us when, in fact, almost nobody thinks like us!

That's important to remember when living in Africa. You have to change the way you think about some things if you are to function here with minimal frustration.

I try to help people with my little airplane to get over some of the obstacles in their lives and spread a bit of joy around while I'm at it....but Dr. Anoza, I have to admit that spreading joy hasn't been easy lately.

Africa wasn't prepared for independence. The Europeans just packed up and left...Right now, it's not easy for anyone living here."

Just as Dr. Anoza is about to respond...Richardsen arrives at the aircraft. He's out of breath and sounding desperate as he introduces himself;

"Hello...Sorry for this unannounced intrusion. My name's Richardsen, Donald Richardsen...I need your help... I desperately need to get back to Léopoldville to my office and family at the American station there. I'm with the U.S. State Department.

I just found out I was 'stood up' and no longer have my chartered plane or pilot and... I believe I'm being targeted by someone or some group who doesn't like my being here today! Can you help?"

Gadden response is accompanied with an understanding and widening sympathetic smile;

"You say you're being targeted?"

"I know so!" Richardsen exclaims;

"A Russian diplomat who I finished meeting with was murdered less than a half hour ago... just outside the airfield. I was nearby and saw it happen!"

Gadden replies;

"Mr. Richardsen; I understand where you're coming from. I also need help! I've been targeted and dodging local gunfire on most takeoffs and landings much too frequently!

Take a look here at my airplane!...you can see there are a half dozen bullet holes in the tail section that I picked up today!"

Renegades

Gadden continues;

"I believe I saw your plane takeoff about 10 minutes ago. The two Russians in that gray car over there…I heard them talking to your pilot. They had a spirited and pervasive "conversation". Your pilot jumped into his plane like a scared jack rabbit and took to the air as fast as he could. The two Russians stood by, laughing as he took off.

However, you are definitely in luck today Mr. Richardsen! I can help you. I'm headed to Mopti airfield and you're welcome to come along. It's a short flight to Mopti. *Air Mali* has a flight out of there in the late afternoon to Léopoldville.

Climb aboard! We'd better leave now. I'm a bit uneasy about seeing those two Russians as well.

Captain Gadden climbs into the left front seat of the cockpit. He starts the engine and turns to the rear seating area and speaking over the idling engine makes a quick introduction;

"I forgot to introduce you two. Mr. Richardsen… meet Dr. Amelia Anoza from Chicago. She's been working the Sahel region with me offering her medical services."

Amelia, who quietly listened to Richardsen's story, shares her thoughts;

"I am very worried Mr. Richardsen. The political situation in Africa is fluid and tenuous. Escalating forces seem to be building and leaning towards armed conflict in several regions.

Along the Sahel today there are massive shortages of food, water and medical care…and now the possibility of civil wars! It's too much to comprehend."

Captain Gadden lines up the aircraft in the center of a worn path of dirt and grass that roughly resembles the outline of a runway. He eases the throttle forward.

He shouts above the engine noise as they pick up speed; "We're a harder target to hit from the ground if we stay low. The snipers usually position themselves at the end of the runway."

The Cessna clears the area without incident and sets a course towards the Mopti airfield. Richardsen turns to Amelia;

"I have lost a good friend today. We shared a vision of building a framework of peace here…he was killed by his own countrymen! You're right Dr.Anoza; It's too much to comprehend."

Chapter 11 – *Envoys in a Foreign Field*

Chapter 12
Back in the USSR
January 24, 1961- Over northern Siberia

The 1942 Doolitle Raid on Japan was successful but because of a shortage of fuel 11 of the 16 crews were forced to bail out over China and 4 aircraft crash landed near the Chinese coast. The only surviving bomber No. 40-2242 made a "wheels down" landing in Siberia at Primorskrai Airfield; near Vladivostok. The crew was interned by Russia for just over a year before being released. The aircraft was flown by Russian pilots from Primorskrai to Semenovka Airbase and finally ordered to Moscow and incorporated into the 65th Air Wing, a Special Forces attachment known for its use of unique designed aircraft. The aged bomber was eventually retired from service in 1960 and scheduled to be scrapped. Then, a last minute and questionable "under the table" offer was accepted by a lower level government official for private ownership as a cargo aircraft to deliver mail and supplies to the distant and isolated Russian towns and villages in northern Siberia.

Now,the Soviet Union; in a period of de-stalinization triggered by Stalin's death in 1953 is experiencing new freedoms and a less repressive era under the leadership of Nikita Krushchev.

The reprieved U.S. Army Air Force Mitchell B-25 Medium Bomber is now a less dignified bare metal civilian cargo plane. The U.S. Army's olive drab paint originally identifying the aircraft was removed and Soviet markings added during its service with the 65th Air Wing. Only a faded partial outline of a red star can be seen from a distance on the side of the fuselage. Now there's an added display of earned scars; small dents and scratches highlighted with smatterings of varied colored mud deposited during takeoffs and landings from a long list of undeveloped rural airstrips in the Soviet Union. The original 1700 HP Wright radials were replaced years ago with Soviet built engines. The extra fuel tanks added for the Doolittle raid are now bare metal inside and prone to leaking. Russian aviation fuel, because of its poor production quality, is highly corrosive and dissolved the rubber lining material inside the fuel tanks.

The civilian crew and new owners are Sergey Ramzin; a 60 year old retired Soviet Air Force and Aeroflot transport pilot and his 21 year old son Yury, a former employee apprentice of the Soviet Aircraft Design Bureau.

It's 22 degrees Fahrenheit inside the cockpit. With his heavily gloved hand, Sergey wipes an accumulated layer of frost from the inside windscreen. He looks through the small opening in an effort to spot a land mark river to confirm they are still following the planned course. It's mid-afternoon but there's only the dim twilight of the Siberian winter barely revealing details of the land below.

Their flight path continues through a strong low pressure front…a massive front producing a continuous collection of local snow squalls with a strong headwind and accompanied rough air.

Onboard is a cargo consignment for delivery to the far northern Siberian village of Verkhoyansk.

Verkhoyansk is known as "Stalin's Death Ring." because of its reputation as a place where Stalin sent his political exiles. The −76F (-60C) climate challenges the survival rate for both man and machine. Mercury hardens in thermometers. Oil and fuel in an unattended aircraft thickens. Upon landing aircraft engines are always kept idling and never shut down unless a hangar or auxiliary heating units are available.

At low Siberian temperatures air no longer retains any humidity…water vapor instantly changes to a form of ice dust. The result is a unique fog existing wherever there's human activity. This phenomenon gradually draws liquid from the body through the lungs making constant thirst and coughing common symptoms shared by Verkhoyansk and all Siberian natives. Bronchitis and pneumonia are common medical problems.

The natural wildlife provides additional challenges for survival. One week ago Verkhoyansk was attacked by a pack of 400 wolves; killing 100 horses and thousands of reindeer.

The cargo list for Verkhoyansk declares fifteen crates of live chickens, four crates of live turkeys, spare parts for the village electric generator, medical supplies, several bags of mail and a dozen assorted dry good packages.

A premium product carried onboard is stored in one of the extra fuel tanks originally installed for the Doolittle Tokyo raid. Instead of fuel, the tank now holds 94 liters (25 gallons) of *Moskovskaya* vodka; an early Russian brand introduced in 1894. A less expensive vodka in one of the other tanks is also available and used on more than one occasion for deicing the aircraft's main wings before takeoff.

Sergey turns to Yury shouting;

"I am lost! I must know where we are flying. Try the radio …there is a navigation beacon near Batagay....I see nothing below…only snow and fog."

There's no other way to describe the cockpit environment than *cold and deafening*. With no sound suppression material or insulation; there's no relief from the thunderous volume and vibration of the two engines as well as the stinging bite of -60C arctic air passing over the thin outside aluminum skin. Conversation is difficult if not impossible.

With his gloves removed Yury carefully rotates the tuner on the navigation radio with incremental precision while intermittently pressing the headset firmly against his ears… straining to hear the identifying sound of the Batagay radio beacon. The only sound received is a constant stream of static.

"I hear nothing Sergey!…Nothing at all. There may be a problem with our radio."

Unexpectedly the aircraft enters an isolated pocket of clear and open sky. Suddenly the sun shines brightly and a town is visible below.

Sergey shouts;

"Yury look! That's the Yana River! Batagay is directly ahead…I see the runway lights at Batagay airport."

Sergey's smile broadens;

"We'll land and wait till morning…maybe the weather clears by then…but tonight we have good hot cabbage borscht, *Moskovskaya* and maybe we invite one of those chickens in the back to our dinner! What do you say Yury!"

The mood in the cockpit has changed from prolonged tension to immediate jubilation as Sergey turns on the landing lights and the retired American Mitchell bomber touches down on the

Renegades

frozen partially iced runway of the Russian Siberian airport.

As the plane taxis towards the flight office...the airport manager, Victor Kologrigov comes running towards them. He's carrying a large lantern; illuminating his hooded parka and a home-made leather mask protecting his face.

Sergey opens the cockpit side window and hollers;

"Victor...Victor my friend, I need a warm hangar for my American beauty. I have *Moskovskaya* for you!

Victor jubilantly responds; waving the lantern high in the air; excited and looking forward to seeing his friends again at this isolated outpost. He points to the hangar closest to the main building and walks briskly towards the wooden structure. The main hangar door is suspended on a single guide rail. Victor pushes the heavy door along the rail and signals Sergey to taxi the plane inside.

As Sergey opens the throttle a cloud of snow is thrown backward and then blown forward by a strong gust of surface wind. Victor covers his face from the cloud of blowing ice and snow. The aircraft taxies slowly into the sheltered hangar and comes to a stop. The twin engines are shutdown. Victor closes the hangar door.

The aircraft's lower entry hatch opens and two tired crew members climb slowly down its attached ladder. Both walk with a noticeable stiffness caused by the hours of confined flying time spent in a cold cockpit.

Evening Dinner

In this region of Siberia the December sun neither sets nor rises but remains hidden below the horizon. The snow has stopped but the outside temperature drops ten degrees. Yury and Sergey sit at a small table near a huge stone fireplace in the office and living quarters of their friend Victor. The dinner of borscht, chicken and vodka is shared with conversation on the changing times in the Soviet Union.

"Life is better without Stalin!" Victor exclaims

"Kruschev is closing some of the gulags...and some he is leaving open! There are still many prisoners being held at Verkhoyansk...Things do not change very fast in Siberia...this is why I live here. I am far and away from the politics and dictates of Moscow."

Sergey laughs loudly as he puts down his glass of vodka.

"Victor, Victor…you can never get far enough from Moscow …unless you leave the motherland!"

Sergey pauses and takes another sip of vodka than continues;

"I share this confidential information with you Victor because I trust you like a brother. I have spoken to no one about this. My son Yury and I are planning an extended "vacation"; a "change of residence" from the Soviet Union. The KGB has been watching us because of some loyalty infractions in the past. This is why Yury was dismissed from the Aircraft Design Bureau. I am getting more uncomfortable as time passes. The KGB is relentless.

Yury, has remained unusually quiet during the evening dinner looks up and turning to Victor says;

"There is no future for me here…I know that. I need freedom. I want to go to a university…to have control of my life. This is important to me and for my future. My father and I have a plan. We are working on it now and waiting for the right time."

Victor nods in agreement…and waves his hand through the air acknowledging the difficult future and limited opportunities in the Soviet economy.

"I understand what you say Yury. I am loyal to you and your father."

Sergey asks;

"Victor, perhaps you can help us. Have you ever visited the Verkhoyansk gulag?"

Victor answers;

"Oh yes, I know the administrator there; Andrey Ivanov. I know Andrey quite well. We are working together on a special project."

Sergey continues;

"Did you know they are holding an American there…he was captured and held prisoner with hundreds of Germans during the war. For years he was transferred to different gulags and became a forgotten misplaced number in the Soviet penal system. I first met him when unloading cargo a month ago. He

Renegades

was working at the airport with several other prisoners."

Sergey's Russian speech becomes slower and more studied as he attempts to correctly pronounce the American name;

"His name is..."*Mik-Konnell*"... "*David Mik-Konnell*". He says he was a pilot...a captain in the American Army...and claims to have flown the first bombing mission over Japan! He's also trying to escape...to go home and enjoy freedom...like we want to do Victor! We have talked with him only once ...I told him of our plan to go to America. The rescue of an American pilot could be very valuable in our plan."

Suddenly, there's a strange silence in the room.

Victor begins to laugh ...slowly at first...then his voice crescendos to a loud uncontrolled boisterous confession.

He hollers; "Sergey! And Yury!...I must tell you!

I am also planning an escape to the United States....to Miami Beach...with my friend Andrey, the gulag administrator. Andrey is not in agreement with the so called 'loyalty crimes' assigned to new prisoners sent to him. They are all young Russian writers, artists and scientists. Many have families with them. They are all creative, educated at universities and all seek freedom for their lives.

I told Andrey...tell the prisoners we'll all leave together'...and with the American pilot!"

Sergey surprised, shocked and without words on hearing Victor's disclosure; hesitantly nods in agreement and finally is able to reluctantly ask;

"Victor, tell me please... how many prisoners are you including in this escape plan of yours?"

Victor with a casual response replies;

"I say, probably about 100!"

Sergey immediately asks;

"...And how are they...and you going to get to the United States?"

Victor instantly displays a large confident smile;

"We will fly there of course!....I told Director Ivanov about you and Yury and how you would be able to fly everyone to the United States of America in your airplane...this would not be a problem...would it?"

Chapter 12 – *Back In The USSR*

Hey Brother Alan,

How goes it at the airplane factory? Have you got your new "swing wing" TFX/F-111 flying yet?

Well, I made it. These are the final weeks of flight training at Luke Air Force Base's "Fighter Pilot U". After graduation I'll be headed to an F-100 squadron; the 27th Tactical Fighter Wing at Cannon...back home to New Mexico.

But the road along the way... especially here at Luke...has been a challenge...but not with the flight training. Stay with me on this letter brother. I just need to "talk it out" and clear my head of some of the issues I've encountered.

I learned on the first day at Luke you definitely have an advantage if you have a "thick skin". The instructors are all seasoned fighter pilots but most of them really want to get back to their regular fighter squadron assignments. They are type "A" personalities; aggressive, self-confident, intensively controlling and blunt with instructions that we were expected to perform with perfection. The instruction is not padded with any pleasantries but delivered with continuous severity in dialogue peppered with sarcasm, cynicism and personal degradation. I understood their style, attitude and reasoning completely. One switch out of a hundred in the wrong position at the wrong time in a flight can result in a mission failure.

The training hours were intense. Debriefing a single sortie can last 16 hours. Training consists of flying 2 to

10 sorties a week. But…I had no problem here. I loved the flying.

I was aggressive in my attitude to flight training supporting the often quoted mission statement; *"Fly, Fight and Win…and don't forget it."* No problem here either. I was especially good at handling the complexities of aircraft recovery no matter what emergency situation the instructors threw at me.

So where did I run into problems?

What I had trouble with was adapting my religious beliefs to the social situation. A lot of off duty vocabulary emphasizes profanities. God is an often used expletive.

Alcohol in excessive amounts is a tradition.

I just couldn't handle that so I stayed away from quite a few of the squadron activities.

Other pilots began to notice the difference and my lack of participation. Some didn't care. Some were curious about me and others were actually hostile. Some even wanted me to reconsider my career choice.

A few instructors took me aside and offered their "guidance" …making sure I understood the importance of living the correct "fighter pilot life style."

It was emphasized that my lack of social participation would affect my professional advancement. I was expected to conform and participate in all the activities and culture of the fighter pilot world. Not participating gave the impression that I was "holier than thou" or thought of myself as "too good" to associate with my fellow squadron members.

Military pilots all have tactical or radio call signs for protecting their identity from the enemy. Naming ceremonies are memorable events in a squadron conducted by the veteran squadron members. New pilots are known as FNGs…NG is for "new guy"…F is a profanity. The names usually reflect a physical characteristic or some personality trait of the pilot. I was lucky…at my naming ceremony…my given call sign was "Padre". Needless to say brother, I became tagged with a name I never wanted to be called…a "Holy Joe."

So, I had a major problem and I asked myself; How do I handle it? How do I survive and save my career? I knew I had to take a more proactive approach. My core belief has always been and will continue to be;

A Christian is to be in the world but not of it…to be different but not separate from it.

I made a conscious decision to do what I thought was right and God's will and perform my duty to the best of my ability… a 110% commitment.

It worked. I was named "Top Gun" in air to ground combat. - I dropped my bombs more accurately on the target than anyone else in the squadron.- When I became a flight commander the squadron began to realize while I was different…I wasn't "that bad" and that I was a good pilot and team player even though I didn't participate in every squadron event. I excelled in my flying assignments above everyone else - I had to do this so that I could just be considered equal. I couldn't just be mediocre. Pilots will never follow or respect men of mediocre presence.

"Padre" earned the respect of his peers but it's an ongoing story…it's been and probably be a continuing challenge for the rest of my career.

Anyhow, that's my story. I'm glad I'm here, graduating and moving on to Cannon and more flying. There's some talk of the training at Cannon is for preparation of a short term deployment to Southeast Asia.

Bill Delaney, my friend and roommate from the first day at the Academy has once again drawn the same assignment. The odds of that happening are astronomical!

We're both flying the new F-100 Super Sabre. It's one fantastic airplane.

Alan, I'm looking forward to seeing you again. Hope all is well. Good luck on the "Swing Wing".

Have there been any leads or developments on Mom's accident?

Take Care Brother,   Roger

Chapter 14
The Fort Worth Renegades
June 8, 1961- Plant #4 office meeting

The TFX – F-111 Tactical Fighter

A proposal meeting is in progress at General Dynamics with all new members of the recently added Purdue team and the existing ten engineering staff members. The two cultures of "new" and "old" have not come together.

"It's a waste of time and time is our most valuable asset! The proposal must be focused on providing the right airplane for the mission and with hard data!" exclaims Alan McConnell;

Everyone around the table sits quietly on the sidelines and listen as the temperature of the meeting dialogue rises. Tom Robinson lights his *Estate* pipe and begins puffing faster than usual.

Team Manager Ronald Esterbrook raises his eyebrows and sits back in his chair while listening to the outburst from the young, newly hired engineer.

McConnell continues;

"The whole concept of a shared aircraft between the Air Force and Navy is flawed. I've spent a lot of extra time listening to the five member team of the Navy group…according to each one of those members the plane the Air Force is proposing is too big and too heavy for the carriers and it doesn't even meet the mission requirements the Navy wants…I won't even mention the high degree of inter service rivalry between the Air Force and Navy group this project has created. The Navy needs its own airplane…it's that simple."

McConnell's dialogue continues to build in passion and confidence but is abruptly interrupted by Esterbrook who responds in a monotone and condescending voice;

"Mr. McConnell, Mr. "*Stormy*"! You…and your so called "*Renegades*" have to learn something here early on. We don't make the rules. Secretary of Defense McNamara asked us to design a multi-role, multi-service fighter bomber…and it is our

122

job to design such an aircraft and meet the specifications of both the Air Force and Navy…For your information and review…"

Esterbrook pauses for second as he opens the project file and begins to read;

"On June 14, 1960, the US Air Force SOR 183 - which is *Specific Operational Requirement* 183; defines a new tactical fighter for a nuclear strike role. *SOR* 183 specifies an aircraft that can operate from unprepared forward airfields and have an unrefueled range of 3,800 miles and fly at Mach 1.2 continuously for 460 miles.

One of the major features of the aircraft specified under SOR 183 *is* having 'variable geometry' or 'swing wings', in which the wings pivot out in a straight-wing configuration for low-speed flight and pivot back into a delta-like configuration for high-speed flight. As you know this scheme had been tested by the Bell X-5 and Grumman XF10F-1 Jaguar experimental aircraft in 1950 and represents the leading-edge concept in aircraft design.

For everyone's added information; Defense Secretary Robert McNamara will release the RFP…which is a *Request For Proposal* in August or September…He is determined to promote a commonality multi role aircraft between the U.S. armed services. We have limited time to prepare a detailed study in preparation for submitting that proposal. No doubt, Boeing will be our major competitor again. We need to work together on this project as a team."

There is continued silence around the table. Esterbrook continues;

"This brings me back to Mr. McConnell and his *'Renegades'* group…you have got to join the rest of us here…I'm not seeing any evidence of a team effort being generated for this project!

That's all I have to say. End of discussion. Let's take a 30 minute break and meet back here."

On A Cafeteria Break

Alan McConnell pulls a chair over to the table next to one of the senior team engineers on the TFX project; John Davies. John is first to speak;

"Hey Alan…I'm glad you pulled your chair over here. I haven't had a chance to talk with you since you arrived. I want you to know there are a lot of the "old timers" here that agree with your view on the project. We want to work with you...and

your team. Competition to win this TFX contract is going to be tough. It's not only going to be a technology based decision ...from my experience Alan, I smell a major political battle percolating on this one which will finally decide who is awarded the contract."

Davies takes a fast sip of coffee and continues;

"By the way, I don't know if you realize what a promoter Gretchen is for your team. She rolled out a PR agenda on each of us "old timers" about your ability and your whole team approach...she converted everyone...including me!

There's a special and wonderful quality in her positive spirit that is pleasantly contagious...I can't put my finger on it. She's attractive looking and all...but it goes beyond that. She has a powerful and unusual ability to speak to the personal concerns of others...I found it amazing and actually spiritual when I listen to her. I wanted to share that observation with you...perhaps you've noticed that before?"

McConnell nods slowly in agreement and sits back in his chair;

"At Purdue her influence on our team was always positive as was her technical advice. Her personality is open...but yet she's hard to get to know. There is something...it's hard to describe...I don't know if this is an "on target" descriptive...but '*other worldly*' may not be too far off the mark...and I mean that in a good sense...she always seems to speak above the turmoil or controversy of the moment with a wider perspective...no matter what it is."

Davies silently considers the description and agrees;

"Yes, yes...I would say that is entirely accurate...most accurate indeed Alan!"

Chapter 15
MAF over the Congo
July 28, 1961 - Meeting Dr.Carlson

The African continent is erupting and the Congo is its flashpoint. Rebel insurgents take advantage of the country's instability and invade and occupy the country.

The medical situation escalates from "urgent" to "critical." 700 Belgian doctors flee from the government run hospitals and clinics. Only 200 doctors from the World Health Organization and missionaries remain in the entire country to serve the medical needs of millions.

The *Protestant Relief Agency* with aircraft support provided by *Mission Aviation Fellowship* formed *"Operation Doctor"* in an attempt to restore the loss of healthcare services to hundreds of remote villages.

MAF pilot John Gadden, and Dr. Anoza are joined by an American physician from Redondo Beach, California; Dr. Paul Carlson. Carlson responded to an urgent appeal for doctors to volunteer and serve four months in the Ubangi Province. He was returning to the government hospital in Libenge.

Dr. Anoza asks Carlson about the conditions there. Carlson shakes his head but manages a controlled smile adding;

"Primitive...very primitive compared to the facilities and equipment back in the states...I performed surgery on patients with no blood pressure pump. We had none that worked, so we operated by 'pulse and a prayer' most of the time!...then there's the frustration of providing proper aftercare. Lack of postoperative nursing care and training can completely undo the success of an operation and recovery of the patient. It's more than a challenge."

Carlson pauses for a moment then quickly adds;

"But you know Dr.Anoza...I love the work and the people here. I don't know if I can go back to California!"

The pilot finishes loading the aircraft with medical supplies. Gadden announces; "Everyone onboard...we've got to go!"

(Dr. Paul Carlson was killed by Congolese rebels –November 24, 1964)

The Challenge of the Sahel
August 21, 1961

The Sahel is the transition region between the Sahara Desert to the north and the wetter regions of equatorial Africa to the south. It extends 3,100 miles from the Atlantic in the west to the Indian Ocean in the east. The Sahel is one of the poorest, environmentally degraded areas on Earth. Relief agencies report 300,000 children under the age of five will die each year directly or indirectly from malnutrition in this area.

A young, tall man…an American in his early twenties wearing a Chicago Cubs baseball cap dismounts from his olive green, 1942 *Matchless G3/L* motor cycle. The engine is a 16 HP, 349 cc air cooled machine developed for use by the British army during the Second World War. He stops to survey a small oasis of trees and plants 100 miles south of the city of Khartoum in Sudan.

Jean Paul Boyer was born of American missionary parents in Haiti, raised in East Africa and is a graduate student at the University of Arizona's College of Agriculture. He's spending a year traveling along the entire length of the Sahel documenting and collecting soil samples and seeds found native to each climate zone area.

His thesis explores a new field of study; a*gricultural genetics* that guides his personal search…a *quest* for a certain vital genetic structure in seeds that would provide the highest growth potential in the harsh Sahel climate.

As he kneels down to collect a sample; the drone of an approaching aircraft is heard. The small aircraft circles twice and lands a short distance from the oasis. The single engine plane belongs to *Mission Aviation*  *Fellowship.* Two figures, a man and a woman, emerge from the plane and walk toward Jean Paul. He instantly recognizes John Gadden the MAF pilot.

Gadden approaches Jean Paul;

"Mr. Jean Paul…it looks like you're keeping busy! Your

parents asked that I keep an eye on you and make sure you're not getting into any trouble! How's it going young man?"

Jean Paul finishes sealing a plastic sample bag;

"I still have a long way to go before I can return to the states and to school. I'll be able to take a closer look at the collected samples when I finally get back to the university lab. All is going as well as can be expected. I'm pleased with the samples I've collected so far. My faithful *Matchless* motorcycle is still running well. I just make sure it has enough oil and gas and it keeps on going!...it's a long hot ride along the Sahel and the desert is not friendly to machinery!"

Gadden sympathetically agrees;

"Yes, I know. Airplanes and their air cooled engines don't like this hot weather and all the blowing sand that goes with it...the calm, dense air of a cool evening is better."

Gadden turns to Dr. Anoza;

"Doctor, I'm sorry, for some reason I'm always slow on proper introductions...

Jean Paul let me introduce you to this fine lady I have been flying with...Dr. Amelia Anoza...she's from Chicago and has been providing and directing medical support all along the Sahel region."

Amelia looks directly at Jean Paul. She recalls the briefing with Gabriel in Chicago and the importance of Jean Paul for his future contribution to God's mission. Amelia replies;

"Jean Paul, I have heard many favorable comments about you and your project as I travel the Sahel. The local natives talk of meeting you and are quite interested in your search for a "super seed" as they call it. They have also taken many of your suggestions on increasing their crop yield and it has worked out quite well for them. You have made many friends and gained their personal respect. I believe you have a following Jean Paul!

As you know, the food and water situation along the Sahel remains critical and when you add the increased political tension and social unrest it makes for a very volatile situation. Be careful Jean Paul...your work is very much needed but these are dangerous times in Africa. I'll mention my concern to your guardian angel in my morning devotions!"

Jean Paul nods...adding;

"Thanks Amelia, sounds good…I can always use some extra protection. But you know…it's not the local natives or the environment that I worry about.

I've been running into a small group of unfriendly looking Russians!...three or four of them. They've even followed me and sometimes stopped and questioned what I was doing. They said they're with the Russian Embassy. I don't know exactly what they want. They're most interested that I'm American…I don't argue with them especially since they're all wearing sidearms!"

Gadden is quick to reply;

"Yes, I've seen them too. An American Special Envoy with the State Department…Donald Richardsen had a recent encounter with Russians.

I have several flights with medical supplies scheduled for delivery in this area all next week. I'll stay in touch Jean Paul."

Gadden and Dr. Anozi return to the aircraft and continue their flight.

Chapter 15 – MAF Over The Congo

Chapter 16
A Peacemaker's Final Words
Republic of the Congo
September 18, 1961

The United Nations charter a *Super
DC-6B*, a modern four engine airliner
owned and operated by *Transair Sweden*. The flight lists ten
passengers and six crew members; Captains are Per Hallonquist
and Nils-Eric Aahreus, First Officer; Lars Litton, Flight
Engineer; Nils Garan Wilhelmsson, Radio Operator; Karl Erik
Rosen and Purser; Harald Noork.

The aircraft departs Leopoldville airport at 7 p.m. while
another aircraft, a decoy DC-6 departs minutes earlier and flys a
different route.

The reason for the additional security measures is to insure the
safety of its important passenger; United Nations Secretary-
General Dag Hammarskjöld. Hammarskjöld, 56 years old, is on
a special UN mission to negotiate a peace between two warring
factions.The Republic of Congo has just declared independence
from Belgium.

The opposing side are secessionist forces in the province of
Katanga supported by mining executives, hundreds of
mercenaries, and several officials from the American and
European governments, all of whom were in favor of
maintaining Africa's colonial order.

It's just after midnight on a still autumn night. The aircraft,
flying 6000 feet over a heavily forested terrain, is only 4 miles
from its destination and on final approach to land at Northern
Rhodesia's N'Dolo Airport

Hammarskjöld is preparing to meet with secessionist leader
Moise Tshombé, who recently declared the mineral-rich
southeastern province of Katanga an independent state.

The men will meet in N'dola, a neighboring British colony of
Northern Rhodesia, because of the ongoing fighting in Katanga.
The stakes are high because of the large deposits of mineral
wealth and radioactive uranium found in the disputed area.

Aboard the aircraft Hammarskjöld stares out the window into
the darkness as the plane prepares to land. He is tired and

nervous. The probable success of the mission is uncertain. So far, it has only proven to be physically dangerous and politically divisive. As the landing gear is lowered; Hammarskjöld is totally unaware of the deadly air attack that has been planned and is about to take place.

Under Fire

Several miles away at an undisclosed location; a pilot's radio transmission from an unidentified and armed military aircraft is being monitored;

"I see a transport plane coming low,"
"All the lights are on."
"I'm going to go down to make a run on it."
"Yes, it's the Transair DC6... It's the plane...."
(a long pause follows...then the sound of gunfire)
"I've hit it!"
"There are flames... It's going down... It's crashing!"

Onlookers at N'Dolo Airport glance upwards and see two planes streak across the sky. One of them has fire lapping around its engine and wings and plummets to the ground.

The DC-6 hits the ground and breaks apart, spilling thousands of gallons of aviation fuel. A huge fire ball is seen from a distance.

The next day the crash site is located and visited. Thrown clear of the explosive fire, the lifeless body of Hammarskjöld is discovered at a distance several hundred feet from the aircraft. Many claim the fuselage of the plane is riddled with bullet holes.

A witness who first came upon the crash said two Jeeps filled with men in fatigues were already there and ordered him to leave, but he observed bullet "holes the size of my fist" in the plane. He described the scene to investigators as looking "as if it had been sprayed with bullets and there was a whole row across the aircraft."

Many pointed to the Soviets as responsible for the attack. The Soviet Union had earlier attacked decisions by the Secretary General; criticizing him for his ongoing independent action. But it was not until the United Nations intervention in the Congo that he incurred the full force of Soviet verbal attacks.

The Soviet campaign against Hammarskjöld reached its peak with an angry speech by Premier Khrushchev. Khrushchev severely attacked Hammarskjöld for not having used military force in support of Patrice Lumumba, the Soviet backed Congolese Premier. Mr. Lumumba was later slain.

Mr. Khrushchev repeated a Soviet demand for Mr. Hammarskjöld to be replaced as Secretary General by a three-man executive council representing the Western, Soviet and neutral camps.

The only survivor of the crash is an American security officer who claimed just after the aircraft was first hit, Hammarskjöld gave his last order to the pilot…to abort the landing and return to Leopoldville.

The world is informed of the crash and loss of the respected and notable peacemaker. The media and public are stunned.

Hammarskjöld's words; spoken earlier in his final address broadcast over United Nations Radio were revisited and digested with a more poignant meaning;

"….Our work for peace must begin within the private world of each one of us. To build for man a world without fear, we must be without fear. To build a world of justice, we must be just. And how can we fight for liberty if we are not free in our own minds? How can we ask others to sacrifice if we are not ready to do so?...Only in true surrender to the interest of all can we reach that strength and independence, that unity of purpose, that equity of judgment which are necessary if we are to measure up to our duty to the future, as men of a generation to whom the chance was given to build in time a world of peace."

A Phone Call
Roger and Alan McConnell
October 29, 1961

Roger: *"Hello Alan?...This is Roger."*

Alan: *"Hey, how's it going brother!...*
Where are you calling from?"

Roger: *"Still here at Cannon...but I'm deploying*
tomorrow to Southeast Asia...I can't give any
details...but I'll be out of country for four months.
I wanted to call before taking off."

Alan: *"Appreciate it Rog...I was just thinking*
...That's a long flight you've got ahead of you."

Roger: *"No!, just a walk across the 'Pond' brother*
...no problem."

Alan: *"Roger?"*

Roger: *"Yes"*

Alan: *"You be careful...Okay?"*
Roger: *"Just give a ring on the 'ole cowbell'*
once in a while for good luck...and add a short
prayer while you're at it."

Alan: *"Got you covered brother. Have a good*
flight."

Chapter 17
"Go West Young Man"
Cannon Air Force Base
New Mexico – *Operation Sawbuck*
October 30, 1961   0300 Hrs Local

There's a lot of early morning pre-flight activity at Cannon Air Force Base. The flight line has a dreamlike appearance as pilots walk toward their aircraft in the predawn darkness. The revolving airport beacon atop the control tower fires two quick white flashes of light followed by one green signal. The outward stream of coded signals attempt to reach an open sky but are instantly and severely diffused by a heavy layer of ground fog.

Large flood lamps illuminate the flight line aiding crews for eight F-100s preparing for takeoff. Fuel trucks complete their fueling operations and pull away from the aircraft. Some F-100s present themselves in their original unpolished aluminum skin while others have received the battle paint of olive green camouflage.

Each F-100 is fitted with four external wing fuel tanks. The tanks provide 1070 gallons additional fuel to the internal tanks 1190 gallons.

Still, the flight to Thailand requires a total of at least 20 midair refuelings. The first leg of the flight from Cannon to Hickam Field, Hawaii is 3,000 nautical miles. The second leg, from Hickam to Guam is another 3,300 miles with a final 2,700 mile leg to the Royal Thai Air Force Base at Takhli, Thailand. The first midair refueling is over the Pacific...just past Santa Barbara, California.

Takhli is about 150 miles northwest of Bangkok. There is an immediate threat of a civil war in neighboring Laos by a communist inspired insurgency. It is feared that the Vietnam Conflict may spread to Laos and then to Thailand.

Operation Sawbuck is the F-100 mission is to provide combat-oriented recon missions over Laos.

Roger McConnell is already strapped into the "Hun" with the J-57 jet engine idling. The crew chief pulls the wheel chocks and signals McConnell that he's clear to taxi. McConnell checks his instruments and eases the throttle forward.

He immediately notices a difference. The supersonic fighter no longer feels light and agile with the full and added weight of the external fuel tanks. He makes a slow turn left onto the taxiway and looks back and to his left and spots his wingman, Bill Delaney. The radio comes to life; It's Delaney...

"Good morning *Padre*....this is *Prof One*...what are you doing out here on this dark and dank New Mexico morning?"

McConnell replies;

"Just out for a morning stroll...headed out West... been thinking about Hawaii...You want to come along?"

"*Prof One* is with you all the way *Padre*."

As the two aircraft exit the taxiway onto Runway 22 Delaney pulls alongside McConnell...their wingtips are only three feet apart.

"*Prof One* is ready to roll."

McConnell looks down the lighted 10,000 foot runway;

"Roger *Prof One*...lookin good...let's do it!"

McConnell pushes the throttle to its full forward position, lighting the engine's afterburner. Delaney adds afterburner thrust and the two aircraft roll down the runway in perfect formation.

A normal throttle setting for the F-100 produces 8700 pounds of thrust. Full throttle, at military setting gives 10,200 pounds of thrust. The afterburner setting just forward of military position pushes out 16,000 pounds of thrust...but there is a tremendous penalty payed on the amount of fuel consumed.

From a distance and in the morning darkness only two fiery plumes of exploding jet fuel from the afterburners are seen streaking down the runway accompanied by their signature powerful and thundering sound...then almost magically the flames rise into the air and pass through a thick layer of morning fog...and within seconds are gone.

Chapter 17 – *"Go West Young man"*

Chapter 18
Meet Mr. Jennings
Bureau of Intelligence and Research
U.S. State Department –
Washington D.C.
December 6, 1961

Jeremy S. Standvok is a former CIA operative reassigned from a fieldwork assignment to the office and position of Assistant Secretary for the State Department's Bureau of Intelligence and Research. During his last Eastern European-Soviet assignment his cover identity unraveled and extraction from the Soviet Union was immediate and necessary.

Standvok stares blankly out the side window of his office; finishes the short end of a *Marlboro* and extinguishes it in a large souvenir ash tray displaying a color rendered photo of the *Lincoln Memorial*. He asks himself why the CIA didn't give him another field assignment...
Why the transfer to the State Department?

Standvok is in an unsettled state; trying to come to agreement and accept the "period of adjustment" needed to perform the regulated duties and routine functions of a bureaucratic assignment. He picks up the phone, punches the intercom call button and buzzes Lloyd Jennings, the young research analyst assigned to his department.

"Jennings...I need to talk to you...bring along your notepad."

Jennings is in his late twenties, tall and wears a pair of "bookish" wire rimmed glasses. His hair is unkempt and noticeably longer than his contemporaries. His rogue appearance is further defined with his independent and matchless research expertise that's applauded and recognized by upper level members of the State Department. The incredibly thorough detailed process of his investigative work has consistently produced concise, detailed and accurate analyses of the changing political landscapes of foreign governments. Department policy makers greatly value his contribution to policy making.

Jennings is prompt and professional to reply;
"I'm on the way sir."

Standvok is finishing some handwritten notes as

Jennings enters the office. He opens a file folder, briefly reviews a couple pages and looks up;

"Hello Lloyd...have a seat...relax for a minute. I was just looking at your job description;

It *says Lloyd Jerome Jennings, Research and Policy Annalist...*" Standvok pauses;

" I don't want to read on...frankly Lloyd, I find your job confining and maybe a little too structured for any real advancement in the State Department...As your supervisor, I want to see you move ahead of your contemporaries. You have a strong following here. Your job evaluation is above average...it is in fact above excellent!"

Standvok pauses for only an instant before continuing;

" I want to ask you something....how would you like to work with me on a special assignment that's slightly off the beaten path...and in fact would be off the record and radar of the State Department. It would definitely be a departure from your normal *Library of Congress* sojourns."

Jennings is typically slow to answer but his curiosity is aroused;

"Yes, I work for you sir...you're my boss!...I'm not particularly looking for an adventure but what do you have in mind?"

Standvok draws the remaining *Marlboro* from the pack, lights up and sits back in his chair;

"A mission to the Soviet Union Lloyd...A rescue mission to save lives. How would you like to add that to your job description!

Let me explain some history...I worked in Moscow. Before it was 'my time to leave' I was a mid-manager for the *Aircraft Design Bureau.* The position offered many opportunities to access information on new aircraft design projects and personnel assignments as well. I noticed that when certain projects were completed there was always a secret "cleansing" by KGB of selected suspect members of the project team. Many were removed from Moscow and sent with their families to gulags in Siberia. One particular gulag; *Verkhoyansk* received a majority of scientists as well as many free thinking writers that were considered threatening to the Party.

Chapter 18 – Meet Mr. Jennings

Now, just yesterday, the Secretary and I discussed an envoy's classified report from Africa. Special Envoy Donald Richardsen was given information from a reliable source... a soviet diplomat... who claims an American is being held prisoner at the *Verkhoyansk* gulag in northern Siberia. His name is David McConnell; an Army Air Force Captain and member of the *Doolitle Raiders* mission that flew the first strike against Japan. McConnell was presumed dead following reports a year later that his B-17 was shot down on a mission over Germany. That was nearly 20 years ago.

He has two sons Alan and Roger. Alan is an engineer with General Dynamics. Roger, his younger brother is an Air Force Academy graduate and fighter pilot serving in Thailand. They have no knowledge or information regarding this new development.

I recommended the State Department refer the report to the CIA for a rescue mission and bring McConnell home along with some of the Soviet scientists and other so called 'criminal' prisoners.

I tried to sell the program to the decision makers upstairs...but was voted down with no further review allowed. They believe Richardsen's report reflected a carefully structured fabrication by the Soviets...communicated to Richardsen to create an enticement for a U.S. rescue mission...an anticipated response that would provide a provocative incident and reason for a soviet confrontation.

Damn it Lloyd, I was ticked when they tried to sell me on their non-intervention reasoning. Sometimes I think we've got some *pinkos* calling the shots in the Department.

"Pinkos sir?" Jennings asks.

"Yes, Lloyd...communist sympathizers...I spotted them when I was at the meeting. Where are the patriots? Patriots who will speak up loud and clear. For God's sake, an American...an American hero is held captive and we're supposed to sit on our asses and look the other way!"

Lloyd remains serious in his expression and quiet for a moment before responding;

"Sir, let me check and research your findings and

Renegades

Richardsen's report as well...I need some time to make a decision. It's just the way I work sir.

I believe we should attempt to free McConnell...if he's a prisoner in that gulag...but let me pursue what diplomatic channels may be open. I have several contacts."

Standvok nods politely and agrees;

"Okay, I understand but remain sensitive to the situation. We don't want to tip our hand as to the intent of our investigation. Remember...officially, any rescue attempt is off the table."

"Sir, Yes sir...completely...but coincidentally I have several additional bits of information garnered from a CIA intercept this morning that further validates your story. The soviet diplomat, the one Richardson talked to regarding McConnell, was murdered by the KGB in Mali.

However, an official memorandum from Moscow states the soviet diplomat ...Nikolay Komarovsky is alive and enjoying retirement from the diplomatic bureau following 40 years of faithful service!

A more revealing dispatch states his post in Africa was immediately filled by a KGB officer; *Devlin Sherkov Makarovich.*

State Department resource files describe Makarovich as a young aggressive and ruthless individual looking for quick advancement in the Soviet government hierarchy. His loyalty and services remain with the KGB."

Standvok looks inquisitively and with some suspicion at Lloyd and asks;

"Very good Lloyd...Very good indeed but tell me how you knew about my interest in the Richardsen report? We never talked about this before."

Lloyd responds with a casual non-revealing expression saying;

"As I had just said...a coincidence sir...that's all...a most remarkable coincidence to be sure."

Four Hours Later
Library of Congress
Thomas Jefferson Building
Room LJ220

Chapter 18 – *Meet Mr. Jennings*

Lloyd Jennings arrives at the Jefferson Building...one of the three Libraries of Congress in Washington D.C. He walks with a relaxed stride up the stairs to the second floor and enters the *African and Middle Eastern* section. The reading room offers a comfortable nineteenth century atmosphere and place to study. It's a favorite place of solitude for Jennings when researching his assignments.

Today, however, it serves as a special meeting place. Lloyd Jennings has another identity. *Lloyd Jennings is Angel Barrattiel.*

Barrattiel *is the angel of support. His intellectual information, practical solutions and creative assistance are of unsurpassed value. His outward appearance and personality remain very human and ordinary. Gabriel has contacted Barrattiel and scheduled a meeting.*

Gabriel has taken the appearance of a research specialist working at the Library. Upon arrival he greets Barrattiel and finds a quiet location in the corner of the reading room;

"Greetings Barrattiel...I am most excited to meet you today. I deliver a message and an assignment carrying the full authority and direction from our Lord.

The Lord is pleased with your work Barrattiel ...but warns of new and increased activity from the *other side* to destroy the efforts and plans of our Lord to help mankind.

There is a plot underway...to capture and take as hostage the Lord's most active and faithful servants. These are specially selected followers needed to fulfill God's *Miracle* event. They will be taken and held secretly in a Siberian gulag in the town of *Verkhoyansk*. It is essential Barrattiel that they are freed from this prison."

Barrattiel asks;

"Who are the hostages you speak of?"

Gabriel replies;

"The Lord will let you know. You will know who they are when the time is right."

Jennings asks;

"Can you tell me any details of the plan, the M*iracle* you speak of?...this would be helpful."

Renegades

Gabriel replies;

"The message I deliver is;

The Lord foresees an approaching era of great upheaval; an examination of traditional values, acts of violence and conflict that have no borders. The earth's environment will be active with extreme and destructive natural forces. It's a time when the entire world will be severely challenged. The Lord wants to give the good earth and all its inhabitants another chance ....a chance for peace. There will be no repeat of a biblical flood and it is not the right time for His second coming.

*Instead, God will guide the earth through the perilous times. He will perform a miracle, a powerful event for all on earth to see and experience...this will be a "**breakaway**" event to reset the world on a new secure and anticipative future.*

The Lord has given us an assignment...an assigned task to support His mission and make the necessary preparations for that special and miraculous time."

Gabriel continues;

"Remember Barrattiel ...in the early times of the Biblical Old Testament; God continually performed miracles directly on Earth. There were great floods and the healing of individuals but as time progressed the Biblical New Testament brought a change as to how God interacts in the world....for many centuries since there have been no direct miracles."

Today miracles are created through His orchestration and interaction with followers guided by their faith and prayers..."

Gabriel pauses and adds;

"and our assistance; the vast army of angels under His personal command.

Barrattiel, know that God reigns at all times but prefers to remove Himself directly from earthly problems. Gabriel places both hands on Barrattiel's shoulders;

"Continue your good work *Mr. Lloyd Jennings* ...I must go now. Know that the Lord is forever present and supporting you in all places and at all times."

Chapter 18 – *Meet Mr. Jennings*

Chapter 19
Takhli Royal Thai Air Force Base
Central Thailand
Mission 33
January 16, 1962

Takhli is a Thai Air Base but in 1960 through diplomatic negotiations a mutual agreement was reached allowing the United States to upgrade five Thailand air bases to meet USAF needs. The agreement reflects a continuing history of cooperation and good relationship with the Thai government.

In 1959 Communist forces were in a civil war inside Laos. There was fear that the war would spread into neighboring Thailand. F-100 Super Sabres of the 524th Tactical Fighter Squadron from Cannon AFB, New Mexico began flying combat oriented recon missions in the spring of 1961 to monitor the situation.

Captain Roger McConnell completes his 33rd Mission and shuts down the F-100's engine. His wingman, Captain Bill Delaney guides his aircraft to the next service stall and parks the aircraft.

The temperature is over a hundred degrees and the heavily humidified air is further thickened by a mid-afternoon "monsoon" rain. McConnell removes his helmet and stands up in the cockpit and surveys the flight line. The downpour of rain is ending…leaving in its departure a rising and lingering cloud of fog like steam over the tarmac taxiway.

The four month tour of duty is nearly over and not what McConnell had anticipated. The recon missions were about as eventful as any airline commercial flight…There was never an adrenalin rush or situation encountered that incorporated his newly honed combat training. Once or twice a few rounds of small caliber ground fire added a few small dents to the underside of the main wing…but that was all. Many of the sorties were so routine some pilots started taking unnecessary chances to cure the monotony.

The crew chief, Sgt. Frank Coleman, places the egress ladder in position and calls up to McConnell;

"Say Captain…Colonel Runyon wants you and Captain Delaney to report to Ops as soon as you're debriefed. How was your flight sir?"

McConnell climbs down from the cockpit, steps onto the tarmac and with his crew chief continues to walk to the rear of the F-100.

"Sargent…I haven't had too many situations that I absolutely needed afterburner on these sorties…except on takeoff and that's always worked fine…but when I'm flying at altitude just under Mach 1 and engage the throttle to afterburner…it doesn't light on first try. It usually takes three or four attempts with the throttle setting before I can get ignition."

Coleman takes out his flashlight and shines it directly inside the dark innards of the rear exhaust;

"It might be the burner nozzles. They look okay but I'll have to get inside and take a closer look. It could also be a linkage problem to the throttle control."

McConnell's wingman; Captain Delaney, carrying his flight gear, joins McConnell;

"You two are looking mighty serious at that exhaust…I bet you're talking 'afterburner'….right? Some of the pilots report no problems…others report intermittent ignition and another group have total failure…it's all random… anything else going on?"

Roger holds back a smile and asks;

"Colonel Runyon wants to see us. You haven't been scaring the natives and going supersonic over any Laos villages lately have you?

Bill returns the question with a half- smile;

"Hey, you know me Rog…I always fly high, fast and straight as an arrow!"

One Hour Later – Headquarters Building

Captains McConnell and Delaney enter Colonel Runyon's office. The colonel and two other officers are present.

All are seated at a long conference table that at first glance seems too large for the small office. The room is quiet except for the steady hum of the window air conditioner.

Chapter 19 – *Takhli Royal Thai Air Force Base*

Runyon is quick to acknowledge their presence;

"At ease gentlemen…have a seat. I'd like you to meet two pilots you'll be working with on a recon mission for the next couple weeks. Meet Captain Mike Salizar and Lieutenant Scott Shepard…they're with the 553rd Reconnaissance Wing flying the EC-121 Warning Star. Their 121 is based at Korat. The EC-121 is the military version of the four engine commercial airliner …the Super Constellation. But this aircraft is not for carrying passengers; it's specially equipped with a new radar system, communications equipment and a host of counter measure electronics. An onboard crew of 25 airmen operate what is literally an airborne command center. Their mission here is to acquire operational experience and qualify the electronics. The aircraft is configured to gather intelligence information on enemy activity in the North.

The Pentagon sees our military involvement in Southeast Asia increasing dramatically in the next couple years. We'll need to know what the North is doing when our aircraft are airborne and enroute to a target. The EC-121s are capable of providing real time information on all aircraft as well as ground based troop movements. They are also capable of transmitting electronic jamming signals to disrupt enemy radar.

The problem with the 121 is that it's slow…300 knots…and unarmed. It's vulnerable and an easy target for enemy aircraft. The 121 requires protection.

I want you two…McConnell and Delaney to fly escort for Salizar and Shepard.. These missions will be six hours in length and operating very close to the North Vietnamese border. It's not known how the North will react to your presence if detected. You are to protect the aircraft and crew at all costs.

This mission is *top secret* and not to be discussed or shared with anyone. I have a detailed mission profile providing support information for your review and study. The document must remain in the Headquarters building. Plan on a full briefing tomorrow at 1300 hours. At that time I'll have a full disclosure of mission objectives, midair refueling, flight plans and opportunity for any discussion and questions.

However, for now gentlemen…I must apologize but I'm off to another meeting on the other side of the base. I'd like you to continue to study the mission profile material as preparation for tomorrow's briefing.

Before I leave though; McConnell and Delaney…I need to talk to both of you."

Colonel Runyon reaches into his briefcase, pulls out a file folder containing two sets of transfer orders. He hands the orders to each of them adding;

"After the completion of your current assignment…you're scheduled to rotate back to the states…but instead of returning to Cannon …you'll be headed to California…you've been accepted for advanced flight training at Edwards Flight Test Center.

"I don't know what connections you have but you two managed to pull an exceptionally good assignment…my congratulations. You'll have an opportunity to fly some of the most advanced cutting edge aircraft to come off the drawing boards!"

"I'll expect to see you both here tomorrow at 1300 hours."

Did You Say Colonel DevlinTomb?

McConnell and Delaney sit down at the conference table with Salizar and Shepard and begin to review the mission.

McConnell scans the flight plan;

"The sortie looks straightforward ….we'll be flying subsonic …we'll have to add a couple auxiliary wing tanks…and looks like we'll need one mid-air refueling... Both aircraft will be fully armed but I really don't anticipate an encounter with any opposition. "

Salizar looks up from the flight plan and replies;

"Don't count on it guys… Did you ever hear of a North Vietnamese pilot called Colonel Devlin-Dinh Ton?

According to unnamed sources, the CIA recorded Ton's name as "Toon" which was later and incorrectly changed to "Tomb". Supposedly, as the rumored story goes, 'Colonel Tomb' tangled with two Navy fighters and won. A self- proclaimed Ace…he is said to fly a MiG-17 with the numbers 3020 on the side of the fuselage and a burning American flag painted on the tail. Further rumors say he speaks English and loves to engage in combative banter with Americans during an encounter. "

Chapter 19 – *Takhli Royal Thai Air Force Base*

McConnell listens and his mood changes with heightened interest when hearing the name "Devlin" mentioned again.

He replies;

"I wonder if this Colonel Tomb or whoever his name is… really exists…it may be a fabrication of Hanoi; propagandists who want to scare American pilots.

Shepard replies with a sharp directness;

"I knew the two Navy pilots that were shot down. I went through flight training with both of them. These guys were good…really good pilots. It wasn't propaganda that knocked them out of the air.

Chapter 20
The Spirit of San Jon
Plant 4 – General Dynamics
February 2, 1962

The General Dynamics TFX design proposal is sent to the Department of Defense (DOD). A month later it's announced t the entries from the other aircraft companies including General Dynamics are all unacceptable; rejected by the Air Force and Navy.

On September 29th 1961, a second proposal request from the DOD is sent to General Dynamics, Boeing, Lockheed, Northrop, Grumman, McDonnell, Douglas, North American and Republic. The Air Force's version of the TFX is designated in the proposal as the F-111A...and the Navy's version the F-111B

General Dynamics's top management team wants the second proposal to take a different approach. A management change is announced; Alan "Stormy"McConnell is named new team project manager.

McConnell and his team create and submit an exhaustive and detailed new proposal. Seven other proposals are submitted by the other aircraft companies. Only Northrop declines to re-enter the competition.

However, the Air Force and Navy again reject all the newly submitted proposals. Only this time; Boeing and General Dynamics are the only companies asked to submit a revised third proposal with more design data. It's also announced that the final submission would be reviewed and the contract awarded to the company based on a point system for (1) aircraft performance, (2) cost and (3) Air Force – Navy commonality.

The McConnell team revises the original proposal only slightly but simplifies the entire style and structure of the presentation to favor the point system evaluation.

The revision proves successful. Finally, a decision is announced; General Dynamics wins the competition and the contract to build the F-111.

Project Manager Alan McConnell asks and receives the corporate endorsement to build a new "fast-track" production facility guided by a new agile management system to accelerate *the process of designing, building and testing the prototype aircraft. A new hangar building is authorized, built and completed in record time.*

The new unmarked hangar is painted in a non-discrept grey color and located near but separate from Air Force Plant 4, the main assembly line at General Dynamics. The hangar is unofficially tagged "Renegade Werks" by employees.

Alan McConnell walks through the side door of the *Werks* and passes through several electronic security stations. Accompanying McConnell is General Walter A. Swenson, Commander, Tactical Air Command (TAC). They have just left the main assembly line in Plant 4 and where they completed the inspection and progress of the F-111A mockup. They walk through a connecting underground tunnel to the new *Renegade Werks* hangar.

A second security station issues security badges allowing entrance to the production staging area. Two large automated doors open sideways...McConnell and the General enter the voluminous hangar.

Bathed in bright arc lamps is the now familiar shape of the F-111 directly in front of them. The aircraft is painted all white with no markings except for a red signature script just below the cockpit;

"The Spirit of San Jon?"
The General asks;
"What have we here Stormy...Is this another mockup?"
McConnell smiles and replies;

"No, you won't find any mockups here General. At the *Werks* we only build and fly airplanes. This is the F-111X you're looking at. It's at least 2 to 3 years ahead in design and production technique than the mockup you just inspected...and this aircraft will begin flight testing in another 10 months. The next step, the most important one, is for us to develop an integrated system able to migrate what we have successfully developed and tested here to manufacturing the aircraft on the main production line at *Plant 4*. We hope to reduce the development time it takes to get a new aircraft design into full production in terms of years. That's what the *Spirit* is all about."
The General notices the major modifications in the design and

Renegades

walks closer to the aircraft.

"Alan, this is unbelievable what you've mange to accomplish here!"

Alan interrupts:

"No, it's not me alone General…it's the design team that's come together and made the difference."

The General continues with a close visual inspection of the aircraft and asks;

They walk closer towards the aircraft…Alan explains;

The *Spirit's* primary feature on this "X" model is its electronic warfare capabilities; in other words…onboard radar jamming coupled with a host of selective countermeasure systems. The terrain following radar has been redesigned and upgraded as well. The majority of the electronics are installed in the weapons bay. When all the electronics are up and firing; the *Spirit* transmits a circular half mile cloak of electronic invisibility. Any object or other aircraft within that cloak is invisible to all frequencies of radar detection. The F-111 with its speed, acceleration, the variable sweep wing design, terrain following radar and invisibility profile offers 21st Century technology.

I didn't mention the special attention given to the propulsion system. The twin engines are upgraded with the special design refinements by Paul Lancer…of one of our team's engine specialists.

Each engine produces 25,000 lbs. with three stage afterburning thrust. Spirit will fly at Mach 1.3 at low level when on terrain following radar and close to Mach 4 at high altitude."

The General whistles quietly to himself and nods in approval;

"I'll take a couple dozen Stormy…let me know when you schedule the first flight…I'd like to see this puppy fly!"

Alan replies;

"You're at the top of the list General!"

Chapter 20 – *The Spirit of San Jon*

Chapter 21
Gretchen and the Coronado
Edwards Flight Test Center
February 12, 1962

Gretchen Summers has been temporarily assigned by General Dynamics to the Convair 990 Coronado design group that's conducting advanced flight tests at Edwards Flight Center in California. The test is with a new 990B modified aircraft designed for supersonic flight.

Gretchen has shown special interest in Convair's new 990 airliner. Its high bred engines powered the Air Force's first supersonic bomber the B-58 "Hustler".

The powerful engines and speed pod wing design earned the 990 the title as the world's "fastest airliner" with a cruising 0.89 Mach number.

However, the resulting high fuel consumption at near supersonic speeds made it economically unappealing to the airlines that preferred the more conservative fuel sipping appetite of Boeing's 707 and Douglas's DC-8 jetliners.

Today's 990 flight is with an experimental "B" model. The 990B flight test is to measure speed and fuel consumption with a new turbofan design modification. The engines should have sufficient power to reach Mach 1.00...the speed of sound.

Tom Wentworth, the command test pilot, is at the controls. The 990 approaches the test area at 30,000 feet. Gretchen is onboard as flight engineer...monitoring the engine console and data recorders.

"I love this airplane Gretchen...the way it flys...it's a pilot's airplane all the way..." confesses command pilot Tom Winworth as he reaches altitude and throttles the engines to cruise.

Co-Pilot Ed Dolan agrees and adds;

"If we could get a better handle limiting the fuel appetite of the *990* ...Boeing and Douglas would be looking at us from the tarmac as the airlines and our 990s speed overhead! France and England are working on a joint project to build a supersonic liner...called *Concorde*...but that first flight is at least 5 years away."

Edward's Flight Test Director's voice over the radio interrupts

150

the conversation;

"Hello Dash One…this is Edwards Flight Center …you'll be entering the test sector in 30 seconds. Prepare for dash."

Winworth replies;

"Roger Edwards, 30 seconds to dash."

There's a period of extended silence interrupted with the occasional sound of radio static …then Edwards announces: "Dash One, recorders to high… All Okay. Maintain current altitude and heading…We've got a solid track on you…..cleared for dash in 10 seconds…….5, 4, 3, 2,1. You're on the mark Dash One…You are Go!"

Winworth pushes the four throttles slowly forward;

"Roger on that Edwards…Dash One is go!"

Gretchen is at the flight engineers station, on the intercom and announces the engine readings;

"All four running at 70 percent……."

"Coming off the 75 percent mark."

"80 percent…now 85."

"This is Edwards…we're tracking you at Mach 0.91."

Winworth announces on the intercom;

"Hold on everyone …we're going throttle up…all the way."

Gretchen watches the bank of white needle indicators as they slowly and uniformly progress forward."

"94 percent…."

"Approaching 97…98….on 99 percent now."

A radio transmission breaks into the intercom

"This is Edwards…You're supersonic Dash One!"

Winworth replies;

"We're taking the engines to 102 percent Edwards. Keep us on your tracking."

Gretchen calmly continues her reports;

"We just passed 100 percent….all engines running well."

An added quality of tension is noted in Gretchen's voice;

"101…and starting to see a temperature rise in each engine.

"102 percent!"

"This is Edwards Dash One…we're tracking you at Mach 1.2!"

Winworth replies;

Chapter 21 – *Gretchen and the Coronado*

"We're throttling down Edwards and coming home."
There's a short period of silence before Edwards resumes communication;
"We can confirm the Mach 1.2 reading Dash One. Congratulations, your 990 has an unofficial world's record for the fastest airliner ever built and the first to achieve supersonic flight!"
Winworth replies with a dispassionate tone of voice;
   "From the initial flight deck fuel readouts we've been monitoring here...it looks like we set a world's record for fuel consumption as well. We were looking for better results in that area Edwards."

Post Flight Coffee
   Following the flight debriefing the crew stops at the *Flight Line Café*. Coffee and burgers are shared. There's a spirited discussion on further options of how to optimize the 990's fuel consumption.
   The technical discussion ends and Gretchen asks;
"How long have you both been flying?"
Dolan Replies;
   "Too long Gretchen! Tom and I both earned quite a few flight hours before joining the military and the Navy's flight program. We had our private license and received training and tremendous amount of flight time and experience on overseas assignments with *Mission Aviation Fellowship*...MAF.
   If you ever want to know how aviation can contribute to improving the lives of others...look no farther than the work MAF is doing."
   Winworth adds;   It was a calling...Dave and I both discussed how the Holy Spirit or maybe it was an angel...led us to MAF. It was one of the best "flying times" of our lives Gretchen. Have you ever had a feeling of being guided by a cause much larger than your own personal goals?"
   Gretchen smiles and replies;   "Yes, oh definitely.... I know exactly what you mean and am most familiar with the MAF organization!"

Chapter 22
Scrambled Eggs!
Near Korat, Thailand
March 23, 1962

The test flights of the C-121 have been successful and uneventful. Flights over the Tonkin Gulf off North Vietnam experienced no enemy aircraft encounters.

With the final mission completed; the EC-121 is 10 miles from its home base, Korat Royal Thai Airbase and on final landing approach.

The F-100 escort fighter jets flown by Captains Roger McConnell and David Delaney are in radio communication with C-121 copilot Scott Shepard and are about to break off formation and return to Tahkli.

"Take care Scott...Have a good flight back to the states. We're breaking off now." McConnell announces.

Scott replies;

"Good luck McConnell, appreciated your assistance. I'm headed for flight training....looks like I'll be flying B-52s."

McConnell chides;

"You really want to fly one of those big ugly airplanes Scott, You'd look better as a Hun driver!"

Scott laughs;

"The needs of the Air Force McConnell...it's all about the needs of the Air Force. Take care."

The Two F-100s bank sharply and leave in tight formation. They are at cruise altitude and facing a sun that's intermittently visible through a thickening cloud cover.

McConnell notices a small bright reflection interior to the sun. He lowers his helmet visor and looks directly into the sun. Instantly he calls Delaney, his wingman.

"Hey *Professor*...Bandit, check 12 high in the sun. Fights On!

Two seconds later a MiG-17 flys 200 feet overhead...the jet wash from the close encounter shakes the F-100.

McConnell calls out;

"I'm after this guy! Going to afterburner...stay with me *Professor!*"

McConnell surveys the surrounding sky for a 2nd MiG. There's none in sight...he's flying alone...The most dangerous condition for a pilot; being a lone aircraft in a combat scenario.... an easy target without a wingman!

McConnell asks himself; *Why is he alone?*

McConnell maneuvers into position directly behind the MiG and throttles out of afterburner. He arms his guns, checks the aiming reticle and fires a short burst. The tracers pass to the left of the target.

The MiG banks hard right then soars skyward in a steep vertical climb directly into the sun.

The side of the MiG has the ID *#3020* and there's a *burning American flag* on its tail! It's the legendary *Tomb*.

McConnell continues to engage the MiG, goes vertical and lights the afterburner. His helmet headset crackles then screams with a high pitched sound of an incoming radio transmission.

There's an unfamiliar voice...somewhat foreign ...It's the legendary *Tomb*;

"Hello McConnell... I have a message from an old friend of mine...maybe you remember meeting him...it goes like this...

The tone and inflection of the voice impersonate a person from the past with a chilling unreality;

' *'What's going on here neighbor? Was there an accident? You say a car was hit by a pickup near Clovis and nobody knows who it was? I can tell you who it was McConnell!...I can tell you!'*

The message was like a recording...a replay of the actual encounter years ago along the ridge of San Jon in New Mexico. McConnell is temporarily confused and distracted by the message.

Then, without warning...the afterburner suddenly shuts down. McConnell moves the throttles in and out of the afterburner detents several times in quick succession in a desperate attempt to relight the afterburner's spray rings. The aircraft loses airspeed and is unable to maintain the steep climb.

McConnell backs off from the climb and heaves the F-100 into a steep left banking descent. The F-100 begins to gain airspeed but *Tomb* has already taken advantage of the situation and maneuvers behind McConnell.

Wingman Delaney breaks radio silence;

"He coming up fast on your tail!…Get out of their now Rog!"

Just as Delaney completes his warning a continuous stream of munition tracers from the MiG find their mark in the F-100's left wing and fuselage section.

In the cockpit McConnell feels a slight "thump" like running into another aircraft's jet wash. The aircraft remains controllable. McConnell keys the mike button;

"I've been hit, going to dump ordinance."

He looks to his left and sees the MiG has broken off and headed towards Delaney. Before he can transmit a warning… a rocket is fired from the Soviet fighter. The missile reaches its target. There's an instant, tremendous explosion. Delaney's aircraft is blown apart. There was no opportunity for ejection.

McConnell looks at his altimeter. He's flying at 14,000 feet. There's a solid overcast at about 7000. The ground is completely obscured.

Without warning, another shudder and the engine seizes. All instrument readings and hydraulics are lost. McConnell knows he has no choice. He's got to punch out. He secures his visor in the down position, squeezes and engages the left and right side armrest ejection seat handles. The *canopy ejection initiator* fires. The *Plexigla*s canopy is blown skyward then thrown backward …caught in the powerful slipstream.

Almost simultaneously with the canopy release… the ejection seat fires propelling McConnell from the disabled fighter. There's the loud explosive sound, a sudden rush of cold air and G-forces pushing McConnell into his seat.

Twenty seconds later, McConnell' senses are startled by the sudden shock of the ejection seat falling away and his chute opening. He looks around and at the cloud cover below and wonders *what am I doing here!...hanging from a nylon canopy over a Laotian Jungle!*

He utters a short desperate prayer …

"Don't forget about me now Lord…I haven't forgotten you!"

Within 5 minutes McConnell enters the thick overcast covering the landscape below and obscuring all visual cues and eliminating any sense of motion. The result is a full dose of spatial disorientation. Suddenly McConnell breaks out of the

Chapter 22 – *Scrambled Eggs!*

overcast.

He's two hundred feet above a tree line. There's no time to maneuver the chute away from the approaching trees. He crosses his legs and breaks through a top layer of branches. After continuing to pass through several more layers; he finally comes to a stop.

A monsoon rain is falling lightly. McConnell surveys his situation. He is hanging from his parachute shroud lines 20 feet directly above a large watery, algae filled pond.

He unsuccessfully attempts to release himself from the harness. McConnell uses his survival knife and cuts himself free but continues to hold onto the harness straps. He sets himself into a swinging motion...back and forth in an increasing arc. If the branch continues to support him he may be able to produce enough forward momentum to throw him onto the solid grass area surrounding the edge of the pond.

Just at the right time, after several energetic final swings and at the farthest point of the arc he lets go of the harness. McConnell sails through the air and with remarkable agility and coordination lands feet first and standing upright on solid ground. He's surprised and pleased with the successful aerobatic maneuver.

Suddenly a slow steady clapping sound is heard ...directly behind him. A voice is heard;

"Well done Mr. McConnell...You were always the great athlete and such a showman...always so upright, uptight and religious at the Academy! What in the Master's name are you trying to prove Mr. Righteous?"

McConnell turns and can't believe who is standing in front of him...it's Devlin Sardoz from the Academy; the officer who engineered the plot to have him dismissed from the Academy. He's dressed in Air Force fatigues.

"I'm not trying to prove anything Devlin" McConnell replies;
Devlin continues;

"You're such a damn fool McConnell. Look where you're religion has taken you. Is this your reward? You've lost your wingman, your first air combat encounter, your aircraft and now you're separated and lost in this god-forsaken jungle. I don't see any rewards here McConnell or any that are forthcoming for you.

However, let me continue…for some reason…perhaps, because of my large reservoir of pity for you that I've found a grain of respect and am able to offer a much different future for you.

Let's make a deal. If you allow me; Not only will you be rescued and survive this despicable experience; I will release a plethora of rewards upon you….rewards of notable rank, respect and delivered with a notable increase of lifetime monetary gain. These are all rewards you really deserve…right? Think about it…a true second chance on life!"

An instant response from McConnell is returned in a sarcastic combative tenor;

"You go to Hell Devlin…Go back to where ever you came from… and get out of my jungle! I don't need you or your worthless offer!"

Devlin returns an offensive sneer in response and adds;

"Oh! that *Go to Hell* phrase is so colloquial McConnell…I hear that so much. I expected more from you…but if that's your decision...so be it!

On to scenario number 2! I call it *payback time.* I have a trick to show you. Look at my hands…Nothing you say…look again!.... **Look at my hands!"**

McConnell looks closer. Sardoz continues;
"See what I have!… Oh goodness, look what has magically appeared! I have your survival radio!"

McConnell reaches for his vest where the radio is attached…it's gone.

"Mr. McConnell…how very careless of you! As long as I have your radio I might as well check and see if it's working properly."

Sardoz turns the switch on….There's an instant puff of white electrical smoke and a short lived burst of flame from the front panel. Sardoz smiles sadistically adding;

"My, my…this certainly is not your day McConnell…another tragic loss!

Sardoz looks briefly at the radio then casually tosses it into the pond. He looks away for a moment then turns again to McConnell with a face and words of uncontrolled anger:

Chapter 22 – *Scrambled Eggs!*

"You ruined my life at the Academy and a valuable position of influence within your military. Now it's payback time Captain McConnell!

There are many crawling serpents in the jungle and they're all waiting for my command. It will be a long, memorable night for you. I have asked for a long and painful resolution to your life.

Before I leave you… I want you to forever know and remember the source of power commanding all activities on your earth. He is my Master; he is the prince of all who worship him…he is Lucifer!"

McConnell says nothing but stares directly at Sardoz until he silently and gradually fades into complete transparency.

The Tahkli Base Command Center

Sir, we've had no radio contact from Captains McConnell or Delaney for the last hour. They departed the C-121 on schedule and were returning to base according to the 121 co-pilot, Scott Shepard.

The day officer, Captain John Banner, glances at the base's local radar and sees no aircraft on the display;

"Make the call to *Airborne Search and Rescue* and let them know we've lost two aircraft. Pass the word to all our forward air controllers and ask for volunteers to join the search. All aircraft should monitor 243.0 MHz…the transmitting beacon frequency on McConnell's survival radio. It only has a 60 mile range but we may get lucky. Contact Shepard again and ask for the approximate coordinates of their aircraft when McConnell and Delaney broke formation for the return flight to Tahkli."

Banner walks over to the window overlooking the base and main runways. He looks to the sky above and notices the setting sun.

The color of *Darkness* is black and lonely

Night falls in the jungle. A low hanging cloud cover remains. There is no moon or stars or any other source of light. The darkness is total and enveloping. McConnell is alone. He finishes eating a small portion of emergency rations…then begins clearing a small circular area around him and lines the perimeter's edge with a collection of wood and dried leaves.

McConnell sits down on the ground. There's an overwhelming need for sleep. He decides to close his eyes for just a moment. McConnell easily falls into a deep sleep.

Suddenly he wakes up. The sound of rustling grass is all around him. He reaches for his flashlight and searches the area.

The batteries in the emergency flashlight are weak; the bulb shines dimly… the throw distance is greatly reduced. He looks closer at the moving ground. His eyes strain to focus on several approaching objects.

There are snakes… A lot of snakes!

McConnell is able to distinguish the reddish gray color of the *Malayan Pit Viper*. The species has a reputation for being bad tempered and quick to strike. Their venom from a single bite causes severe pain and ultimate death. McConnell is unable to count the massive number of snakes as they crawl through the tall grass and begin to encircle the campsite.

He retrieves matches from his emergency pack but drops the entire sealed metal container while attempting to open it. Finally, McConnell lights a match on the first try and carefully transfers the fragile flame to a dry leaf on the edge of the makeshift fire barrier. The flame takes hold and rapidly spreads to the more substantial wood branches. He walks along the circling barrier lighting other sections of the perimeter. Soon there is an entire protective circle of flames surrounding him.

The crawling population of snakes end there advance as they reach the fiery edge of the burning perimeter.

A couple smaller vipers slither through the barrier. McConnell spots them and quickly grabs a long, narrow tree branch…about 6 feet in length and skillfully picks up and tosses each of the small snakes high into the air and outside the barrier.

The entire night is spent tending the fire and maintaining control over the invading snakes. When morning arrives, the sun rises and shines brilliantly through the overhead tree foliage. The cloud cover has lifted. The sky is blue.

The snakes seem to respond in unison and mysteriously retreat

Chapter 22 – *Scrambled Eggs!*

into the jungle again. McConnell lies down and closes his eyes.

He suddenly awakens again. There's another sound…a voice is heard;

"Hey *Padre*…Come and get it!"

The *Professor,* his wingman and friend, is hard at work preparing breakfast.

"I don't want to burn these eggs!" Delaney exclaims.

McConnell is stunned. He must be dreaming. He hollers out;

"You're alive! How did you do it! I saw your plane explode. There was nothing left. There was no chute!"

Delaney is tending a fire beneath an improvised bamboo grill that holds a large black metal skillet of scrambled eggs and a kettle of hot coffee. He looks directly at McConnell;

"Rule Number Uno Padre, you can't kill a spirit!...especially an angel! After all these years together...you must have had some notion I was your guardian!

McConnell's mind, still reeling answers;

"I'm all confused. Maybe I have a fever and am hallucinating this whole conversation!"

"In that case Rog, enjoy some of my special "*Hot Fevered Scrambled Eggs and coffee!* …it's really the best breakfast in town my friend…my good and faithful friend!"

Delaney pauses before continuing.

"We'll have a good breakfast and then I'll get to work and send you on your way back to the base."

Delaney continues;

"How do you like Laos? We've both seen Laos from the air. It's a beautiful country isn't it? It's a tragedy to know what will happen here in the not too distant future. In case you haven't already guessed from all the political dialogue and our recon missions here…a long term war will be fought in Vietnam and right here in Laos as well. Over a nine year period …270 million bombs will be dropped on this peaceful looking countryside…That's a bombing every eight minutes for nine years. God's land will be forever cratered Roger."

McConnell shakes his head in disbelief;

"No…no…That's impossible…I don't believe it! That's insane!"

Delaney looks at his friend and sees the painful concern written on his face and the strong emotion in his voice.

Delaney suddenly realizes and regrets disclosing his knowledge of the future. He makes a mental note to be more selective in sharing disclosures of future events. He immediately changes the subject.

"Sorry I couldn't join you earlier Roger…I wanted you to have an opportunity to put Sardoz in his place rather than me. I know how strong your faith is…and you could handle him...and you did!

Demon Sardoz is one unhappy, disbelieving spiritual dude this morning!

Delaney serves his scramble eggs and adds;

"In addition to getting you back to base…my purpose in seeing you this morning is very timely and important. I have a message from Gabriel…an angel of the highest order. **The Lord has a special mission for you and your brother to perform.**

A Miraculous event will take place in the future…a "breakaway" event which will alter the path mankind is on and guide the world to another more enlightened and peaceful journey.

However, certain elements and actions must be completed and performed before this event happens. You will be given an assignment to support the Lord's plan.

Delaney does not deliver any further information. McConnell is about to ask several questions but Delaney ends the conversation abruptly announcing;

"Well it's time for me to leave and time for you to return to civilization again…It's quite easy; just follow the trail!"
A narrow path which McConnell had not noticed earlier is suddenly visible.

"You're only a short distance, about a half hour's walk, from a local medical clinic and an American doctor who can help you. So, for now we'll part company.

For your knowledge…The "professor", your wingman and friend…of human form no longer exists. He was killed by the missile from Tomb's MiG. I will no longer be able to return to a human form with that identity. You'll just have to get used to knowing me as a spirit Roger! We'll stay in touch and meet again…I promise…It is so written. I am your guardian."

With those closing words, Delaney closes his eyes, lowers his

Chapter 22 – *Scrambled Eggs!*

head and is gone. McConnell walks to the spot where Delaney was standing and looks around the area. All is quiet.

McConnell begins his walk along the newly discovered trail. A short time later he sees the medical clinic. A group of young children are playing nearby…they run to greet him.

Chapter 23
Mr. President
Los Alamos National Laboratory
New Mexico
A Visit by the President - December 7, 1962

President John F. Kennedy arrives at the Los Alamos Scientific Laboratory for a briefing on the progress of a classified program. *Project Rover* is one of the Lab's newer projects; to build and test a nuclear rocket engine for future deep space exploration.

Before leaving the Lab, Kennedy asks for an impromptu visit with Dr. Kashi Verma, the lead scientist and director of the Advanced Laser Applications Group. Her program is a new and classified top-secret project.

Dr. Verma greets the arriving President...her voice is reserved, calm and welcoming;

"Good Morning Mr. President...This is such a wonderful surprise and honor. I appreciate the opportunity to meet you and tell you about our work here at the Lab."

Kennedy smiles, nods in recognition and replies in a friendly, thoughtful tone;

"Dr. Verma...I am most pleased to finally meet you today. I have followed your progress from Washington and am impressed with your accomplishments...not only in the development of more powerful lasers but in finding new applications for this technology. Your leadership is to be commended and is very much appreciated by this President."

Dr. Verna is slightly embarrassed by the President's praise but returns the compliment...thanking him for his support;

"Mr. President, your personal endorsement of this new program has made the difference. We are able to make substantial progress in our research program because of the continued funding from Washington...which we greatly appreciate!

You will be receiving a report, probably next month, on our first test of an airborne laser...it's scheduled for next week.

The airborne test, on a specially prepared aircraft, will include a new area of interest in addition to our focus on weaponry. We have discovered and will be running preliminary tests on the use of focused laser beams to affect the weather. They offer a completely 'clean' alternative to traditional cloud seeding.

The technology is in its infancy but with more development time, I believe lasers will eventually produce enough power to modulate the weather in areas of high contrast, such as California or Chile, where flooding and droughts occur in the extreme.

Under certain conditions lasers would be able to create new clouds where there are none by inducing condensation. The process is really quite straight forward; naturally occurring water vapor in the air is condensed into droplets...ice crystals form, mimicking the natural process that create clouds.

Alternatively, rainfall could also be triggered to 'empty' the atmosphere and increase the potential for dry weather. We performed this in our laboratory. We created clouds in a large test tube, but are unable to take the next step. The lasers we are using today are still not powerful enough and there are so many technical parameters we still can't control.

It seems as though every time I think I have done everything with lasers, something new comes up. For example, there are potential applications in the biomedical field. By changing the color of the laser, we could identify and selectively kill cancer cells, with little or no collateral damage."

Dr. Verna pauses from her delivery of technical details and expresses a personal concern;

"Mr. President, the only worry I have is the long research and experimental time that's necessary to bring these break through developments to fruition."

There's a subtle twinkle in Kennedy's eyes that seem to communicate an understanding of her concerns but also a hint of his continuing support... and the telling of one of his favorite stories;

"Dr. Verma your concern reminds me of the great French Marshal Lyautey, who once asked his gardener to plant a tree. The gardener objected that this particular tree was slow-growing and would not reach maturity for a hundred years. The Marshal replied, 'In that case, there is no time to lose, plant it this afternoon.'

I say to you...plant your tree today Dr. Verma...by all means plant your tree!"

Kennedy is abruptly interrupted by an aide; reminding him of

164

the time and tight schedule of events still ahead. The President concludes the visit with a closing exchange of pleasantries and leaves the laboratory.

Dr. Verma returns to the laboratory.
The lab's assistant director, Phillip Conrell approaches her and anxiously asks;

"Kashi, how did it go? How was your meeting? We were all excited seeing him arrive this morning."

Dr. Verma's reply is buoyed with enthusiasm.

"I must tell you it was a most memorable experience. He seems so young...but yet very confident and knowledgeable. He possess an optimistic spirit, a strong positive sense for the future of our country.

You know Phillip, I believe John F. Kennedy is exactly what the country needs now...I am most excited with this new President!"

Chapter 23 – *Mr. President*

Chapter 24
Generally Speaking
Forth Worth
May 4, 1963- 11:00 AM

"Mr. Alan McConnell, Good Morning...this is Tactical Air Command Headquarters...I have General Walt Swenson on the line. Are you able to speak to him at this time?"

Alan replies; "Yes, by all means!"

There is a short pause. The general's voice explodes over the phone;

"Stormy!...good morning! Did you finish building that airplane of ours yet?"

Alan replies;

"We're still working on it General."

The General continues;

"Well, maybe this can help get the 'one-eleven' flying a little sooner. I want you to know I followed up on your request to have your brother; Captain McConnell assigned to General Dynamics and the F-111 project."

Your brother is currently assigned to a flight test program at Edwards. He's putting the new F-4 Phantom through its paces. He'll be finishing up with the program in late November.

I talked to *Assignments* and they agreed; he's a perfect fit and well qualified for the F-111 program.

So, the final word is...you can look forward to having your brother in Fort Worth come January...next year."

Alan is elated;

"That's outstanding! I truly appreciate your help General, thank you. Roger and I have a strong working partnership when it comes to flying.

Progress on the *"Spirit of San Jon"* is continuing on an aggressive schedule with activity currently centered on the engines. We've been making some modifications to upgrade its performance.

Rollout for the *Spirit* is November 15th .

The General replies;

"Very good...I'll see you again on the 'first flight'. Be sure to confirm the date with our office Alan. You take care."

Chapter 25
A Troubled Road to Bourem
The African Congo
May 4, 1963- Late Evening, 11:00 PM

Scientist and agronomist Jean Paul Boyer is only eight kilometers from the town of Bourem. The front head lamp on his *Matchless G3L* motorcycle is dim making it necessary to reduce his speed accordingly. The road, *RR32*, is a neatly drawn straight line on the map with no deviation. In reality; the road needs significant repair and in some places is totally buried under drifting sand. He had hoped to reach Bourem earlier in the day but the motorcycle ran into engine problems. After 2 hours breaking down the engine and cleaning all its individual parts he was able to get underway again.

Now, once again the steady sound of the small single cylinder 350cc engine is running smoothly and offers a pleasantly reassuring tone from its exhaust.

As he continues down the road, another higher pitched sound is heard coming from behind and rapidly approaching. It sounds like a jet engine. The whine of its turbines becomes louder and reach a deafening intensity. Jean Paul looks back. A hundred feet above the road and approaching is a large twin engine jet aircraft. It turns on its landing lights. The strong and focused beams of light are directed on the road ahead. In a matter of seconds the aircraft is directly above him. Jean Paul can clearly see the support struts, hydraulic lines on the landing gear and a large red star on its wing. He slows down and pulls over to the side of the road. The aircraft touches down and reverses its engines.

Almost immediately a dozen armed soldiers exit the aircraft. Jean Paul lowers the cycle on its side and drops to the ground. The soldiers are yelling in Russian and rush toward him.

One of the soldiers calls out in English;

"CIA!...CIA! We see you!...Stand up right now!....Place your hands above your head!"

Jean Paul remains low to the ground and attempts to crawl away from the motorcycle and into a large area of high grass. He reaches the edge of the road. Without warning, he suddenly feels a sharp sting to his shoulder. He cannot move...he rolls on his side. A strong light shining in his face is all he remembers before becoming unconscious.

KGB operative, Devlin Victor Dudorov smiles and continues to shine his flashlight on the wounded young man. He quietly orders:

"Take him onboard and have the wound tended to…we have a long flight ahead of us. We will have plenty of time to question him when we reach Verkhoyansk ."

Inside and unconscious is another American, David Richardsen, the son of the U.S. Envoy.

Devlin talks to his aid;

There is something about these two that I intensely dislike. I was immediately offended by them. They reek of a strong destiny, of some vile scheme which I cannot identify. They are dangerous beyond comprehension; I understand why my Master instructed me to take appropriate action.

Standing nearby is a military soldier and lower ranking demon who participated in both abductions. He asks:

"What about the American government? Surely, they will ask about the disappearance of these two?"

Dudorov laughs and casually replies;

"I have taken care of that. Do not forget, this is Africa and these are revolutionary times…I have begun and strategically placed in proper channels a rumor that will eventually elevate to a credible news story;

African rebels have taken hostage of two Americans and transported them to one of their camps at an undisclosed location.

Of course, The Soviet Union will officially announce support and agree to join the United States effort in finding the two Americans!

Instruct the pilot to takeoff now. A long flight is ahead of us."

Renegades

Chapter 26
Poetry and Power
Amherst College
October 26, 1963

President Kennedy accepts an invitation to participate in a ground breaking ceremony of the Robert Frost Library at Amherst College.

On board *Air Force One* he prepares his speech and directs his thoughts toward Frost's poem, *Poetry and Power*. He underlines two sentences in the typed speech that has been drafted.

"The men who create power make an indispensable contribution to the nation's greatness, but the men who question power make a contribution just as indispensable...for they determine whether we use power or power uses us."

"When power leads man toward arrogance, poetry reminds him of his limitations. When power narrows the area of man's concern, poetry reminds him of the richness and diversity of existence. When power corrupts, poetry cleanses."

He reads further and edits the speech's content and scratches out a paragraph with his pen;

In soviet Russia, Chairman Khrushchev has informed us, 'It is the highest duty of the Soviet writer, artist and composer, of every creative worker, to be in the ranks of the builders of communism, to put his talents at the service of the great cause of our Party, to fight for the triumph of the ideas of Marxism – Leninism.'

He continues reading leaving in the words and paragraph;

'In a democratic society, the highest duty of the writer, artist and composer is to remain true to himself and to his vocation, letting the chips fall as they may.

In serving his vision of the truth, the artist best serves his nation. And the nation which disdains the mission of art invites the fate of Robert Frost's hired man...the fate of having
Nothing to look backward to with pride
And nothing to look forward to with hope.

168

I look forward to a great future for America…a future in which our country will match its military strength with its moral restraint, its wealth with its wisdom, its power with its purpose. I look forward to an America which will not be afraid of grace and beauty…which will protect the beauty of our natural environment, which will preserve the great old structures and squares and parks of our national past, and which will build handsome and balanced cities in the future…

I look forward to a world which will be safe not for democracy and for diversity but for distinction.'

For a moment Kennedy's thoughts drift abstractly to another term of office and what he would do in 1968 upon completing a second term of his presidency. He muses that he'd be too old to begin a new career and too young to write his memoirs.

He places the outline of his speech to the side and retrieves the daily briefing folder handed him before takeoff.

Kennedy skims the daily summary of world events. Terrorism threats at key bases around the world are on the rise. Reports confirm terrorist activity has increased in Europe. For just a moment he foresees how "terrorism" could evolve into a world-wide threat to democracy presenting a greater challenge to defeat than the events of World War II.

He is about to close the file but notices a singular unsigned unofficial looking note clipped to the top of the file. A small embossed silver cross is on the upper left corner of the note paper. The message is written in a careful and artistic script and not conforming to any of today's writing styles. The note reads;

> *Mr. President,*
> *On The 22nd Day of November:*
> *"Put on the whole armor of God so you may be able to stand against the devil's schemes."* Ephesians 6:11

The steward working on *Air Force One* watches Kennedy from a distance in an adjoining compartment as he reads the note. He is pleased to see Kennedy remove the note and place it in his shirt pocket. However, there is disappointment and concern for being unable to provide a more direct warning.

Renegades

However, the powers of angels are limited especially when they are in human form.

Kennedy hears a change in the sound of the engines and looks out the window of *Air Force One.*

It's Indian summer and the ground below is a golden and orange pallet of colors. The view offers a sense of peace and calm. The aircraft landing gear lowers, locks in place as *Air Force One* completes the final approach to its Massachusetts destination.

Change is the law of life. And those who look only to the past or present are certain to miss the future" – John F. Kennedy

170

Chapter 27
A Morning Call
"The world will never be the same again."
November 22, 1963 - Fort Wort, Texas

A Phone Conversation:
"Gretchen, this is Alan. We missed you at the planning meeting this morning. Are you Okay?"
Gretchen answers;
"No Alan. I must see you. Please come."

Gretchen's Apartment

Alan arrives at Gretchen's apartment...he knocks at the door. There is no answer. He attempts to open the door. It's unlocked. He slowly opens it, walks in and calls out;
"Gretchen...Gretchen...are you here?"
The living room shades are drawn. Gretchen is sitting on the floor in a darkened corner of the room. Her legs are crossed... her face entirely covered with her hands. She looks up on hearing Alan. She appears distraught almost beyond recognition ... overcome with a severe and disfiguring appearance of sadness written on her face and reflected in her eyes...a distant, hurt look. Tears fall slowly down her face.
Alan kneels down at first...then sits quietly next to Gretchen. There is a long period of silence. Alan remains quiet then finally asks in a voice of sympathetic concern;
"Gretchen...My good friend Gretchen...What has happened here?"
Gretchen attempts to compose herself...she begins to relate her story;
"You know Alan...it's our President...President Kennedy. He spent the evening here visiting Fort Worth and departed for Dallas this morning.
Air Force One was parked a short distance from our hangar. Earlier this morning, I walked from my office to the reception area. Reporters and other employees gathered on the tarmac waiting to see the President board the aircraft.
President Kennedy and his wife arrived and stepped out of

171

the limousine. There were cheers from everyone there. The two waved and looked so well and happy together… like they were departing for a holiday.

President Kennedy walked right past me…we exchanged only a fleeting glance, our eyes met for what must have been less than a second."

Gretchen becomes emotional again and breaks into tears;

"I saw it in his eyes…it was very clear…so very clear. I saw his future. I saw it happen. I saw our future change. The world will never be the same again. Evil…pure Evil has won a battle."

Alan is more confused and replies in concerned desperation;

"The President is fine. I heard the news… he just landed in Dallas. You're not making sense Gretchen! I don't understand. Tell me. Tell me please…what did you see?"

Gretchen is impatient and uncharacteristically intolerant in her response;

"I don't think you'll ever be able to understand Alan. You are a gifted engineer but you are so blind and dutifully ignorant to the world that surrounds you.

We live in two worlds; a spiritual one and temporal one that are in constant warfare with each other…a war between good and evil. You are lost and concerned with only your day to day obligations and the schedule of your temporal world…you are totally unaware of an Almighty God and the works of the Holy Spirit in the spiritual dimension you're living in."

Gretchen pauses for a moment. She wipes her eyes and continues;

"Listen carefully. Let me explain it to you in terms you might better understand.

You are viewing the world through an imperfect prism that reveals light as only a single band. You are unable to see the real full rainbow display…a splendid multitude of lights in many colors…a full and complete spectrum.

If you continue to recognize only one band of light Alan…you will remain forever blind to God and all things spiritual.

I am a part of God's many colored spiritual world. I am

Chapter 27 – *A Morning Call*

fighting for the *'Good'* Alan. I am your guardian angel. Can you comprehend that?

Today *'Good'* succumbed to the powers of Evil. A battle was lost. The world will not be the same.

Please…wake up to the moment Alan. Be aware of the total world which surrounds you…not just half of it. The Lord and his angels need you and your faith…We need your help now!"

Alan's absent and confused state is drawn to Gretchen's eyes…those eyes which always seem to radiate a strong and powerful truth with a vulnerable innocence. He turns away and attempts to gather his own thoughts.

He looks about the room and mentally challenges the reality he sees and contemplates the concept of faith…accept faith in a world with a God he cannot see or measure?

Alan returns his attention to Gretchen. Who waits in patient anticipation for Alan's response.

In a slow, thoughtful and painful manner…Alan replies;

"I am so sorry Gretchen…but I am unable… and cannot believe in God."

Alan pauses and continues to look at Gretchen. The words that follow are spoken with sincerity and meant to soften his reply;

"…I believe in you Gretchen."

Gretchen replies with a sad but consoling smile;

"If you believe in me Alan…than you must also believe in God. Ponder these things in your heart. Continue to consider all that I have revealed to you today."

A First Report-Dallas, Texas

CBS Television is ten minutes into the live broadcast soap opera; *As the World Turns.* A "CBS News Bulletin" slide abruptly breaks into the broadcast at 1:40 pm. The voice of television news anchor Walter Cronkite is heard. He reads the following:

"Here is a bulletin from CBS News. In Dallas, Texas, three shots were fired at President Kennedy's motorcade in downtown Dallas. The first reports say President Kennedy has been

seriously wounded by this shooting."

A short time passes. Regular programing is interrupted. Walter Cronkite is seen "live" on camera as he's handed a news bulletin. After looking it over for a moment, he takes off his glasses and makes the official announcement:

"From Dallas, Texas, the flash, apparently official: President Kennedy died at 1 p.m. Central Standard Time."

He glances up at the studio clock and then continues

"That's 2 o'clock Eastern Standard Time, some 38 minutes ago."

After making that announcement, Cronkite pauses briefly, puts his glasses back on, and swallows hard to maintain his composure.

Chapter 27 – *A Morning Call*

Sidebar: The Shot Felt "Round the World"

Notes From: "Our Ambassadors Association for Diplomatic Studies and Training"

Democratic Republic of Congo
Brandon H. Grove, Jr.

"Much has been said about the shock and grief that followed not only in our country but all over the world. Kennedy was the post-war symbol of a revitalized America, a leader determined to move forward at home and abroad on the issues of his day.

His style, wit and elegance, his wife and children, captivated the media who made him larger than life and ignored his foibles....When he died, so, once again, did American innocence and a large piece of our native optimism....As individuals, we seem to have shorter time for being young."

Sudan
William M. Rountree

"One of my embassy officers leaned over my shoulder and told me that my secretary was on the phone saying that the President had been assassinated. I said that couldn't be true, the President was there. He said, "No, she means the President of the United States". I left immediately for the Embassy and turned on the radio....Even as I listened to those early reports before President Kennedy's death was actually confirmed, Many local Sudanese, this was late at night, came to the Chancery door to express condolences. Many of them were weeping.

Within hours, every taxi in Khartoum had a black banner on its radio aerial. It was evident that people were not merely giving lip service, but felt his death very deeply and emotionally."

India

"We had a memorial service for him in the Anglican

Renegades

cathedral in Bombay. The crowd was tremendous. The church was absolutely packed, and there were people outside, and everyone wearing white. White in India is the color of mourning. People stopped you on the street to say how sorry they were. No, the outpouring from India was absolutely tremendous. President Kennedy grabbed the imagination of the world, certainly of the Asian world in a way that perhaps no one else had done, as far as I know, up till that time....We were joined by the love of many, many thousands of people in Bombay over the death of President Kennedy."

Japan
Elden B. Erickson

"I was going to be the chief rapporteur for the Japan-U.S. Ministerial Conference. I had just gotten to Tokyo the day before and was staying with a USIA friend. He was called during the night and told about the attempted assassination–at that point he hadn't died. He and I went down to the press club and watched the tickers come in. It was really a very exciting moment. The conference was canceled and I immediately went back to Osaka. There was the most remarkable outpouring of sympathy I have ever seen in my life. The Japanese, who never show emotion, would come up to you and cry and say how sorry they were to hear about the President. We had a service in Osaka and one in Kobe. Both were absolutely jammed packed. It is hard to think that Japanese, who are unemotional normally, would express themselves like that."

Yemen
Robert Theodore Curran

"I was in Aden (Yemen)...the morning we heard about it. The first reports were that he'd been shot but not killed, and by the time we got back to Taiz, we knew that the President was dead. Not only were the Americans struck, but the Yemenis were terribly, terribly affected. And we had a condolence book at the chargé's house, Jim Cortada's house, and I think it took us three days to accommodate all the people who wanted to express their grief.

Guests cried and tore their hair. I suppose there were two reasons. One is that they saw America as kind of being the "great hope of the world," as it were. And I think Kennedy came across generally to the world as a new spirit in international relations.

So it was a very, very sad time, and the Yemenis were casting around for some way to honor the fallen President, and they fixed on the city water system for Taiz. And after a debate, the Kennedy family agreed, so there exists still in Taiz the John F. Kennedy Municipal Water System."

USSR
Ralph E. Lindstrom

"I remember learning about it on the Voice of America (while in Moscow). Roger Kirk was living in the same building with me and he came up to tell us that Kennedy had been assassinated. We rushed down and listened to the commentary on Voice of America. And insofar as the Soviets were concerned, Khrushchev personally came over and signed the condolence book in the embassy and was crying. They're very impressed by death, perhaps because at that time they didn't believe there was any place else to go. I think insofar as the man on the street was concerned, I was traveling at that time, and we talked to taxi drivers, and the typical line was that Kennedy had been a great man. They didn't say so while he was alive. But then they'd say that (Lyndon) Johnson is a very bad man. No real basis for that, just something they didn't like about Johnson's looks. It seemed to be almost a standard thing you'd pick up all across the Soviet Union. But they clearly seemed to be very sorry to see Kennedy perish that way."

Colombia
Lawrence P. Taylor

"It hit me like a sucker-punch in the solar plexus, but what was, I think, more interesting is the effect it had in the community. I'll never forget it. I think that community and every community I knew of or later heard about in rural Colombia

Renegades

seemed to be as affected by that event as America was, and I still remember the endless lines of mules and horses and people that walked out of the countryside to come in and tell us, who were the only Americans they knew, how sorry they were and that in this Catholic country they all burned candles on the night after, when people knew that he had died.

The whole countryside, as far as an eye could see, was full of candles. There's no electricity out there, but every little hut for as far as the eye could see had lit a candle in remembrance of President Kennedy. It was, in a depressing sense, kind of a magical moment."

Chapter 27 – *A Morning Call*

Chapter 28
Revelation on the Yard
Yards Park, Washington D.C.
December 28, 1963

Jeremy S. Standvok, is a former CIA operative reassigned to the State Department as Assistant Secretary of Intelligence and Research. He walks with Policy Annalist Lloyd Jerome Jennings through Yards Park...a location not far from the Washington Naval Yard and the Capitol building where they conducted a monthly security briefing. The park area is active during the summer months with tourists and concerts...but is quiet now, almost isolated. Standvok and Jennings sit down on one of the benches.

Standvok looks about the park and in the direction of the Naval Yard remarking;

"I like to visit this area. The Yard has a lot of history Lloyd. That great Navy sailing ship; the three masted heavy frigate *Constitution* came to the Yard in 1812 to refit and prepare for combat action. You could understand wars and conflict back then...you knew how to plan a battle and fight the enemy. It's all changed now.

Standvok's mood becomes visibly more solitary and negative;

"You know Lloyd...DC in the winter sucks! This is not the greatest place to be stationed...its grey, its cold, and there's too much concrete and hard nose politics."

He turns directly to Lloyd and asks;

"So, Mr. Jennings; where are we at with our Siberian rescue of Captain McConnell. Is he really alive and a captive prisoner? What's going on?"

Jennings replies with his usual studied and precise manner;

"Yes, he's there; a gulag prisoner, he's alive...but his physical condition is marginal and deteriorating. Something else I found out...and especially disturbing...two other Americans have recently arrived and placed with the other prisoners there. The Russians are going to great lengths to cover up and isolate themselves from this abduction they planned and executed.

We've had two recent reports wired from Africa and special

envoy Donald Richardsen. His son was on assignment for the Peace Corps and another young man, Jean Paul Boyer, a university student, was conducting some independent agricultural research along the Sahel. Both disappeared near the same location on the same day. Richardsen says the local newspapers report one of the Rebel armies responsible.

Standvok sits up straighter;

"This is getting more interesting."

"...and that's not all." Jennings continues;

"Listen to this bit of information I gleaned. The total population of prisoners confined at Verkhoyansk is slightly over a 100. All are writers, religious leaders, scientists and engineers confined there because of not buying into the Soviet Party line."

Standvok shakes his head in dismay;

"Khrushchev knows how to handle citizens alright...lock up your best and brightest in Siberia! Damn!"

Jennings continues;

"There's more. I could not believe this! The director of the Verkhoyansk Gulag is Andrey Ivanov. He's asking for political asylum for himself and the 100 prisoners! He's looking to escape but needs support from the United States. He says this is a *Human Rights* issue which demands our attention...

Accordingly, he observes; the United States has an unwritten obligation and right to intervene."

Standvok takes out a cigar from his inside coat pocket and begins to light it.

"This is new information Lloyd. You did good young man! Let me begin conversation with some of my old friends in the CIA and our leadership in the State Department. *Let's see if we can generate new interest for a rescue mission!*

The two McConnell brothers need to be brought into the loop. They should be contacted immediately and told about their father. Where are they now?"

Lloyd refers to his notes;

"Air Force Captain Roger McConnell is an Air Force Academy graduate, a pilot who completed a tour of duty in Thailand, reported to Edwards Air Force Base Test Flight Center and just graduated from the program there. What's interesting is his new assignment.

Chapter 28 – *Revelation on the Yard*

He was just assigned as the Air Force representative and certifying test pilot for the General Dynamics F-111 program. His brother, Alan McConnell, everyone knows him as *Stormy*, is the lead engineer in charge of the F-111 project. The two brothers will be working together."

Standvok gazes upwards into the grey sky…blows a single, circular smoke ring into the air that quickly dissipates in the brisk wind…then replies;

"I'll contact the two brothers and give a call to Langley. My friend, Air Force General Sam Billington is the Associate Director for Military Affairs. He heads up the CIA group coordinating, plans for executing all worldwide activities. Sam's a World War II veteran and runs an aggressive program.

Meanwhile Lloyd, I want you to get a message to Andrey Ivanov, the Director of the Verkhoyansk Gulag…let him know we're working on a plan. We'll be in touch.

By the way…tell me Lloyd how do you ever get in touch with Ivanov?

Who is our contact in Siberia?…that's one Hell of a place to be assigned."

Lloyd replies with a half-smile;

"We have an *unofficial United States –Siberian Ambassador*…His name is Victor Kologrigov, the manager and custodian at the Batagay and Verkhoyansk airports. He has a shortwave radio and our special frequency."

Standvok replies;

"Okay Lloyd…I won't press on. We all have our own special assets to protect…Let's get back to the office."

Edwards Flight Test Center

January 19, 1964

Hello Alan,

    Glad we had a chance to talk on the phone the other night. Sounds like your thoughts on religion and faith are evolving. The world starts to take on a different perspective. I was especially interested in listening to your experience. with Gretchen and her spiritual identity. I had a similar experience and can verify that angels really exist! Right now it seems two angels are very interested in monitoring our activities and preparing us for some kind of assignment. I don't pretend to understand what's happening. We'll have to wait and see what develops. I delayed reporting to Edwards after the crash in Laos and the loss of Delaney. I needed some time to process all that had happened.

    I've finished the flight testing for the F-4 Phantom project yesterday. I can tell you for a fact…it's one mean machine! An opposing enemy would in no way want or should attempt to challenge this aircraft in combat!

    By the way, orders are in hand for my assignment to Fort Worth and joining you and the F-111 flight test program.

    Brother…you've certainly learned how to maneuver this many layered Air Force bureaucracy. A large number of qualified pilots were interested in going to Fort Worth…but your connection with General Swenson at TAC made the difference.

    I'll be leaving in a day or two and driving to Fort Worth in the Vette.

Take Care… Roger

Chapter 29
Here, There and Everywhere
Early afternoon - January 24, 1964

St. Peter's Dome Trail – New Mexico

Angels Michael and Gabriel walk together along the wilderness trail and reach the dome; the highest point in a small group of 8000 foot peaks on the eastern edge of New Mexico's Jemez Mountains. They slowly climb the steps of an unoccupied watchtower used during the summer to spot forest fires. The temperature is -20 degrees. The door is locked but is easily opened by the angels. The tower offers a welcomed respite from the outside wind and cold.

Michael is the first to speak;

"The weather here mimics the climate of Siberia; an area of concern and activity as we prepare for a rescue mission there. It is a terribly hostile and dangerous corner of the world. Is everything in place Gabriel?"

Gabriel offers assurance;

"Yes Michael…all segments of the mission have come together now. The entire prison population, their families as well as all the guards are included in the rescue. Only the activities of the *"other side"* remain a troublesome source of constant resistance. Yet, they have no knowledge of the Lord's plan and of the Miracle that will take place."

Michael does not reply, only nods politely in acceptance. The response is unemotional but serves as a positive expression of confidence which Gabriel has seen many times before.

Verkhoyansk Gulag, Siberia

Prison Director, Andrey Ivanov, is conducting daily rounds of the prison facility and enters the mechanical room to inspect the boiler there. Accompanying him is Victor Kologrigov the manager of the Batagay airport .

Andrey checks the main steam pressure gauge on the boiler…he taps its glass face with his index finger before taking a final reading. He records the result in his log while informally asking;

"So Victor, tell me the details of the latest radio communication you've had with the Americans?"

Victor replies;

"They're working on a plan to airlift the entire prison population to one of their bases on the Aleutian chain. We will be contacted next month with the exact details."

Andrey shakes his head;

"I am not very encouraged with their progress. Time is running out. I don't know if I'm able to maintain the secrecy needed to execute the American plan...whatever it may be!

There's been more interest from Moscow in recent days since we added two new prisoners. They abducted two Americans, David Richardsen and Jean Paul Boyer...for what reason I do not know! Richardsen is the son of a special presidential envoy! That will go over '*big time*' with the Americans if the Russian connection is discovered!

Boyer is just a college student on some kind of university agricultural project! Once again Moscow provides me with no information on what's going on! The KGB questioned them both and then flew back to Moscow.

There's another issue as well. This facility is scheduled to be shutdown...closed and boarded up in 90 days. When this happens the prisoners will be sent to another location two hundred miles south of here.

Stay close to that airport radio of yours Victor. Let me know as soon as you hear more details of the *American plan*."

General Dynamics -Fort Worth - Texas

The road trip from California and Edwards Air Force Base was a long all night drive.

For Roger McConnell the open road offered more time to reflect on the Laos crash and the spiritual revelation of his former wingman.

The trip to Fort Worth also offered an opportunity to appreciate the Corvette and put it through its high end performance paces on the long, wide open roads.

Chapter 29 - *Here, There and Everywhere*

The only consequence was a "pullover" by a radar armed Texas Ranger who clocked McConnell "flying" at over110 mph.

However, the officer also owned a "vette" and after a short conversation showed some understanding and mercy by offering an undocumented verbal warning...and no ticket.

Arrival

It's early morning and McConnell pulls into the parking area of Hanger 4 and the *Renegade Werks* at General Dynamics, Fort Worth. It's a cool and bright start to the day. Roger, in civilian clothes, approaches the military security post at the entrance to Hangar 4.

McConnell's disheveled appearance reflects the all night, non-stop drive from Edwards. Unshaven and wearing his aviator sunglasses, a bright colored, flowered, short sleeved Hawaiian Luau shirt complimented with a wrinkled pair of khaki shorts. The combination presents a more than casual appearance to the uniformed guard at the security check point.

Roger introduces himself. The guard remains expressionless; standing rigidly stiff in stature and manner .

"My name is Roger, Roger McConnell. I just arrived and haven't processed through yet. Could you call my brother Alan, Alan McConnell...he's expecting me."

The guard looks suspiciously at McConnell and asks for his driver's license. Roger pulls out his wallet and in a clumsy uncoordinated fashion searches through a collection of plastic credit and identification cards.

"I have it here...somewhere!" After some time Roger exclaims;

"Here it is!"

He hands the license to the guard who carefully examines the identification and says;

"California...Hmmm...I thought so!"

With a suspicious nature; he visually surveys McConnell again and asks with a directed sense of disdain;

"Tell me exactly...what is your intended purpose visiting here today Mr. McConnell?"

Roger takes off his sun glasses, rubs his eyes and the stubble of his overnight beard. He replies in a matter of fact tone;

186

"I'm the new test pilot for that secret airplane you've got parked in the hangar. I'll be putting it through its paces for the next couple months Sergeant. I want to see the airplane and I'd like to see my brother. Is that a problem?"

McConnell presents his military ID.

"I'm a little tired right now Sergeant. Could you call my brother and let him know I'm here?"

The guard, momentarily stunned, stares blankly at McConnell then becomes apologetic;

"Yes...Yes by all means...sir! There's no problem here...Sir, I'm sorry. "I'll call right now...Captain McConnell."

The guard dutifully returns the military ID card and picks up the phone and connects directly with the hangar's project office.

A minute passes.

Suddenly, Alan walks through the main hangar entrance door and enthusiastically greets his brother.

"Roger...you made it! Good to see you!"

An energetic handshake is accompanied with light laughter; Alan exclaims;

"Well, we did it...we're back together again...like the old days! Let's not waste time. Follow me Rog. Let me show you the *Spirit*."

The brothers walk past the security post and through several more security doors, down a long hallway to the entry door of the *Werks*.

Alan remarks;

"By the way... you really look like hell Rog!...where did you get that shirt!"

They both laugh.

Alan places his ID badge over an electronic device. The door automatically opens.

The gleaming white F-111, *Spirit Of San Jon,* is bathed in bright arc lamps and dominates the first view from the hangar's entry way. Its wings are swept back to their full 72 degree angle.

Roger exclaims;

"It looks like some kind of arrow...ready to be fired Alan!" Roger immediately strides towards the *Spirit* admiring its sleek aerodynamic lines. He makes a quick walk around the aircraft

Chapter 29 - *Here, There and Everywhere*

Alan follows close behind. Roger stops for a moment and peers inside one of the engine's twin air intakes...and studies it for a moment.

"I can see you've been busy Alan...the intake includes what looks like a variable spike to control inlet air and prevent compressor stalls...very impressive...shows some real serious engineering...and then this whole variable wing design ...unbelievable!"

Roger turns away from away from the aircraft and looks at Alan and recalls the first glider flights from their high school days taking off from the cliffs of San Jon, New Mexico;

"Did you remember to solve the *center of gravity* problem we had on the last flight together?...the one that crashed? "

Alan responds;

"Better than that... '*Spirit*' automatically adjusts the flight controls and compensates for the *center of gravity* change when the wing's sweep angle changes. You're going to like this airplane Roger!"

The two brothers spend another hour inspecting the aircraft then walk to Alan's office...a short distance along the outside perimeter of the production area.

They enter the office. Alan shuts the door and immediately tells Roger;

"I received an unusual call a couple days ago from the State Department in Washington. A director there...identified himself as Jeremy Standvok the Assistant Secretary of Intelligence and Research. He asked if we could meet. I agreed of course but had no idea why he was calling me....or what he wanted to talk about. He said it had nothing to do with my work here but refused to discuss any details till we met."   Roger asks;

"Sounds very mysterious...strange to be sure. Did you meet with him?"

Alan nods;

"Yes, last night. We met at the house. You're going to be blown away...especially if it's true."

Roger becomes more serious;

"Okay, what's up?"

Alan swallows once and reveals the startling news;

"Dad is alive...there are reports that he's imprisoned at

Verkhoyansk, a Siberian gulag. There's a CIA plan underway to conduct a rescue mission...and bring him home."

Central Intelligence Agency-Langley, Virginia
National Clandestine Service – Special Ops Meeting
Deputy Director of Operations – Stewart O'Sullivan

The Special Ops planning team held two previous meetings. The 15 member team includes Air Force Generals Samuel Billington, General Walt Swenson, Colonel Johnathan Devrose, USMC and Jeremy Standvok, from the State Department . Deputy Director Sullivan summarizes the progress of the rescue mission planning;

"Last week we had the endorsement and approval from the President to proceed and execute a rescue mission of an American held captive in the Siberian city of Verkhoyansk in the Yana River Valley near the Arctic Circle.

Initially, the rescue was for Army Captain David McConnell; one of the original *Doolittle Raiders*.

As of yesterday evening two additional Americans have been added to the rescue attempt; David Richardsen and Jean Paul Boyer.

The list just keeps increasing. Now, as of an hour ago; I have new information and another new directive from the President. The rescue operation takes on a new initiative greatly increasing the mission's complexity and risk.

It seems the Gulag at Verkhoyansk is especially unique in that its prisoner population is composed entirely of highly talented Russian rocket scientists, engineers, writers, religious leaders and artists...all who have lost favor in the Soviet system because of their vocal and written support of religious and human rights issues.

The prison director, five security guards and 122 prisoners each submitted a brief dossier reflecting a history of their vocational background, accomplishments accompanied with a personally signed request for political asylum and entry into the United States. The dossier information was transmitted to us daily in 5 minute coded broadcasts for over a month using a

Chapter 29 – *Here, There and Everywhere*

short wave radio system. The signal was received by one of our U.S. based MARS stations in California. All communication has been entirely through short wave radio transmission. Because of coded protocol; we have confidence that no intercept or interpretation of these messages was accomplished by the Soviets.

We believe an airlift rescue of this large number of individuals is possible because of the prison's remote location in Siberia, the use of radar evasion tactics and the added support of a new electronic stealth aircraft. An F-111 protype would serve as an escort aircraft for a high performance *Convair 990*. Also, a small, highly trained team of 20 Marines would accompany the mission and provide ground support as needed.

The *Convair 990* is a commercial airliner currently in service with several American and foreign carriers. Its unique capability is its speed. The 990 uses the same engines as our operational *Strategic Air Command B-58 "Hustler"*…a Mach 2 bomber designed and built by Convair.

The 990…because of its "Hustler" engine heritage and other new and added design modifications allow the aircraft to cruise at just under Mach 1.0…the speed of sound. A recent flight test at Edwards clocked the 990 at a record speed of Mach 1.2.

We have the hardware and mission planning to complete the assigned rescue. However, we need to incorporate an intensive 40 day flight test program for both the F-111 and 990 aircraft to confirm and certify the reliability, performance and confidence level of these new designs and flight crews to successfully perform the mission. Both aircraft currently at Fort Worth are scheduled to be flown to Cannon Air Force Base, New Mexico to begin flight tests. Cannon also provides a more remote and secure location for a mission rehearsal exercise.

Another development…we are working under severe time restraint. A rescue must be attempted soon because of the deteriorating physical condition of Captain McConnell who is seriously ill and in need of medical attention. Secondly, as time progresses, there is an increased probability of the undercover details of the mission being detected by Soviet intelligence.

There is also another operational factor. The winter weather conditions of snow, ice and local temperatures can reach

Renegades

minus -94 degrees Fahrenheit.

From this point forward we will meet daily. The initial detailed *Top Secret* mission plan hereafter is ***Operation Sabre Canyon.*** We'll continue this meeting tomorrow at 1300 hours."

Chapter 29 – *Here, There and Everywhere*

Sidebar: General Dynamics F-111 and Convair 990

General Dynamics F-111	Convair 990 *Coronado* Enhanced
Crew: Two	Four
Capacity: 0	149 passengers
Length: 73ft 6 in	139 ft 9 in
Wingspan: Spread 63 ft	120 ft
Swept 32 ft	
Height: 17 feet	39 ft 6 in
Empty weight: 47,200 lb	113,000 lb
Loaded weight: 82,000 lb	253,000 lb
Engines: 2×PW TF30-P-100	4 × GE CJ805-23B

Performance

Maximum speed:	1,650 mph	621 mph
	Mach 2.5	Mach 1.2
Range:	3,700 mi	4,300 mi
Service ceiling:	66,000 ft	41,000 ft
Rate of climb:	25,890 ft/min	3,250 ft/min

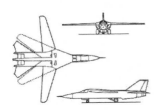 

Chapter 30
First Flight – *The Spirit of San Jon*
Tuesday, February 4, 1964
Time: 0735 hrs / 7:35 a.m.

Preflight Meeting

Alan walks from his office to the aircraft assembly area. He carries an extra set of flight manuals and checklists for the flight to Cannon. He'll accompany Roger and occupy the right seat next to his brother in the Spirit of San Jon as Navigator and Weapons System Operator.

Several days earlier, Spirit successfully passed a full series of ground engine run-ups and high speed taxing tests certifying its readiness to begin flight testing.

If all preflight systems checkout; the crew will fly a relatively short 360 mile ferry flight to Cannon at subsonic speed.

Before the flight this morning Alan schedules a final pre-takeoff meeting with the Renegade Team to discuss any last minute technical items.

Roger McConnell sits in the cockpit running through the preflight checklist. On seeing Alan approaching the plane...he nods and returns a "casual" military salute.

The four member *Renegade* design team is assembled and standing near *Spirit's* wingtip. Alan begins;
"Good morning everyone!"

"This is the day we've been waiting for...the first flight."

Tom Robinson, the specialist in radar and computer electronics, is wearing his favorite heritage ensemble; the original and well-worn Purdue crested sweat shirt and is about to light his marble bowl estate pipe.

Alan instantly spots Tom and hollers;
"Hey Tom, there's 30,000 pounds of fuel onboard *Spirit* this morning!...you're standing right next to a fully loaded outboard pylon tank!"

Tom immediately extinguishes his lighter;
"Sorry boss..."

Alan continues;
"The team is scheduled to fly this afternoon aboard the

990 to Cannon Air Force Base. We've been assigned to the 27th Tactical Fighter Wing and continue conducting the flight test program at Cannon. In addition, we'll be evaluating the 990's performance as well.

Tomorrow morning a joint mission briefing is scheduled at 0700 hrs with the Air Force. This will provide everyone with answers as to why there's been so many unscheduled changes to the test program and the last minute 990 addition.

Alan pauses for a moment.

Roger McConnell climbs down from Spirit's cockpit and joins the meeting.

Alan continues;

"I know you've all been bothered, confused and overworked by the stream of last minute changes in the program. I'm really sorry for that...and not being more candid on what's going on. I think tomorrow's meeting at Cannon will clear the air.

Roger and I need to get underway but before we leave I'd like to make one last check with everyone...are there any items we still need to discuss?

Tom.....how are things looking this morning for *Spirit*?"

Tom Robinson, *the electronics specialist;*
"Electronics, avionics and countermeasures, the flight computer ....are all *Go* Alan!
Just one item...remember the TFR system, the *Terrain Following Radar* will not provide accurate returns when flying over water or through heavy rain storms."

Paul Lancer, *Jet Engine Engineering*, looks up from his note pad;
"Alan....just remain advised on compressor stalls...if you're above Mach 2.35 in level flight... you'll lose 100 percent thrust on both engines and need to *restart* at subsonic speed and descend to a lower altitude.I've been struggling with the compressor stall problem and refining the inlet design for some time.

The *TF30* is the first afterburning turbofan engine ever built. All previous published engineering performance data and documentation on inlet geometry is based on older turbojet engines. The turbojet numbers just don't hack it.

The engines are two different breeds. We're writing the "first edition" performance book on high Mach, afterburner- turbofan engines. It's all new, unchartered country Alan.

Regardless, the *Spirit* that you're flying this morning with the TF30 engines are the latest design in performance and reliability. They'll bring you home. "

***Donald Gibbs**, the aerodynamicist is hunkered down under the Spirit's wing armed with a flashlight in hand shining its beam on the innards of the wing spars and an area towards the main wing box...the pivot point of Spirit's variable sweep wings. He steps away from the wing and stands facing the group;*

"I'd like to back track for a moment Stormy...and add some additional thoughts on the compressor stall issue.

I spent quite a lot of focused time and energy working with Paul on compressor stalls. I added a variable spike to the inlet area. The spike moves forward and backward with the changes of airspeed, wing sweep and engine thrust. It won't solve the airflow problem completely but adds a high dividend of reliability...it's part of the answer we were looking for.

...Other items; some changes need to be made in the exhaust nozzle geometry...its creating some excess drag...we're working on a design change to clean things up there.

I'm always poking around with my flashlight checking for metal fatigue cracks. We're using high strength D6AC steel where needed. I'm anxious to see how it's holding up after we log some extended flight time.

Otherwise Stormy...*Spirit* is ready to fly...You have my endorsement. Have a good flight!"

Alan concludes listening to the reports adding:

"Gretchen isn't here this morning. She's assigned as Flight Engineer with the 990 crew flying to Cannon.

Okay, Well... I guess it's time to go. Joe Sandquist is the test pilot from Convair who will be flying chase this morning in a F-106. He'll follow *Spirit* all the way to Cannon and keep an eye on us."

Chapter 30 – *First Flight*

*A pushback tug has already pulled Spirit out of the
hangar. Once outside the tow bar is unhooked from the nose
gear while another service technician finishes his inspection;
closing and locking the various electronic access bays.*

First Flight

*Roger and Alan leave the hangar and climb aboard Spirit. The
Fort Worth morning temperature is 47 degrees, under clear skies
with a light wind indicating 4 knots from the north. The sun is
breaking over the horizon.*

*They settle into the two seats, close and lock the clam shell
Plexiglas canopy. The seats are comfortable appearing almost
theater like upholstered in a royal looking red fabric. Compared
to other military aircraft the cockpit of the F-111 is pure luxury.
Roger and Alan wear standard military flight suits, G-suits and
helmets with attached oxygen masks even though the cockpit is
fully pressurized. There are no bulky parachutes or harnesses.*

*Two bright yellow levers in the cockpit protect their destiny
in case of an inflight emergency. If the yellow levers are pulled;
an explosive cutting cord shears the entire cockpit section from
the rest of the aircraft, a rocket engine fires propelling the entire
section to the safety of a higher altitude accompanied with a
timed deployment of a recovery parachute. If all works as
designed...the entire capsuled cockpit with crew land gently and
safely back on earth.*

Roger exhibits a natural familiarity with the F-111 and
immediately gets to work demonstrating a practiced routine as he
goes through a series of ordained startup protocols;

"Okay Alan let's light these engines and get underway."

The engines come alive, the increasing whining sound fills
the cockpit as the turbines gradually gain rotational speed
...Roger continues monitoring their startup and talks to Alan
over the intercom;

"Say Stormy, I was just thinking about this yesterday...have
you ever flown in a military jet before?"

Alan answers;

"No...this is the first time...It's also the first time I've worn one of these flight suits. What's with all the pockets! I brought along some corrected sun-glasses and was sure I had them in the right leg pocket...there are enough pockets in this flight suit to keep me looking for the entire flight!"

Spirit travels smartly along the taxiway, turns onto the main runway and comes to a stop. Its variable wings are fully spread to their take off position.

Alan looks off the right wing and watches the "chase" Convair F-106 pull into position and stop about 5 yards distant. Sandquist, at the controls, looks toward Alan and offers a "thumps up" gesture.

Meanwhile, Roger reviews the items on the pre-takeoff checklist;

1. *Canopy hatches – **closed and latched**.*
   The unlocked warning lamp is out.
2. *Canopy latch handle lock tab –**Flush**.*
3. *Anti-collision light – **ON**.*
4. *Wings, flaps and slats – **Set for takeoff**.*
5. *Ground roll spoiler brake switch – **BRAKE**.*
6. *Speed brake switch – **IN**.*
7. *Control system switch – **T.O. & LAND**.*
8. *Control system switch – **NORM**.*
9. *Takeoff trim – **Checked**.*
10. *Warning and caution lamps – **Checked**.*
11. *Pitot heater, engine inlet and anti-icing switches – **Climatic**.*
12. *Fuel quantity and fuel distribution – **Checked**.*
13. *Translating cowl switches – **OPEN**.*
14. *Translating cowl switches – **AUTO**.*
15. *IFF master control knob – **As required**.*
16. *Takeoff data – **Checked**.*

Roger places the checklist aside, lowers his head and doesn't move or say anything.

Alan looks at his brother and becomes concerned;

"Roger...Are you alright!"

Roger raises his head and turns to Alan;

Chapter 30 – *First Flight*

"No problem Alan...all set to go!...just offering a short prayer...you remember...for a good flight."

Alan does remember what he said on the San Jon Ridge on July 4th as they prepared for their glider flight nine years ago...Alan replies;

"There's nothing to worry about Roger...you know that...it's a solid plane, perfect to the specs...we'll have a good flight."

Roger smiles back ...answering;

"I know! You designed a fine airplane...but remember...God controls the winds...I've got to check in with Him too!

Okay Alan...we've got an immediate clearance for takeoff. We might as well go!"

The runway ahead looks infinite as it seems to stretch without end into the horizon. Roger closes the four remaining items on the checklist;

1.   *Brakes* – Set.
2.   *Engines –**Checked and set for takeoff.***
3.   *Flight instruments – **checked and set for takeoff.***
4.   *Brakes – **RELEASE***

Roger advances the throttles to full "military power" and then to "full afterburner". He checks the dial and tape readouts ...everything looks normal and stable.

Now there is the regular soft thumping as the landing gear passes over the seams in the concrete but these details on the runway soon become lost with the increasing speed.

The engine noise in the cockpit is only a distant whining. Roger provides the readouts over the intercom;

"One hundred knots"

Another cross check on the instruments

"One hundred forty"

"One forty two"

Roger pulls back gently but confidently on the control stick.

Spirit becomes airborne for the first time and begins an easy, graceful climb with the Texas landscape rapidly dropping away.

He raises the landing gear handle.

The landing gear position indicator lights and the warning light in the landing gear handle go out. The landing gear doors close and lock. The throttle is retarded..taking the engine out of the high power, fuel consuming afterburner position and into reduced military power.

Roger looks to his right and just off the wingtip Sandquist maintains the F-106 in perfect formation.

Sandquist opens his radio communication channel;

"Say *Spirit* you're looking good...gear is up and all door panels sealed nicely. Everything looks A-OK from out here. Gentlemen, I'm going to back off now and give you some maneuvering airspace."

Roger replies;

"Copy that...I'm not going to make any changes in wing sweep this flight...I'll save that for another day at Cannon."

Two digital readouts on the right hand side of the instrument panel quietly display the aircraft's exact longitude and latitude.

Roger goes on the intercom;

"Alan, were coming up to 20,000... I'll level out and practice a couple maneuvers and get to know this lady."

Roger begins to perform the ritualistic maneuvers known to all pilots seeking acquaintance with a new aircraft. There are banking turns to the right and left at different angles, steeper as confidence builds. Then lazy eights...slow flight...with gear up and down.

From a distance Sandquist continues to monitor *Spirit*;

"Still looking good *Spirit*."

Roger returns to level flight sits back in his seat and asks Alan;

"Hey brother, how'd you like to take the controls?"

Alan replies;

"I thought you'd never ask...Okay if I try a 360 roll?"

Roger shrugs his shoulders, smiles;

"Why not?"

Alan takes hold of the control stick. *Spirit* is no longer a conceptual object of Alan's making... no longer a collection of two dimensional connecting lines on a blueprint. All the calculations, formulas, equations, wind tunnel testing, minute design changes have come together into a living flying machine that precisely responds to the control handle resting in Alan's hand.

Alan moves the stick gently, initiating a gentle roll to the left.

Chapter 30 – *First Flight*

The earth does a somersault. Roger is surprised at the immediate response…much quicker than he anticipated for a forty ton airplane.

Now another to the right…this time *Spirit* finishes it roll with wings level instead of a cocked angle. There's a sense of exhilaration that's hard to resist.

Alan rolls again and again, each time more precisely. Finally Alan completes a hesitation roll, halting at eight points. After three attempts the eight point roll is performed perfectly.

Roger responds;

"Hey, I'm impressed Alan…outstanding, that last roll was right on…Can I have the airplane now? We're about twenty minutes out from Cannon."

Reluctantly Alan answers and takes his hand off the control stick;

"You've got the *Spirit* Roger."

Chapter 31
The Brothers Petrov
Pushkin Square, Moscow
Aragvie Restaurant
February 5, 1964

Moscow on a winter night is a very grey city and becomes even more austere under a solid cloud cover and a moonless sky. There are no neon lights or bright colors to offer relief from its somber pallor. Snow is beginning to fall.

Off duty, dressed in civilian clothes, Soviet Air Force Captain Alexi Petrov and his younger brother Lieutenant Mikhail Petrov are seated at a small table overlooking the Square.

The restaurant windows are fogged at the edges. It is a biting cold outside. Two older women dressed almost entirely in black walk the streets looking for food items in short supply.

The brothers each hold a cup of *Sbiten*, a hot Russian winter beverage of water, berry jam, honey and a combination seasoning of ginger, cloves and cinnamon.

"I feel very uneasy about tomorrow's flight..."
Alexi says to his brother;
"You know, Airchief Marshal, General Viktor Orlov, *The Wolf!* ...He called me personally to the Defense Headquarters and handed me orders assigning us on what he described as a 'special mission'.

We are to transport prisoners from the Verkhoyansk gulag to an undisclosed location for what he termed 'final processing.' I've heard many rumors of these 'special flights' from other pilots. I felt like asking the General if I could be reassigned to another mission but knowing his unbending character, short temper and stories of the retribution dispensed to other pilots...no way!"

Mikhail replies;
"A good choice brother...but I've also heard rumors about those flights. The KGB is in charge. Prisoners from the gulags are taken on a *special flight* and thrown overboard!

The 'final processing' is 'out the cabin door' at 10,000 feet over the Siberian wilderness!"

Alexi shakes his head replying;
"I don't want any part of these KGB dealings....I am not the

200

only one with this opinion."

Alexi has no further comments and is hesitant to continue in a public place but in a quiet voice, almost a whisper says;

"Please listen to me Mikhail…this mission has taken on another meaning as well. You will not believe this…I experienced a very strange event. I find it difficult to talk about. I have shared this story with no one until now.

It happened yesterday, the same day I received the orders…that very evening there was a noise outside my home. I opened the door to investigate and could hear footsteps and movement… the sound of someone walking through the snow. It was quite late and very cold. I went outside and sitting on one of the large rocks in the garden area… a man dressed in a long, black raiment. He wore a Russian *kamilavka*…you know, a tall, black stovepipe hat with no brim. A black veil covered his face. I recognized it as the vestment of an Orthodox monk. His head remained bowed as I walked towards him. Then, as I approached …he looked up and through the veil I could see his eyes. They seemed to hold a spirit of calm and understanding. I said nothing. Then, he quietly began to speak with a deliberate slow cadence as though he was reading a scripted message.

He said to me;

'You are a good man and there is no reason for any concern of the mission I was ordered to perform.'

He continued speaking;

'Listen and follow the commands coming from the heart…the commands are from the Lord."

Then he lowered his head, turned and walked away. He must have gone only about three or four steps before he disappeared …completely gone. It was all very strange. I could not sleep most of the night. It affected me deeply."

Mikhail replies;

"Brother…Now, I will not sleep tonight! I am not as religious as you Alexi but I do believe in a God. This flight to Verkhoyansk takes on a different meaning which is not clear."

Alexi abruptly changes the subject;

"I want to talk about the details of the mission. It is a long and difficult flight to Verkhoyansk…about 4,800 Kilometers, with a midpoint refueling…it's 10-11 hour flight.

We'll takeoff tomorrow afternoon, 1500 hrs. I've looked at the nav charts…the airfield runway at Verkhoyansk is too short…instead; we'll land at nearby Batagay airfield."

Chapter 32
Operation Sabre Canyon
A Change of Plans
Cannon AFB, Wing Operations
1000 hrs. 10 a.m.
February 5, 1964

Operation Sabre Canyon - CIA Deputy Director Of Operations –
*Stewart O'Sullivan, Air Force Generals Samuel Billington,
General Walt Swenson, Colonel Johnathan Devrose, USMC,
USAF Captain Roger McConnell, Jeremy Standvok and Lloyd
Jennings from the State Department.*
   *From Fort Worth; Alan McConnell, the entire General
Dynamics team including civilian Convair Coronado 990 pilots;
Tom Winworth and David Dolan.*
   CIA Deputy Director Stewart O'Sullivan is the last to enter
the briefing room. He immediately steps to the podium and
announces;
"This is a *Top Secret* meeting. All information and discussion
this morning is confidential, secret and not to be shared.
   Good morning. I'm Stewart O'Sullivan, CIA Director of
Operations. I apologize for delaying the planned 0700 start time.
Because of significant and new developments affecting this
mission; I needed to meet with military advisors earlier this
morning.
   The original purpose of the planned briefing this morning was
to discuss, approve and initiate a rescue mission of three
American citizens and prisoners held in a remote Siberian Gulag
in the city of Verkhoyansk.
   Over 100 prisoners; former soviet citizens were to be
extracted. These prisoners were highly respected Russian
citizens who had worked in high level soviet defense and space
projects. They were all sent to this one particular gulag for
internment because of their outspoken vocal and written political
beliefs.
   The prisoners have sought and formerly applied for political
asylum and freedom in the United States. It was our intention to
extract them from Siberia as part of the American rescue
mission.

203

However, I regretfully need to report the communique I received late last evening was anything but encouraging. One of our key assets in Moscow intercepted orders detailing an event to take place in four days.

The orders outlined steps for immediate closing of the Verkhoyansk Gulag. It also directed that all the prisoners, including three Americans be transported to four separate secret locations selected by the KGB.

After I informed upper level military planners, the CIA and the Secretary of State of the new developments, **Operation Sabre Canyon** was cancelled.

The planning, training and coordination for a rescue mission of this magnitude could not be accomplished in the limited time available.

General Billington draws attention as he stands up and walks to the front of the room. He stands next to O'Sullivan and says;

"I was part of the decision process and regretfully agreed to the cancellation. There is just not enough time to pull everything together. There is no option for failure in the execution of a bold mission that this represents…The Soviets would…"

Alan McConnell stands up, interrupting the General in mid-sentence…his voice is loud and defiant;

"General, excuse me…but we can do this. We can perform this mission successfully if given the opportunity…We're talking about saving American lives."

General Billington looks incredulously at McConnell…startled by the sudden, unexpected outburst.

An uneasy silence fills the room.

CIA Director O'Sullivan is equally stunned by McConnell's interruption.

General Billington continues;

"Alan, I can understand your immediate reaction and disappointment on this decision…your father was one of the prime reasons for initiating this mission…but you have to look at the bigger picture…"

McConnell again interrupts;

"I'm afraid I'm unable to see 'the bigger picture' General but I do see the alternative picture that's drawn; the lives that are going to be lost!"

Chapter 32 – *A Change of Plans*

McConnell gathers his files and notes and places them in his brief case. The room remains silent and focused on McConnell as he walks towards the door...stops for a moment and looks at his brother.

Roger slowly stands up and joins Alan. They leave the meeting room together.

State Department Director Jeremy Standvok turns to Lloyd Jennings and whispers;

"Damn, we need more Americans like that Lloyd. I love those boys."

General Billington looks about the room and announces in a quiet and reserved tone;

"I'm sorry the meeting had to end this way...this was not an easy decision...This morning's briefing is officially concluded."

An Angel Over My shoulder

The two brothers leave the Headquarters building and walk towards the officer's quarters. There's no conversation.

Then, from behind they hear a call;

"Alan!...Roger!...I need to talk to you."

Gretchen, out of breath, runs up and joins the two brothers.

"Alan...I was very proud of you and your brother. You both have the "bigger picture" but you need help now. I have a plan...a meeting is set for tonight at 11:00...inside hangar 7 where *Spirit* is now. Can you both be there?

"Okay Gretchen...yes, we'll be there. So tell us...what's up?"

Gretchen smiles and hugs Alan and Roger...then walks on.

Roger slowly shakes his head in an astonished state of disbelief and asks;

"Alan, who is that lady?"

Alan takes a deep breath and answers;

"Rog, let me tell you the full story about Gretchen; the most unusual and spiritually wonderful lady you will ever meet...she changed my life."

Hangar 7 – Evening - 2300 Hours

It's a cold clear night. Cannon is at an elevation of 4,000 feet and the air at night is nearly always exceptionally clear providing a startling view of the heavens with exceptional clarity.

Roger and Alan McConnell approach the security guard stationed at the entry door to Hangar 7. Both are wearing flight suits and their security badges. The young sergeant on guard examines the badges with his flashlight and remarks;

"Kind of late to go flying isn't it sir?"

Roger replies;

"Yes, I couldn't sleep. We're taking off tomorrow morning and just wanted to check out the aircraft to see if maintenance was completed on some of the electronics."

"Very good sir" the sergeant replies.

Roger and Alan enter the hangar. The lighting is dim but the the *990* and *Spirit* are clearly visible.

Alan looks around the hangar and remarks;

"Well, it's 11:00 and…I don't see anybody!"

Just then the hangar entry door opens and the security guard announces;

"Captain McConnell…I have two civilians from Convair. They claim to be *990* pilots and were told to report here tonight? Will you vouch for them?"

"Yes, by all means send them in"

Tom Winworth and David Dolan walk through the doorway.

Winworth appears somewhat confused and upset;

"Damn…What's going on?…I'm sound asleep and get a call from our Fort Worth Project Director, Dick Greenberg. He tells me I should wake up Dolan and make it over to Hangar 7 for some kind of meeting. Something about a mission requiring the *990*. It was my understanding from the morning meeting that the mission was scrubbed?"

Before Roger has time to respond a voice is suddenly heard;

"Alan and Roger…Sorry I'm late!"

The two brothers turn;

Gretchen appears and is standing with another uniformed officer;

Gretchen offers a short greeting;

"Greetings everyone. Both Alan and Roger know about angels…But Tom and David; you may have some trouble getting up to speed. Let me begin.

Tom Winworth responds instantly;

Chapter 32 – *A Change of Plans*

Whoa! Hold on!....What's going on here? Angels! Is this some kind of joke?"

Alan interjects;

"Tom ....David...believe me...this is no joke. Please...listen to Gretchen...Listen to what she has to say."

Gretchen nods and continues but slows the pace of her presentation;

Tom and David...I apologize. It's customary for angels to be more aware and considerate of first encounters. Angels usually present themselves slowly...over an extended period of time.

Let me begin by telling you the Lord has an infinite number of Angels at His command. We carry out His orders. God has a new set of orders for us. Accompanying me this evening is a very special angel to present the Lord's plan.

I would like to introduce Gabriel. Gabriel is an angel of the highest order. He is an Archangel and the principle messenger in God's Administration of the universe."

Gabriel steps forward. He has chosen to appear as a military officer wearing an Air Force, sage colored flight jacket and flight suit...His manner is serious but relaxed;

"I bring you Greetings from our Lord and Savior.

Know that I am an angel. I am a spirit able to appear in any human form I choose. Forgive me if my presence and appearance tonight is not convincing. I may seem too familiar, normal... and unconvincing.

However, I wanted everyone to feel more at ease and comfortable by offering a more normal appearance.

I understand the natural human reluctance and reservations to accept the authenticity of angels in the 20th century...but let me begin.

Open your hearts and minds...and have faith!

Each of you present tonight is very special. You have been asked by the Lord to be a participant in a most extraordinary event; a miracle of God that will have a lasting effect on the future of all mankind."

Those present gaze into Gabriel's eyes and see there are no complexities...a total absence of worldly rules are seen. The eyes are challenging yet forgiving. Gabriel speaks with a

Renegades

measured and commanding voice;

The Lord foresees an approaching era of great upheaval; an examination of traditional values, acts of violence and conflict that have no borders. The earth's environment will be active with extreme and destructive natural forces. It's a time when the entire world will be severely challenged. The Lord wants to give the good earth and all its inhabitants another chance ....there will be no repeat of a biblical flood... and it is not the right time for His second coming.

God will guide the earth through the perilous times. The Lord will perform a miracle; a powerful event for all on earth to see and experience...this will be a breakaway event to reset the world on a new secure and anticipative future.

The Lord has an assignment for each of you... The rescue mission you have only discussed begins now. Your departure is tonight.... It's a 12 hour flight to Siberia."

There is a moment of sustained silence. Roger is the first to speak;

"Gabriel...Gretchen...This is insane! We can't fly a military aircraft without authorized orders, approved and filed flight plans! We would be considered a security threat, renegades and shot down by our own military. Surely, you know we need more time to prepare and further test both these aircraft. What of the 20 Marines needed for protective ground support?" Gabriel instantly replies;

"These concerns have already been addressed Roger. Everything is in order. Both aircraft are ready to fly. Proper documentation was prepared, filed and approved.

Gretchen is your guide and will be of great assistance.

As my final words to you; I ask for the removal all doubt from your hearts and minds. Believe...have faith and be willing to accept miraculous help as events unfold. You will be challenged on your mission but always know the Lord is with you. He is with you always."

With those final words, Gabriel steps backwards and is gone.

Gretchen steps forward. The silence in the hangar seems unnatural. She is about to speak when the hangar entrance door opens and the sergeant looks in.

Chapter 32 – *A Change of Plans*

"Is everything okay here? Nobody told me about your meeting."

Roger answers:

"Yes Sergeant all is well,..but we need your help to open the hangar doors. We have orders for the 990 and our F-111 to takeoff immediately."

The Sergeant replies;

"This seems a bit unusual sir. You came here to check the aircraft and now you've got orders to fly them both out of here! I need to contact base operations to verify your request."

Gretchen interrupts;

"Yes, go ahead sergeant, please make your call."

Roger looks on in disbelief. Gretchen offers a quick nod as a sign of confidence to Roger.

The sergeant goes on his personal radio;

"Hello OPS...this is Sergeant Lorning at Hangar 7. Do you show any departure orders for the two visiting aircraft from Fort Worth...The F-111 *Spirit* and a Convair 990 *Coronado*. They're supposed to take off this morning?"

There's a brief silence...followed by a reply from OPS;

"Yes, both aircraft are cleared for departure...a direct flight to Cold Bay, Alaska ...The orders describe something about running cold weather engine and equipment tests."

The sergeant looks at Roger and Gretchen and says;

"I guess you're set to go! I'll call ground operations for you and have them send someone over to tow you out to the tarmac."

The sergeant leaves the hangar.

Roger looks at Gretchen he shakes his head in disbelief;

"Gretchen, I won't even ask how you did that!"

Gretchen replies;

"Roger this is not a one angel show...there's a lot of us working on this mission and in many places."

Roger and Alan walk toward *Spirit* and climb aboard.

The Coronado crew, Tom and David are on the flight deck and discover a complete printed flight plan computed with the latest weather information. Tom turns on the battery power switch and the instruments come to life. The fuel levels all read 100%.

"That's impossible...something's wrong!"... David quips in disbelief.

Renegades

"Those tanks were reading 30% at shutdown!"
Gretchen arrives on the flight deck and can't help but hear David's remark and answers;
"Nothing is impossible…keep that in your mind and heart David."

The situation is very much the same aboard *Spirit*. Roger and Alan find the flight plan loaded in the inertial navigation system and all fuel levels are 100% in both the internal and extra external wing tanks. The under wing ordinance consists of (4) *AIM-9D Sidewinder* air to air missiles. The sidewinder uses infrared sensors and can be fired at a range of .6 to 22 miles. All electronic and flight electrical systems appear normal and primed for engine start.

The main overhead hangar door opens and a motorized tug vehicle pulls in front of the 990. The driver attaches the y-shaped fork and secures it to the nose landing gear.

As the 990 is pulled out of the hangar. Communication checks are performed between the two aircraft. Tom, in the command left seat of the 990 is first to report;
"Hello Test…1,2,3,4…How do you read *Spirit?*"
On board the *Spirit* Roger replies;
"Copying you Tom...Is everything on preflight checking out okaywith you?"
Tom answers:
"I'm going through the motions here Rog but I'm not sure at all what's happening…and I'm questioning if mentally…I've got it all together!....You know what I'm saying?' This is like living some kind of dream. Too many things happening without any logical explanations. It's like we've tossed reality to the wind!"
Roger replies:
"I know exactly what you mean…
Alan and I have been there before. Gretchen will help. Listen to her. This is all real….believe me!
Tom…listen up! I'm checking the flight plan…We're looking at a direct flight on a true course of 316 degrees with an average cruise altitude of 40,000 feet at 540 knots to Cold Bay, Alaska.
After takeoff we'll be flying over Colorado, Salt Lake City, Twin Falls and Boise Idaho, Oregon and Olympia, Washington …then over the Pacific till we hit landfall on the Aleutian chain

Chapter 32 – *A Change of Plans*

and finally landing at Cold Bay. We'll refuel at Cold Bay and take a look at the weather over Siberia.

The flight time to Cold Bay will be approximately six hours. I'll fly lead...Stay with me in a loose formation.

Depending on our fuel situation...when were over the Aleutians and approaching Cold Bay I'd like to run a test on the *Terrain Following Radar* and give both of us some experience on flying low altitude...and I mean really low...100 feet above terrain. "

Tom replies;
"Say again, did you say 100 feet!"
"You can copy that...The F-111 is designed for deep interdiction missions into enemy territory in any type weather...and especially at night, flying low, supersonic and under the radar."
Tom remains completely silent before finally acknowledging;
"You're really making my day now Rog!"

Cannon AFB - Takeoff!
Aircraft: F-111, Convair 990
Time: Feb. 6th – 0300 hrs. 3:00 a.m.
Temperature 19 F.
Visibility: 60 miles

The *990 Coronado* and F-111 *Spirit* taxi to the holding position at the threshold of Runway 04 and come to a complete stop.

"This is Cannon tower...We have no traffic this morning gentlemen. You're both cleared for immediate takeoff at your discretion. Good day."

The 990 moves off the taxiway and onto the active runway and its engines spool up to takeoff RPM. An outpouring of dark gray smoke pours from each of its four engines; visible even under the night sky. On the radio Tom reports;
"990 is rolling."

The 990 slowly begins its takeoff roll... gradually increasing its speed till at 6000 feet down the 10,000 foot runway the *Coranado* rotates and begins a gentle climb. With its flaps and landing gear retracted the aircraft locks onto a 316 degree course heading at 250 knots and fades into the distance.

Spirit is already in takeoff position. Alan turns off the electronic identification transponder known as **IFF**; "*Identification Friend or Foe*."

Even with the extra fuel load and ordinance hanging on its wing the F-111 with wings fully extended begins to accelerate at a surprisingly rapid pace.

Roger lights the engine afterburner. *Spirit*, despite its forty-five-ton weight; rotates and takes off in *twenty seconds* trailing a 35 foot pillar of fire behind.

Onboard, Roger is able to visually track the 990 by its flashing strobe lights and he banks onto a 316 degree heading. Meanwhile, Alan adjusts the radar height and receives an electronic return on the 990. Within minutes a rendezvous is made with the aircraft.

"Roger maneuvers to a position just off the left wingtip of the 990 and opens radio communication;

"Good morning…everything OK?"

Tom replies;

"We're A-OK Spirit!"

Roger reports;

"*Spirit* is also looking good Tom. I'm going to maneuver about a half mile ahead of you. Keep radio communication to a minimum and just follow me all the way to Cold Bay!"

Roger advances the throttle and Spirit moves forward and ahead of the 990…its distance gradually increasing. The weather remains clear and calm.

Aircraft: F-111, Convair 990
Elapsed Mission Time: +02:10 hrs.
30,000 feet – 540 Knots IAS
Position: Over Olympia, Washington
Distance traveled: 1,170 nautical miles
Distance remaining: 1,560 nautical miles
Destination: Cold Bay. Alaska

Chapter 32 – *A Change of Plans*

Tactical Air Command Headquarters
Langley Air Force Base, Virginia
Thursday morning, February 6
0710 hrs. 7:10 a.m.

It's early morning and Sergeant Donna Ramsey reports for duty. As part of her normal routine she reviews the daily aircraft ordinance requests and notices a requisition for (4) *AIM-9D Sidewinder* air to air missiles. What's unusual is the designated aircraft is not identified as part of the current Air Force inventory....the information available reads; a *'fighter–bomber, an F-111 built by General Dynamics, Fort Worth, based at Cannon Air Force Base, New Mexico.'*

The report further states the aircraft was loaded with ordinance from inventory five hours ago...but is missing several of the required support documents from Cannon's ordinance facility.

She immediately picks up the designated secure phone line to Cannon Base Operations.

Captain Karl Bronski picks up the phone and answers;

"Captain Bronski, Cannon OPS..."

"Good morning sir, this is Sergeant Ramsey at Langley. I'm trying to find information on an aircraft...designated as an "F-111" that's based at Cannon. The aircraft is not shown in our current inventory. However, an ordinance request and load out was completed five hours ago for (4) *AIM-9D Sidewinder missiles.* Do you have the support documentation for this aircraft?"

Bronski does not immediately answer. He looks at the flight operations log, takes a deep breath and feels a formation of sweat forming on his forehead as he answers;

"The F-111 took off over two hours ago....a two man crew are at the controls; Captain Roger McConnell and his brother, a civilian, Alan McConnell, the Chief Project Engineer and designer for the F-111 at General Dynamics.

According to our information...their destination is Cold Bay...Cold Bay, Alaska...and that's not all...a Convair 990 *Coronado* and two of its company's civilian pilots are accompanying them. Both aircraft are running cold weather engine and equipment tests"

Sergeant Ramsey asks;

"Who ordered and signed off on those flights?"

Bronski voice tightens...

'"It was a General...let me check the authorization."

Nearly a minute passes before Bronski returns to the phone ...

"Damn it...Sergeant, I don't know how this got approved... The signature and name are bogus!...The General's name is entered as 'General Dynamics!'"

Sergeant Ramsey's reply is immediate;

"I've got to make some calls Captain...stand by, I'm placing your call on hold. I have to find out what's going on!"

U.S. State Department – Washington D.C.
Bureau of Intelligence and Research
Thursday Morning, February 6
Local Time: 0830 hrs. 8:30 a.m.

Director Jeremy Standvok and Intelligence Analyst Lloyd Jennings returned to Washington following yesterday's meeting at Cannon. A new day begins.

Jennings walks into the Standvok's office and sits down. Standvok, gazing out the window, swivels his chair 180 degrees directly facing Jennings. There are none of the usual morning pleasantries. Standvok is stone serious, terse and tight lipped in his announcement;

"I just talked to both fathers of the two Americans being held in Siberia. They arrived at Dulles just a few hours ago from Africa and are scheduled for a briefing in our office this afternoon. They want to know the status of the rescue mission for their sons.

"I have to tell them the rescue was 'cancelled till further notice' sounding more like someone telling them their home water service is being shut-off because they forgot to pay their bills!

I'm pissed Lloyd... really pissed! We could have pulled a rescue mission together in time...We should have had two aircraft flying today!"

He shakes his head and looks intently at Jennings with a

Chapter 32 – *A Change of Plans*

tightened jaw.

Jennings on seeing Standvok's appearance is unable to contain an ever widening grin. Standvok is immediately taken back by Jennings response.

"What the hell are you smiling about Lloyd?"

He pauses for a moment…looks closely at Lloyd and feels his mood slowly changing.

"Okay…Okay…I'm getting your message Lloyd…you're holding back something…I can tell Lloyd…I know that duplicitous grin of yours?...so what's going on?"

Jennings answers, while continuing his questionable smiling, composure;

"There's a change in the wind Director Standvok!…Our government is waking up this morning and finding threads of reported information of two American aircraft taking off from Cannon Air force Base, New Mexico on a 'unauthorized mission.'

The two aircraft, a General Dynamics F-111 and a Convair 990, are now flying somewhere over the Pacific with a filed flight plan direct to Cold Bay, Alaska … a very 'convenient' refueling point for a nonstop mission to a certain small Russian Siberian airfield named Batagay and a previously discussed Russian gulag!

There's a lot of confusion because of the very high quality, authenticity and reams of forged documentation produced… including command orders for missile ordinance. The orders were accepted into the system and a loadout of air to air missiles was completed for the F-111.

All attempts with radio communication have failed and the F-111's new stealth cloaking electronics seem to be very effective…even against our own radar tracking."

Standvok is immediately elated;

"Damn! I told you I liked those two McConnell brothers! We've got some work ahead of us Lloyd…They need our support. We better make sure nothing gets screwed up by the bureaucracy. If we don't get involved they'll end up being hunted, shot down and labeled as some kind of renegade, turncoat terrorists."

Renegades

Chapter 33
All Roads Lead to Verkhoyansk
Local Time: 1800 hrs. 6:00 p.m.
Thursday, February 6, 1964
Flight 023- Prisoner Relocation Mission

Aircraft: Russian Antonov 24
Elapsed Mission Time: +03:00 hrs.
13,000 feet – 285 Knots IAS
Position: 1 hour from landing at
Napalkovo Airfield for refueling
Distance traveled: 855 nautical miles
Distance remaining: 1,715 nautical miles
Destination:-Batagay, Siberia

The AN-24 is a 44 seat twin engine turboprop passenger aircraft designed in 1957 manufactured in the Soviet Union by the Antonov Design Bureau.

Soviet Air Force Captain Alexi Petrov and his younger brother Lieutenant Mikhail Petrov are at the controls of the AN-24 Transport. Onboard is a ten member Soviet Army security detail specially selected for the "Special Mission" prisoner transfer. The majority of soldiers onboard are Privates; young 20 year olds. They are led by a Master Sergeant Devlin Poplavski.

Poplavski walks forward into the cockpit. The engine noise is quite loud. He grasps Petrov on the shoulder and asks;

"Captain, my men are getting hungry…when will we eat?"

Petrov looks to his side and directly at Poplavski and replies;

"We're about an hour out from Napalkovo. We need to refuel before continuing on to Batagay. There's a small commissary there. The food is not the greatest but out here…not much choice…you know?

Petrov pauses and then with guarded hesitation asks;

"Do your men know about this mission? There have been many rumors about flights like this one…stories of prisoners being mistreated and murdered… and in some cases…thrown off the aircraft. Tell me…Tell me this isn't true."

Poplavski turns his head away from Petrov.…pretending not to have heard the question. He looks out the side window staring at the thickening cloud formations for a moment, then turns and leaves the cockpit.

Mikhail interrupts…he is in radio communication with Napalkovo;

"Napalkovo reports their grass landing strip is ice covered with dropping temperatures and some light snow starting to fall."

Petrov replies;

"Our kind of winter weather wouldn't you say brother! I'm going back to see our passengers and talk to Master Sergeant Devlin Poplavski again. He's got his own agenda and isn't telling us anything!"

Petrov opens the cockpit door into the passenger section. He immediately senses a strong negative aura filling the entire cabin. Sergeant Poplavski is sitting alone at a window seat at the rear of the aircraft. As he walks down the center aisle Petrov can't help but notice the tense nervousness written on the faces of the young soldiers.

Petrov sits down in the empty seat next to Poplavski. There's no recognition by Poplavski as he settles into the seat. Petrov turns and speaks slowly, directly into Poplavski's ear.

"Devlin, I want you to know…this is an order. There will be no violence or questionable activity to any prisoners onboard my aircraft as long as I am Captain. Do you understand?"

Devlin turns face to face with Petrov…smiles politely and smugly replies;

"Of course Captain, there is no problem here. We are all good Russians doing our duty. There is no need for any concern on your part."

Devlin mentally dismisses Petrov…and returns his attention to the view out the window.

Petrov gets up from the seat, walks forward…returning to the cockpit. As he climbs into the left seat Mikhail asks;

"How was the Master Sergeant?"

Petrov replies; "He's in his own world and not letting us in…but I'm afraid I know what his plans are. He's a strange and isolated

Renegades

individual who has his own agenda. There's an evil aura about him that's felt immediately when you enter the cabin. I can't describe it any other way."

The Verkhoyansk Gulag
The message from Moscow
Time: 1940 hrs. 7:40 p.m.
February 6, 1964

Andrey Ivanov, District Administrator of the Verkhoyansk Gulag is in his office. A teletype message from Moscow prints out its message confirming the closing and transfer of prisoners;

"...relocation flight 023 for all Verhoyansk prisoners is scheduled for arrival at 0400 hours. Prisoners are to be transported by bus to Batagay Airport and transferred to the arriving AN-24 aircraft. Master Sergeant Devlin Poplavski is onboard the aircraft and will provide new base assignments for each prisoner. As acting Administrator you will accompany the prisoners to their new location."

He tears the message from the printer and places it in the center of his desk. There's knock on the office door. It opens and Andrey recognizes his friend Pavel Guisha.

"Pavel, you came at just the right time. The KGB is flying a military plane here to transfer the prisoners!"

Gabriel has arrived and assumed an alternate identity as *Pavel Guisha, a Russian airline operations manager from Aeroflot. Pavel is heavily bearded, wearing a World War II 'Telogreyka' winter jacket and military style black fur Cossack 'Ushanka' hat.*

Pavel has developed a close friendship with the gulag administrator Ivanhov... Pavel also claims a special connection as an asset for the U.S. State Department. Pavel announces to Andrey the immediate plan underway for extracting all prisoners from Verkhoyansk and supporting their entry into the United States.

Pavel on hearing news of the approaching Soviet plane shows concern and some added humor;

Chapter 33 – All Roads Lead to Verkhoyansk

"This is an interesting situation Andrey…We now have a race to Batagay between the Americans and Soviets!

The United States is sending two aircraft to Batagay…they are inflight at this exact moment. So, we must begin preparations for transporting the inmates to Batagay before the Soviet arrival."

Andrey is concerned;

"Pavel, we have a new problem. The families of the prisoners are here also. The 100 count of passengers we originally planned on is now close to 200! We may not have enough room onboard the aircraft for everyone.

Everything is moving too fast.…I am worried. I moved the prisoners and families to the dining hall. There are two busses and a truck fueled and ready to depart to Batagay. Two drivers volunteered and also want to be included on *Freedom Flight* as they call it. Sergey Ramzin is a retired Aeroflot pilot and his son Yury…who is an aeronautical engineer. They are here today and ready to go."

Pavel offers support and confidence to Andrey;

"You have done well and prepared for this day Andrey. Do not worry…I will accompany you on the flight but we must leave now; the road to Batagay is still open but the weather is changing. How are the three American prisoners?"

Andrey replies;

"The two young men are fine. However, Captain McConnell has a fever and is very weak. The pneumonia is taking a strong toll on him. Our medical doctor has been tending to him but medical supplies are limited here.

There are 105 detainees. I have a list prepared for you."

Pavel glances at the first couple pages;

George Balanchine	choreographer
Boris Bazhanov	politburo secretary
Grigol Robakidze	author
George Gamow	physicist
Abdurakhman Avtorkhanov	author
Nicholas Poppe	linguist
Victor Kravchenko	engineer
G. M. Dimitrov	politician
Jan Cep	writer

Renegades

Nora Kovach	ballet
Andrzej Panufnik	composer
Vladimir Petrov	diplomat
Ernst Degner	motorcycle racer
Jonas Pleškys	submarine tender captain
Rudolf Nureyev	ballet
Valentin Poénaru	mathematician
Peter Fechter	bricklayer
Petr Beckmann	physicist
Paul Barba Neagra	film director
Ivan Diviš	poet
Anatoly Kuznetsov	author
Miloš Forman	film director
Cornel Chiriac	journalist
Georgi Markov	playwright
Simonas Kudirka	seaman
Ioan P. Culianu	philosopher
Alexander Elder	author
Paul Nevai	mathematician
Stanislav Kurilov	oceanographer
Youri Egorov	pianist

Pavel remarks;

"This list contains so much talent…these appear to be knowledgeable people and valuable citizenry most countries would consider of high value. Yet, the government decides to imprison them in Siberia…why?"

Andrey replies;

"You'll find upon closer investigation, every one of these individuals was judged and sentenced by the state without a jury or trial because of what is described as 'human rights issues'… freedom of the press, speech and religion."

Pavel says;

"I'd like to visit the dining hall and have an opportunity to speak to them. Would this be possible?"

"Yes, by all means" Andrey replies.

"Follow me. I'm very glad you're here Pavel…I feel more confident now. Thank you good friend."

Both men leave the office and walk through a connecting tunnel

Chapter 33 – All Roads Lead to Verkhoyansk

leading to the prisoner area and dining hall. The underground tunnel is dimly lit and cold but still warmer than the -30 F. degree outside temperature.

They reach the prison complex and pass through a series of connecting "airlock" doors used to maintain temperature control within the compound. As they continue to walk Pavel notices the doors of all the rooms and cells are unoccupied and left wide open. They enter the dining area.

The inmates and families with small children are sitting together at the stainless steel tables that fill the room. They are having coffee and quietly talk among each other.

As Andrey and Pavel enter the room; all eyes immediately become affixed on their arrival. Pavel sees the two Americans, Jean Paul Boyer and Donald Richardsen sitting together. They stand up as Pavel enters. Pavel makes eye contact and nods... acknowledging their presence.

As Pavel scans the entire room it's evident from the physical condition of the inmates that the years of incarceration and living in the severe conditions of Siberia have taken a toll.

Pavel attracts the attention of everyone as he steps into the center of the room. He speaks in Russian:

"My name is Pavel Guisha. Like you, I understand and feel your need and decision for seeking freedom...Today, the United States will help you reach freedom. I bring a message of support to each one of you from the United States of America.

America is answering your call for freedom. Two aircraft are enroute to Batagay. One is a transport aircraft ...the other an armed fighter jet to provide protection if necessary. They will be landing in seven hours at the Batagay Airport.

So, we must be ready. We will board our transportation...we have two busses and an enclosed heated truck. We will leave within the next hour and leave Verhoyansk...forever!"

An immediate response of cheers and clapping erupts... continuing for several minutes.

When the room quiets again Pavel concludes by saying;
"Many of you here tonight know of the God that has given you strength during these hard times...Others may have no such recognition or lost their faith along the way and are no longer believers.

Renegades

To everyone listening to me now…know that I am here today because of a loving God who commanded me to do so. He is a God of great love but also a Warrior of great strength who will guide and protect us. The Holy Bible in the book of Exodus says;

'The Lord is my strength and my song; he is given me victory. This is my God and I will praise him - my father's God, and I will exalt him! The Lord is a warrior; the Lord is his name'

May the Lord continue to be with us and protect us on our journey."

Tactical Air Command Headquarters
Langley Air Force Base, Virginia

Permission for a shoot-down is authorized to the Commander of Cold Bay AFB, Colonel Leonard White.

"Hello Colonel, General Swenson at TAC …We have a developing situation; two of our aircraft an F-111 prototype and a civilian transport Convair 990 *Coronado* are enroute to your base for refueling. Indications are that they have intentions to enter Soviet airspace. The 990 has no passengers.

The F-111 is armed with *AIM-9D Sidewinder* air to air missiles. They have refused radio contact and we've lost radar contact. We need to intercept these aircraft, have them land and find out there intention. If necessary, you have a command option for a 'shoot down' if necessary."

Captain Spaulding is on our secured line and will give you all the information we have on their assumed course and altitude. Colonel White listens and replies;

"Damn…We'll look at the situation General and scramble four of our intercept aircraft. I'll keep you informed sir."

Chapter 33 – All Roads Lead to Verkhoyansk

Aircraft: F-111 and Convair 990
Elapsed Mission Time: +04:00 hrs.
25,000 feet – 540 Knots IAS
Position: Over the Pacific
Distance traveled: 2,100 nautical miles
Distance remaining: 625 nautical miles
Destination: Adak Island, Aleutian Chain

Air Force Captain Roger McConnell continues to monitor Tactical Air Command radio transmissions. He turns to Alan;

"We can forget about going to Cold Bay. The radio chatter from TAC is turning downright hostile. We'll not be welcome …they're expecting us.

Let's land somewhere else. There's a small isolated Naval Air Station on Adak Island a little farther up the Aleutian Chain. They just started flying antisubmarine operations with the new P-3A Orion jet turbo props. They have JP-4 fuel. The base is within range. I'll give them a call. We'll find how well the Navy monitors Air Force TAC frequencies.

Alan checks his chart and keys in the radio frequency for Adak. Roger makes the call under the Convair identification;

"Adak Operations…This is Convair 990 and FX-111 test aircraft…do you copy…over?"
"Adak Operations…I repeat this is Convair 990 and FX-111 test aircraft…do you copy…over?"

There is an immediate response;
"Hello Convair…This is Adak Naval Air Operations you are coming in loud and clear. What can we do for you…over?"

"Adak we're running cold weather tests on the fuel systems for two aircraft. The 990 is a passenger aircraft and the 111 is a prototype fighter. Both of us fly out of Fort Worth Texas. These are General Dynamics aircraft. We have a situation here. The sealant on our main fuel tanks has been

Renegades

giving us some problems. We've lost fuel and need to land and take a look."

"Roger Convair...we have no traffic. You're cleared to land ...Runway 23...light and variable wind at 7 knots, visibility 10 miles. Our OPS vehicle will meet you and take you the parking area. Check in with me at Base Ops. I'm Lt. Stebbins."

"Thank you Lieutenant. I'm Captain Roger McConnell, I'm Air Force but on temporary assignment to General Dynamics."

"I guess the Navy can allow Air Force to land here Captain. Welcome to Adak."

Roger closes the comm channel and turns to Alan.
"Damn, I can't believe what I've just done...we're in real trouble now Alan...and digging deeper."
Alan says;
"You were convincing alright...now all you have to do is get the Navy to buy us some gas!"
Roger returns to the moment;
"Let's go down to a lower altitude...and make sure we're not being tracked on radar."
McConnell opens the comm channel to Tom Winworth piloting the 990 flying a quarter mile behind;

"Hello Tom...the situation is becoming more serious with TAC. They're gunning for us...big time. They know we're heading to Cold Bay so we'll continue flying up the Aleutians and divert to Adak Island and the Naval Air Station there.

I just talked to the Navy Ops officer and we're cleared to land on Runway 23. Take a look on your charts, Adak is a small island but...they have two 8,000 foot runways.

Spirit's stealth electronics seem to be working but as insurance I'd like to lose some altitude and drop down to a 'under radar' altitude...about 100 feet."

Tom doesn't reply immediately;

Chapter 33 – All Roads Lead to Verkhoyansk

"...Roger and Alan, you guys always are the bearer of such great news...say again...100 feet?"

Roger replies;

"100 feet it is. Just watch out for the whales!"

The White House – Washington D.C.
Oval Office

"Hello, Mr. President, this is General Swenson, Tactical Air Command. Sir, my purpose in calling is to update you on the two armed rogue aircraft that took off this morning on what we believe is a flight into the Soviet territory."

The President answers;

"You believe...Did you say 'believe' it's a mission to Soviet territory? Can you be more definitive General!

I'd like to know how two aircraft were able to arm and fly out of one of our military bases with no one asking any questions and what in hell's name are they planning to do?

If the Soviets track two aircraft entering their airspace...there will be a retaliatory response that I don't even want to imagine! Where are the two aircraft right now General?"

There is a prolonged silence before General Swenson is able to answer;

"I don't know sir...we lost all tracking on radar... minutes after their takeoff from Cannon. The F-111 prototype has so many new and sophisticated types of electronic countermeasures ... they've been able to effectively evade and cloak their progress and well...we're simply unable to find them. All attempts in radio communication have failed.

They initially filed a flight plan to Cold Bay, Alaska. Radar along the Aleutian chain has detected nothing. Four intercept aircraft from Cold Bay are airborne now and conducting a visual search of a 500 mile area including a projected air corridor into Russian Siberia. They have orders to take down the aircraft if necessary.

226

Mr. President, the two crew members of the F-111are brothers. Roger McConnell is an Air Force Captain and his brother Alan is employed by General Dynamics and is the primary designer for the F-111 program. The aircraft and crew were originally chosen for a rescue mission to the Verkhoyansk gulag in Siberia where their father and two other Americans are being held. However, the mission was scrubbed just a day ago.

The other aircraft ...flown by civilian test pilots is a Convair 990 *Coronado* and was to serve as the transport aircraft for the Americans and other prisoners."

The President answers;

"I was briefed and kept informed of *Operation Sabre Canyon* and its cancelation. It sounds to me like the McConnell brothers decided on a bold independent move to rescue their father. Continue trying to contact them...defer the 'shoot down' order General...cancel it immediately."

The General asks;

"Did you say defer the shoot-down Mr. President?"

"I most certainly did General; that's an order. I talked to the State Department on this matter. Continue to focus all your efforts to establish radio communication with the two aircraft... and keep me informed. We may be able to offer assistance."

Aircraft: F-111 and Convair 990
Elapsed Mission Time: +00:00 hrs.
Location: Arrived Adak Naval Air Base
Distance traveled: 2,100 nautical miles

Adak Naval Air Base
Flight Operations Office

Both aircraft land at Adak Naval Air Station; park and shut

Chapter 33 – *All Roads Lead To Verkhoyansk*

down their engines. A heavy, foreboding cloud cover has moved in. The grey unbroken sky is accompanied with a dropping temperature that seems to accentuate the exceptionally remote and isolated character of the island base.

Roger and Alan walk over to the 990. Tom, David and Gretchen climb down the ladder from the passenger section.

Roger is apprehensive as he greets everyone;
"We need both aircraft fueled...all tanks filled to100%. We're looking at 20 thousand gallons of JP-4. Any ideas? anyone?"
Gretchen replies with a surprising but assured sound of confidence;
"...Just let me do the talking. I can be very persuasive."

The Flight Ops Office is a one story wooden frame structure painted in the Navy's traditional battleship grey. They walk up a few steps, open the door and face a long counter separating them from the main office area. There's a welcoming voice coming from a desk in the far corner of the room.
"Greetings Air Force...you made it in okay!"
The young officer walks up to the counter;
"I'm Lieutenant Stebbins. Our Captain is away for a couple days on TDY. I'm in charge. You mentioned the need to check on some leaking fuel tanks?...I've got a maintenance crew that could take a look and provide some assistance and get you underway. There's a huge low pressure moving toward us. Looks like a major snow. We'll have to shut-down flight operations in a couple hours. The combination of high winds and low visibility makes life here especially miserable for airplanes and pilots. It's two hours away..."

Gretchen steps up to the desk and interrupts the Lieutenant;
"Lieutenant we need JP-4 fuel for both aircraft, 32,000 lbs. for the F-111 and 101,500 lbs. for the 990. We'll be able to provide assistance to your Navy crew on the refueling process."
Gretchen's voice is controlled and softly spoken but delivered with an underlying pervasive tone. Alan listens closely and has felt its power before...he looks at the Lieutenant who responds at first with a terse, affronted reply;
"You can't be serious!...I could never authorize anywhere near the amount you're asking for!"

Renegades

Gretchen replies;

"Yes, you can Lieutenant…you have the authority. You're in charge….and are a leader. You are pleased to provide these exact amounts;

32,000 lbs. JP-4 for the F-111 and 101,500 lbs. of JP-4 for the 990. That's a total of 20,538 gallons."

The Lieutenant cocks his head nervously to left and then to the right to loosen the tightened muscles in his neck. The movement is followed by an almost instant facial expression of total understanding complimented with a friendly smile and ccompliance with the request;

"Yes...yes you're right!" the Lieutenant repeats enthusiastically; "I can do that!"

He carefully writes down the needed amount of fuel for each aircraft and reconfirms the amounts with Gretchen.

Gretchen adds;

"Very good lieutenant… and of course there is no charge to the Air Force…we all work for the same company right?"

The lieutenant replies with continued enthusiasm;

"Yes of course…no charge for our friends in the Air Force! I'll order the fuel trucks to your aircraft immediately...you'll be out of here in an hour!"

Gretchen can't help but notice the startled expressions on the faces of her fellow crew members. They look on with total amazement as Lieutenant Stebbins picks up the phone and orders the fueling operations for their aircraft.

One hour later two completely refueled aircraft taxi to the end of the runway. Alan McConnell updates the inertial guidance system (INS) with Adak's longitude and latitude coordinates. A course for Batagay is entered; 67 degrees 38'56"N, 134 degrees 41'42" E. The two aircraft begin their takeoff roll.

Meanwhile, back at the Flight Ops Office; Lieutenant Stebbins receives a call from Chief Warrant Officer Majewski at the base's Fuel Depot;

"Lieutenant…I need your help. What's the story on those two Air Force planes we just fueled? We loaded a hell of a lot of fuel

Chapter 33 – *All Roads Lead To Verkhoyansk*

on those two birds.

I don't have any paperwork on them at all…who authorized the refueling? Who do I charge it to?...and I hope you have another fuel tanker coming in Lieutenant…we're going to be short for all our birds by the end of the day!"

Stebbins thinks for a moment and becomes confused. Then, he sees his hand written notes next to the phone with the exact fuel amounts. Stebbins suddenly feels very out of sorts. He feels flushed and warm in the face. He looks at his notes again and hesitantly answers;

"I guess it was me…I did Chief…but I don't exactly remember….How much fuel did I order?"

The Chief doesn't say anything at first…then replies;

"Oh Shit Lieutenant…We're up that proverbial 'creek' and we 'ain't got' a paddle between us!"

At that exact moment and 10 miles out from Adak…the lead F-111 aircraft Spirit and Convair 990 bank sharply to the INS course heading…direct to Batagay, Siberia.

Aircraft: Russian Antonov 24
Elapsed Mission Time: +05:00 hrs.
Location: Napalkovo Airfield for refueling
Time: 2200 hrs. 10:00 p.m.
Distance traveled: 1,300 nautical miles
Distance remaining: 1,260 nautical miles
Destination: Batagay Airport, Siberia

Captain Alexi Petrov and copilot Lieutenant Mikhail Petrov finish a large bowl of hot beef and cabbage *Schi* at the Napalkovo Base Mess Hall.

Alexi says;

"Nothing warms one like good Russian Schi. The food has gotten better here. They must have a new cook.

You know, it will be good when we finally land at Batagay.

Renegades

This is a long flight. I must be getting older. I need some rest. They have warm barracks there. Later we can meet Director Ivanov and finalize the details for the transfer of the prisoners."

Devlin and his soldiers eat together at a separate table. During the entire meal there is no conversation. They stand up and quietly prepare to leave.

Alexi looks outside at the AN-24.

The ground crew is finishing the refueling.

It's night and flood lamps light the apron area as the fuel truck pulls away.

Alexi says;

"Mikhail, I remain feeling very uneasy with Sergeant Devlin onboard. His presence is a dark cloud overhanging our flight. I am not a religious person but I feel something evil and disturbing with him.

Even the weather is not normal. High pressures and clear weather almost always dominate the region here…but now this massive storm…accompanying a low pressure front confronts us. Well, we've been here an hour already. we must get underway."

Prisoners on the Move
On the Bus to Batagay

The road to Batagay is a single layer of clay and gravel. During the Summer when temperatures are above freezing rain turns the roads to a deep muddy mixture or they may become flooded making them completely impassable.

The road is at its best when frozen. During daylight hours and when clear and cold weather conditions prevail; the 45 mile trip is normally an hour and 15 minutes.

An early morning snow has begun to fall. The temperature is -26 degrees F. High winds and low visibility slow the progress of the three vehicle caravan to 20 miles an hour.

Mikhail is driving the lead bus. He gazes through a small unevenly cleared portion of the front windshield. The wipers are unable to clear all the snow. The wiper blades ice up and solidly resound with a battering sound at the far end of each cycle.

Chapter 33 – *All Roads Lead To Verkhoyansk*

Standing at Mikhails side is Pavel Guisha.

Pavel turns to the rear of the bus to check on the stretcher and condition of Captain McConnell who remains unconscious with fever...the medical doctor remains by his side.

The inside of the bus is in complete darkness. Pavel approaches McConnell and physically changes into his true spiritual and invisible form as angel Gabriel. He places his hand on McConnell's shoulder. Gabriel recalls the early morning carrier takeoff from the carrier *Hornet* with a much younger and stronger McConnell at the controls. He remembers the courage and concern he had for the safety of each member of the crew. With his hand remaining on McConnell...Gabriel offers a silent prayer for protection and physical strength to combat the pneumonia.

Unnoticed Gabriel reappears in the form of Pavel and is confronted with the sounds of children. Children are crying... feeling the pain of the frigid chill in the air; barely warmed by the overburdened and under-performing heater. Suddenly there's a cry from a passenger looking out of the side window. A call rings out;

Stop! Stop!

Mikhail, who is in the driver's seat, glances at the outside rear view mirror and sees Alexi's bus has gone off the road and into a high snow drift. He stops the bus and turns to everyone in the rear;

"Everyone; stay onboard the bus. Do not leave. I am going outside. The other bus has gone off the road. They need help...We will get underway shortly."

Mikhail walks through the blowing snow, covering his face from the searing cold. He falls and picks himself up several times until he finally reaches the bus.

The bus has traveled 20 feet off the main road, rolled over and rests on its side. Alexi helps the passengers exit the bus through a rear door.

Alexi is visibly shaken.

"The passengers... are all okay but it will be impossible to right the bus and get it back on the road again. I cannot believe this is happening!"

Mikhail says;

Renegades

"It's only a short distance to the airport…another 20 minutes at most…Have your passengers board my bus. We must continue on…without delay!"

The storm continues to intensify and as Makhail walks to the bus he wonders if their small band of refugees will reach the airport or end up being discovered in the days ahead; frozen bodies along the roadside…human collateral of a failed mission.

Then there is also the question…If we reach the airport…will the American planes be able to find and land on the snow packed runway?

The passengers of the now abandoned bus board the remaining lead bus. Pavel meets the passengers as they arrive and speaks to Alexi and Mikhail;

"When we arrive at the airport I will ask for volunteers to open the runway. We must clear the runway and it's lighting as as soon as possible."
Alexi answers;

"I know the airport manager, Victor Kologrigov. He is a very efficient and may already have the runway cleared for us."

Chapter 33 – *All Roads Lead To Verkhoyansk*

Chapter 34
"A Bear in Heat"
Above the Bering Sea
380 Knots

On course to Batagay Convair 990 Pilot Tom Winworth radios
Roger McConnell in the lead F-111 aircraft;
"Roger we're getting a real rough ride at this 11,000 foot
altitude....I've got to reduce airspeed."
  McConnell answers;
  "Understood Tom....Reduce your speed to 200. Continue
flying in our counter measures shadow. We're going to climb to
35,000 to avoid some of the weather associated with the low
pressure ahead of us. Everything should smooth out once we
gain some altitude.
   Tom replies;
  "Very good we'll remain a half mile behind you.... don't go
'cowboy' on me and get too aggressive on your climb out! This
is an airliner with a full fuel load."
  McConnell replies;
  "Understood Tom"
Roger advances the throttle slightly and begins a shallow 1500
feet per minute climb.
Alan is monitoring the ECM...*the Electronic Counter Measures*.
A radar contact suddenly appears on the display.
  Alan studies the green symbol as it slowly advances along the
screen. He turns to Roger;
  "I have a return on an aircraft indicating 400 knots at 30,000
feet....70 miles ahead of us on a parallel heading. Looks like
we'll intercept his flight path....then climb above it ....and
remain behind him by about 80 miles."
  Roger asks;
  "Is he transmitting an ID signature?"
Alan replies;
  "It's a Soviet aircraft... the database identifies it as a
Russian *Bear*, reconnaissance aircraft...a Tupolev TU-95RTS
bomber. The data base says it's a four engine turboprop...a crew

233

of seven and a top speed is 480 knots. They're armed with radar controlled guns and an autocannon in the tail turret. I don't have any information on what might be mounted on their underwing pylons…could be missiles. This particular RTS model just went into production last year. It's armed with the latest radar and electronics primarily used for detecting and gathering *electronic intelligence* on foreign emitters….like the counter measure cloaking signals were transmitting. I guess it's our lucky day!"
Roger reacts immediately;

"Okay Alan, we're changing course 30 degrees for two minutes and then a return back to our original heading. Let's see what the *Bear* does."

A minute passes…
Alan reports:
"No change."

Two minutes pass…
"The *Bear* is still on the same course…no change."

Roger looks at Alan and says;
"Alright, I think we're okay. He hasn't seen us."

Just as Roger is about to bank the aircraft and return to the original course heading Alan interrupts;
"The *Bear* knows we're here Roger!…he just changed course matching our heading…and he's losing airspeed and altitude…300 knots now. We're starting to gain on him. We're at 60 miles now."

Roger breaks radio silence and calls the 990;
"Tom; are you following us okay?"
Tom answers;
"Still have you in our sights and right on your tail…I was with you through the course change….What's going on?"
Roger replies;
"We picked up a Soviet *Bear* on radar…and he's looking at us! It's a reconnaissance bomber on the prowl.
We've got to lose him. Let's increase our climb rate and plan

Chapter 34 – *A Bear in Heat*

to go high and fast…level off at 45,000 and generate some airspeed. Let's see if we can earn some distance insurance…The *Bear* needs four big old heavy props to pull him through the air…Those props limit his airspeed."

Tom answers;

"The *Coronado* can handle Mach 1 for a short dash."
Gretchen is at the flight engineers station and adds;

"I'll monitor the fuel flow…we have a limited reserve…our dash time must be watched. I'll keep everyone updated."

Roger replies;

"Sounds good…I'll hold the reins on *Spirit* to Mach 1. Let's do it!"

Aircraft: Russian Antonov 24
Elapsed Mission Time: +7:00 hrs.
Distance traveled: 1,716 nautical miles
Distance remaining: 855 nautical miles
Destination: Batagay Airport, Siberia
ETA: 0410 hrs. 4:10 a.m.

The small twin engine AN-24 is unable to climb fast enough or gain enough altitude to fly above the snow and ice combination of the low pressure front. There is no doubt when the "24" first meets the front. It's tossed upward a thousand feet and then just as suddenly pulled down by 2000 feet.

Captain Alexi Petrov steadies the control column and calls out to his copilot Mikhail.;

"Oh! Did you feel that brother! We've arrived Mikhail…the battle begins to reach Batagay!"

Mikhail looks out the front windscreen and side windows. He turns on the exterior lights…illuminating both wings and engines and reports;

"The deicers seem to be working…no accumulation on wings."

Renegades

Alexi asks;

"Good...are we in range of the navigation signal from the Batagay beacon? I need a correct heading or we're lost."

Aircraft: F-111 and Convair 990
Elapsed Mission Time: +9:00 hrs.
Distance traveled: 4,280 nautical miles
Distance remaining: 300 nautical miles
Destination: Batagay Airport, Siberia
ETA: 0350 hrs. 3:50 a.m.

Spirit and Coronado are 300 miles from Batagay at 45,000 feet and airspeed reduced to 250 knots.

Roger asks;

"Any sign of the *Bear*?"

Alan looks at the radar screen and selects various ranges and tilt angles;

"No returns. I can't find any traffic. We're all clear."

Roger opens the communication channel to Coronado.

"We're on course and dropping down to 6000 feet.
This will put us about 100 miles out from Batagay.
Roger has you on radar and will have updates with course and altitude numbers throughout the descent and landing. It's going to get a little rough down there when we enter the first cloud layer at 5,000. Stay with us and maintain a descent of 1300 fpm at 250 knots.
Tom in the *Coronado* replies;

"Copy you on that *Spirit.*"

Chapter 34 – *A Bear in Heat*

Chapter 35
Showdown at Batagay
Time: 0100 hrs. 1:00 a.m.
February 7, 1964

One small bus and truck pass through the village of Batagay. There is no activity in the early morning darkness. The bus reaches the airport and follows the perimeter road to the hangar area where the flight office is located.

The airport is enveloped in complete darkness. A figure comes running towards the bus...he's carrying a large lighted lantern; just barely visible through the heavy blowing snow. It's Victor Kologrigov, the airport manager.

Alexi stops the bus and opens the front door and calls out above the wind;

"Victor, what's happening here!...there are no lights, no beacon? The Americans will not be able to find the airport!"

Victor replies with his boisterous, assuring sense of confidence;

"No, No...Alexi! I have just finished some repairs on the generator. I was about to start it when I saw your bus arrive. The runway has been plowed. All is ready for the Americans! Pull your bus into the hangar...the one next to my office, it's heated...everyone will be able to warm up. Follow me...I'll open the door. I am glad you made it...this heavy snow and these winds are very dangerous...you know?" Alexi answers;

"Yes Victor, I know!"

Alexi closes the bus's entry door and follows Victor's lighted lantern as he walks towards the hangar. A single floodlight illuminates the hangar door. Parked outside is a farming tractor with a front plow attached. Victor opens the hangar door and Alexi pulls inside.

As he opens the bus's front door there is a rush of warm air into the bus. Victor appears at the door, pulls back his parka hood and steps up and into the bus;

"Welcome my comrades to *Batagay International*! You must be very cold...so, everyone...I have hot black tea and my special robust Turkish coffee prepared for you. We will wait in the warm hangar for the arrival of the American aircraft."

238

All of the passengers exit the bus. The truck holding the remaining passengers pulls into the hangar. The hangar doors are closed.

Pavel, the medical attendant and two other passengers assist carrying the stretcher with Captain McConnell from the bus to a warm corner of the hangar.

The hangar is filled with crowded activity. There is talking, laughing and music from the speakers of a small stereo player. Pavel asks Victor:

"What is that noise?, the music that's playing...I have never heard anything like that!"

Victor moves his hand in a sweeping wide motion, like he is directing an orchestra and answers;

"It's...*I Want To Hold Your Hand.* We are not the only ones going to America today. A band from England, the Beatles are arriving in New York City. You like the sound Pavel? It is a sound of freedom...yes!"

Pavel laughs and says;

"You are right Victor...It has a wonderful sound and distinctive lyrics expressing fun, freedom...and being young!"

Pavel looks about the hangar and sees Captain McConnell on the stretcher.

"I must check and see how Captain McConnell is doing."

McConnell has regained consciousness after being moved but is totally unaware of recent events and what's happening. He sees Pavel for the first time and asks;

"Who are you? Would someone tell me where I am...and what's going on!"

Pavel smiles and replies, no longer hiding his identity;

"I am Gabriel, an angel sent here to help you. You've been unconscious for nearly 24 hours but you'll be pleased to know we're waiting for a plane to arrive to take you home...back to the United States."

McConnell attempts to sit up but falls back.

He replies with sarcastic emotion;

"What!...an angel!...I don't understand...Have I died?

Pavel stoically and matter of factly replies;

"No, you are quite alive Captain but I have exciting news for

238 Chapter 35 – *Showdown at Batagay*

you that may seem even more incredible and difficult to believe...but what I say is the truth. Your two sons...Roger and Alan are responsible for your rescue and all of the other refugees here as well. Their aircraft will be arriving shortly. You will see your two sons very soon!"

McConnell again attempts to sit up and continue his questioning. Pavel places his hand on his shoulder effectively preventing him from further movement. McConnell feels an immediate physical reaction from Gabriels action...an enveloping sense of calm that welcomes a strong restful sleep. Pavel quietly says;
"It is time to rest...a long journey is ahead of you Captain."
Pavel leaves McConnell and walks to the center of the hangar and pours himself a cup of the coffee. The hangar remains filled with conversation and anticipation. As he takes his first sip of coffee; Pavel is approached by the two Americans;
"My name is Jean Paul Boyer and this is my friend David Richardsen. We don't....."
Pavel interrupts;
"I know exactly who you are. There is no need for introductions."
Both are taken back with the unexpected response...but Jean Paul continues;
"...I don't believe this is really happening.

It all began In May of last year. One night on a road near Borem, a small village in the African Congo; we were attacked, taken hostage, drugged, separated and questioned in a Moscow prison for at least seven months.

Then, we were both sent here to Siberia. We were only in the Siberian prison for a couple weeks when we were told of an escape plan...a rescue of the entire prison including its administrator!"

Richardsen listens quietly and is suspicious of Pavel. He finishes his tea and asks;
"Pavel, you seem to be the one in charge here. Really, who are you? Do you know why we were taken hostage?"
Pavel replies;
"I have a cover identity working for the Russian airline, *Aeroflot* but am actually working as an agent with your State

Department. I have no idea why you were taken hostage. But let us all pray our flight is successful this morning… and you will return home safely."

Aircraft: F-111 and Convair 990
Elapsed Mission Time: +9:30 hrs
Location: 6000 feet - 250 knots
Distance traveled: 4,530 nautical miles
Distance remaining: 60 nautical miles
Destination: Batagay Airport, Siberia
Time: 0325 hrs. 3:25 a.m.
ETA: 0402 hrs. 4:02 a.m.

The F-111 *Spirit* and *Coronado* prepare to land and penetrate the center of the low pressure front. The pilots continue to experience unrelenting turbulence and lowering visibility. Alan turns to Roger;

"We're a 60 miles out from Batagay…according to the INS guidance and we have a weak ADF beacon signal from the airport. Maintain our present 6000 feet altitude. I've been looking at the forward scanning Radar…there are a lot of 5000 foot mountain peaks directly ahead."

Roger adds;

"I can't see a damn thing down there…or in front of us."

Tom at the controls of the *Coronado* calls in;

"We're getting beat up and tossed all over the place with this turbulence."

Roger replies;

"Okay, maintain 6000 feet…reduce airspeed to 190 knots and add some flaps. We're about 25 minutes out from our approach to Batagay. Maintain your half mile separation and follow me in for the landing. I'll give a call when I have the runway in sight."

Chapter 35 – *Showdown at Batagay*

Aircraft: Russian *Bear* bomber
Location: 150 miles East of Batagay
30,000 feet - 400 Knots- circular orbit
Time: 0340 hrs. 3:40 a.m.

Radio Communication:

"*Dobraye ootro!*, this is Soviet Reconnaissance aircraft Bear 95, Captain Helmut Alebekov to Napalkovo OPS do you copy over..."

"This is Napalkovo OPS...you're loud and clear Bear 95."

"Napalkovo... I am tracking two unidentified aircraft; a fighter and what appears to be a commercial jetliner. They're on a direct course to Batagay and preparing to land. I'm circling at a 150 mile radius from Batagay. Requesting a fighter intercept to investigate. Have the intercept flight leader contact me for exact coordinates. Weather over Batagay is a complete whiteout...but a small break, an hour long clearing will be passing through the area."

"Bear 95... Your request for intercept mission is understood. Will scramble four MiG 19's to investigate. The flight leader will contact you prior to takeoff."

"*Spaseeba* Napalkovo!...Bear 95 out."

Renegades

Aircraft: F-111 and Coronado 990
Elapsed Mission Time: +09:47 hrs.
1000 feet - 180 Knots
Over a large plain area and clear of mountains
Distance remaining: 5 nautical miles
Destination: Batagay Airport
ETA: 0400 hrs. 4:00 a.m.

Alan is on the F-111 radar scope;
"Radar's showing a large clearing…a good sized break in the clouds and snow…just ahead us. Talk about good timing…We're 5 miles out and should be seeing some runway lights."

Roger replies;
"I'm looking Alan…dropping the landing gear, adding 10 degrees flaps and turning on the landing lights…..the runway should be dead ahead but I don't see it yet."
Spirit suddenly breaks into the anticipated clearing.
Roger exclaims;
"Okay! I'm looking ahead at some beautiful runway lights brother… that's exactly what we're looking for!"
Roger calls to Coronado;
"Tom, you should be seeing some runway lights now!"
Tom gives a sigh of relief;
"Your damn right I do… they're beautiful! I'm right behind you."
Alan throttles back….

Chapter 35 – *Showdown at Batagay*

The Batagay Aircraft Hangar
"a time to leave!"

Victor peers out of a small window in the hangar door. He wipes off a larger area of the accumulated frost formed on the inside.

"There are two planes!" he exclaims;

"The American planes …They're landing now. I see their lights!"

The F-111 *Spirit* passes over the outer threshold and gently settles on a 4 inch layer of snow.

Aboard *Spirit*... for just a second at touchdown…snow completely covers the front windscreen then is quickly blown away. Roger taxies to the end of the runway and turns *Spirit* a full 180 degrees, lining up to its takeoff position.

Alan looks directly ahead just in time to see *Coronado* touch down. No wheel brakes are applied on the icy runway. The Coronado reverses its engine thrust.

Breaking the silence and darkness of early morning; *Coronado's* four engines slow the jetliner's forward momentum creating a maelstrom of blowing snow in front of the main wings as it thunders down the runway.

The Coronado slows and taxies a short distance to the end of the runway and initiates a 180 degree turn. Both aircraft are parked close to each other, the *990* is in front of *Spirit*… positioned for takeoff with engines idling in respect to the -35F temperatures.

A short distance away the hangar door opens and a long line of nearly 200 passengers emerge and slowly plod through the snow towards the aircraft. Many are carrying improvised luggage; cardboard boxes and large burlap gunny sacks.

Roger and Alan scan the long line of passengers to see if they can spot their father.

Leading the procession is Pavel.

A specially made stairway ladder with hand rails is lowered to the ground from the passenger entrance of *Coronado*. Gretchen, dressed in an orange colored arctic parka is first to emerge from *Coronado*. She climbs down stairway and meets Pavel and the arriving passengers. Despite Pavel's earthly disguise; Gretchen

244

instantly recognizes *Gabriel.*

Gabriel continues his walk towards *Coronado*…and greets Gretchen by her angelic name;

"Uriel…..my *Archangel of Wisdom*…we meet in this most unusual and challenging of times. All is well with you I pray?" Gretchen answers;

"Yes, the Lord is watching over us and protecting us in ways that I do not even see. How are our special three passengers? "

Pavel answers;

Captain McConnell is weak but has tremendous spirit and a will to live. Jean Paul and David are both doing fine."

The passengers approach the boarding ladder. Gretchen and Pavel help the passengers aboard.

Alan and Roger remain in the cockpit of the F-111. Alan sees the stretcher carrying their father;

"Look over there! There he is Rog! There's dad!"

The ailing McConnell is taken aboard *Coronado*. His stretcher is lifted with attached cargo straps by pilotsTom, David and several other passengers. The last few passengers follow and climb up the stairway.

Victor is the last to board but as he reaches out for the handrail he pauses for a moment and notices two small points of light breaking through the fog filled sky. Victor calls out;

"There…look…those are landing lights from another aircraft! "Do you see them?"

Gretchen answers;

"I certainly do Victor!…We must get underway...now!"

Spirit on Guard

Roger McConnell also sees the approach landing lights of the unidentified aircraft. He throttles up *Spirit's* engines and maneuvers to a takeoff position directly in front of *Coronado*. Alan adjusts the tilt angle on the radar in an attempt to identify the aircraft. Alan calls out;

"I have the ident …it's an *AN-24* Russian Transport…a twin engine turboprop; a mile out and lined up with our runway! He's too close…we can't takeoff now."

The AN-24 comes into view… lands, reverses thrust and comes

to a complete stop 200 yards in front of *Spirit*. The two aircraft face each other... nose to nose.

Spirit's comm radio is scanning all frequencies and locks onto a strong signal...a communication channel with the *An-24*. In perfect English; a message is received;

"I am Master Sergeant Devlin Poplavski of the Soviet Air Force. Power down your two aircraft and prepare to be boarded."

As the communication ends, a contingent of armed Russian soldiers exit the AN-24 and slowly march towards *Spirit* and *Coronado*. The contingent also includes the pilot, Captain Alexi Petrov and his Copilot and brother Mikhail Petrov. Master Sergeant Devlin Poplavski is in the lead position.

They walk 100 yards ...about half way between the two planes... and stop.

Roger and Alan in the cockpit of *Spirit* are able to see the soldiers and pilots clearly lit by the combined landing lights shining from the gathered aircraft. Alan sees two persons approaching the soldiers;
Alan exclaims;

"It's Gretchen and Pavel...What are they doing out there!"
Tom, in *Coronado's* cockpit radios;

"Gretchen is out there...she speaks Russian...I couldn't stop her. She wants to talk to them...she has a mind of her own! Pavel is with her."

Roger and Alan watch Gretchen as she approaches the armed military. Pavel stands at a safe distance behind Gretchen. The Russian troops raise their rifles and point them directly at her. Gretchen raises both hands high in the air.... a display to communicate a surrender and lack of arms... she speaks in fluent Russian;

"I am unarmed...there is no need for weapons. I have a message. You must listen."

Master Sergeant Devlin hollers in a commanding tone to his men;

"No one listen to this lady!...I know this person well...we have met before. She speaks with poisoned, twisted and misleading words."

Gretchen immediately replies;

Renegades

"Say no more Devlin...have your men lower their weapons and throw them on the ground. Prepare to surrender."

Devlin reacts with amused disbelief;

"Uriel...Uriel...'*The Archangel of Wisdom.*' You must be losing some of your enlightened intelligence. I am in control here. You and your renegade crew are now my prisoners!"

Gretchen replies;

"Really Devlin...I suggest you look behind you!"

Roger and Alan look on and are unprepared for what they see. Walking out of the darkness and a fog bank is an army of several hundred soldiers. In appearance and stature they are unlike any "earthly army."

They are fierce looking...all wearing shiny metal breast plate armor and carrying long spears with glowing red tips. Others have their swords drawn. Each soldier is twice the size of a normal man. They are best described as what would be imagined as the "*Ultimate Warrior.*" Gretchen's calls out;

"These are God's Warriors Devlin! They are fierce fighters. Do not test the power of their weapons. It is time to surrender. "

The Warrior angels with perfect military execution and cadence encircle the small band of stunned Russian soldiers who one by one throw down their weapons into the snow.

One soldier draws his revolver and fires directly at Gretchen. At the same instant a spear from the Warrior angel is already in flight and intercepts the bullet in mid-flight. There is a small bright flash of exploding light.

Devlin is unable to issue commands...his voice silenced by the power of God.

Gretchen speaks to the Russians;

"We are leaving for a flight to the United States. We have rescued three Americans from the gulag as well as most of the prisoners there. I invite any soldier who would like to join us... follow me on our flight to freedom and begin a new life."

AN-24 Captain Petrov and his brother are the first to come forward. Four of the ten soldiers follow. Gretchen leads the entourage back to *Coronado*.

The passenger doors are closed and sealed. The Warriors that provided protection now quietly return to the surrounding mist from where they came.

Chapter 35 – *Showdown at Batagay*

Devlin is able to speak again and calls out to the remaining soldiers;
"Retrieve your weapons and destroy those two aircraft!"
The first rounds fired hit the rear section of *spirit's* fuselage but the light ammunition is unable to pierce the metal.

Roger sees and hears what's happening as the second round of bullets ricochet off the canopy;
"We don't have a choice. Let's take out their aircraft…He looks at Alan and asks;

"Do you know what happens when you fire an "air to air" missile in a "ground to ground" situation?"
Alan shakes his head and begins to smile;
"Now is a good time to find out!"
Alan places his right hand on the *Armament Select Panel*. The *Master Power* is turned **On.** The *Weapon Mode Selector* has 18 positions marked in clockwise order. The missile's **Manual Launch** mode is selected…then Alan presses weapon select **Button 1**. A red lamp lights indicating the weapon on the pylon wing station is ready to fire.
The **Weapons Release** button is mounted on both the aircraft commander's and weapon officer's flight control grip. Alan grasps the control and says;
"Here goes *one*!"
The **Release** button is depressed.
There's an immediate mechanical sound of the release latches opening. The missile falls on the runway and beneath the snow. Roger and Alan are transfixed… looking for the missile that remains hidden. Alan says;
"Oh shit! Nothing's happening!"
Then suddenly, the propellant ignites and the missile scurries off to the right and off the runway. The missile, traveling beneath the snow, generates a massive rooster tail of flying snow as it travels along an unguided, ground hugging trajectory.
Alan calls out;
"Scratch that…let's try again…the weapon select **Button 4** is depressed but no "ready light" appears."
The missile remains silent… "Damn…everything's too cold…frozen and locked tight. I'm taking *four* off line. .Going to *two* and adding some *UP trim* on guidance control….Okay.

One more time..

Weapon Select **Button 2** is activated…

The red activation light is on…**Firing 2!"**

There's the immediate mechanical sound of the release latches opening. The missile falls onto the runway and beneath the snow. The propellant ignites.

The missile travels a short distance down the center of the runway. Roger looks on;

"…It's going to sail underneath and right past the target!"

Then, all of a sudden the missile breaks loose from beneath the snow, angles up and directly into the underside of the AN-24.

A single loud and massive explosion erupts. The early morning darkness disappears. A menacing, flaming orange, red and yellow fireball of exploding fuel rises into the air. Black smoke and debris spread outward in all directions. A shockwave is felt aboard *Spirit*. A series of smaller secondary explosions follow.

The Russian soldiers are motionless, sprawled out on the snow.

Roger is on the radio to *Coronado;*

"Okay…it's time to go home."

He turns on the exterior taxi lights. The runway marker lights are buried beneath the snow but still offer a diffused visible marker on each side of the runway. Roger releases the brakes and eases the throttle forward. *Spirit* begins to move. Alan activates the ECM electronics.

Additional snow has accumulated during the brief time spent on the ground and *Spirit* responds sluggishly from the added resistance. He continues to taxi very slowly and maneuvers around several smoking debris fields of the AN-24.

With an open runway ahead; Roger advances the throttle to the full afterburner position. Twin daggers of flame emerge from the rear afterburner nozzles touching the snow behind it…*Spirit* picks up speed and within seconds is hurtling down the runway towards takeoff speed. A trail of melted snow marks its path down the runway.

Roger pulls back on the stick. *Spirit* is airborne.

Alan reaches over the center console and raises the gear retract control.

Over the radio he hears Tom report;

"*Coronado* is rolling"

Chapter 35 – *Showdown at Batagay*

Alan turns, looks back at Batagay and sees *Coronado's* dim outline against the snow as it leaves the runway and gains altitude in a steep climb.

Coronado reports;

"We're wheels up and right behind you *Spirit*. Passengers and your father are doing well." Roger is about to ask about his father but is interrupted.

Alan looks up from the radar screen;

"The war isn't over Rog...I've got a contact 130 miles out on an intercept course. Three other aircraft have broken off...reversed their course...may have been low on fuel."

Roger asks;

"What about the remaining aircraft. Do you have an ID?"

Alan looks up and replies;

"It's a MiG-19 and he's at 110 miles and closing fast. Roger radios Tom aboard *Coronado*;

"Tom...I'm breaking off...Alan's picked up a MiG-19 on radar...we're in his sights...we've got to get him."

Tom replies;

"Good hunting *Spirit*!"

Roger banks *Spirit* into a steep turn away from *Coronado* and on an intercept course with the MiG.

He tells Alan;

"I'm going to try a full sweep on the wings...all the way back to 72 degrees. We haven't flight tested your swing wings yet Alan ...what do you think?...Will they hang together okay?"

Alan reports;

"I've ran so many ground tests with heavy loading on this design ...it's solid Rog.

Roger reaches to his left and pulls back on the wing controller moving it to its full aft positon.

Alan and Roger both look to each side and watch the wings slowly retract. The flight computer continuously monitors and seamlessly adjusts the flight controls and trim to the new aerodynamic configuration.

Roger adds more throttle. Airspeed increases to 900 knots. *Spirit* remains rock solid in straight and level flight; going supersonic for the first time. Roger enthusiastically exclaims;

"Good show Alan!...No difference on the flight controls

Renegades

during the entire sweep. A computer!…that's what was missing on our glider's last flight!….
Where's the MiG now?"

Alan goes back on the scope.
"We're nose to nose; closing speed at 1,600 knots; we're 60 seconds to intercept …."
Roger replies;

"Okay, Give me a 30 second count…then I'm going vertical, change direction at the top of climb, drop down and fall directly behind and nail the MiG with a missile shot."
Alan counts the seconds, 27, 28, 29… Bingo!
Roger pushes the throttle full forward engaging both afterburners.

He pulls back on the stick. G forces slam them into their seats as *Spirit* enters a vertical climb.

Roger goes over the top of the climb and begins a rapid descent towards the MiG which is now slightly ahead and at a lower altitude.

The sun is beginning to rise and Alan looks up from his radar screen and to get a visual confirmation on the MiG as they approach from behind.
Roger says;

"He doesn't see us. I'm going in closer. Arm the missiles Alan."

Alan attempts to arm the remaining missiles but there's no response.…no confirmation lights. The missiles are just useless.

Chapter 35 – *Showdown at Batagay*

weight hanging on the pylons. Alan decides to give it one more try.

Suddenly, *Spirit* is violently shaken as if it hit by armament. Roger calls out;

"We've got compressor stalls on Number 1 and 2 engines. Going for a restart."

Spirit immediately loses airspeed. A high rate of descent follows. The MiG spots its injured American assailant and banks sharply to follow *Spirit* in its rapid descent. The MiG doesn't attempt to fire on the crippled aircraft.

Roger continually repeats the procedure for a restart with no success. Alan calls out to Roger;

"Why isn't he firing on us?…we're an easy shot!"

Roger answers;

"He's in no hurry, figures he has time to look us over first; probably studying our design.   Alan, we're out of options. We're unarmed and gliding without an engine…I need more lift…I have to extend the wings."

For what is only a brief few seconds, Roger looks to his left. The MiG is flying in tight formation....just off *Spirit's* left wingtip. McConnell sees the pilot and the red star on his helmet. The Russian pilot raises his visor. He studies with interest the changing sweep of the wings as they go into the full forward position....then looks directly at Roger. The expression is neutral …more inquisitive than combative.

Roger returns quickly to the moment; banks sharply to the right and away from the MiG….Engine 2 finally restarts. He increases the throttle. The MiG attempts to follow.

Roger turns to Alan;

"The weather front ahead of us has some heavy clouds…that's what we're looking for and where we're headed!

What about the terrain radar…what's it seeing ahead?"

Alan calls out;

"Mountains!…6000 feet max."

Spirit enters the cloud bank…suddenly all outside visibility and sense of speed is lost. The sensation is like being suspended in a container of gray liquid. Instruments with their digital readouts and radar images are the only portals to "see" what's outside and ahead.

Renegades

Roger calls out;
Alright, things are starting to look up!…I've got a restart on engine 1 with RPM winding up! Let's see if our TFR, the will relieve our MiG problem…I have a plan! Are you with me brother?"

Alan knows exactly what his brother is thinking;
"I'm firing up the TFR, and setting the altitude for 500t…
The autopilot and auto throttle will take us down to 500 feet above ground level and maintain that altitude above any obstacle in front of us…even when climbing up the side of a mountain."

Spirit is in the clouds at 10,000 feet and losing altitude fast at 5000 feet per minute. Alan calls out;
"The MiG is still with us…and directly behind. He's following our descent on radar…but his reaction time will not be as fast as our computer's flight control…..Right?"
Roger nods and says;
"You have the picture Alan."
Alan monitors the terrain radar and announces;
"We're approaching the target altitude…500 feet."
Roger keeps his hand close to the flight control stick; in a relaxed position about an inch away…primed to take control if the TFR doesn't begin a pullout from the rapid descent.

Alan calls out;
"1000 feet"
Alan lightly touches the control stick and just as he is about to pull it back…the TFR takes control.

Roger and Alan are pushed down into their seats with the high G pullout.

Now they're flying supersonic over a flat plain area at 790 knots through solid ground fog with no forward view.

"Okay, we've got a 4000 foot mountain range directly ahead in 30 seconds. TFR has a solid reading." Alan exclaims.
Once again Roger monitors the instruments and monitors the control inputs of TFR.

Alan reads out the time to first upslope in the mountain range;
"15 seconds, 14, 13, 12, 11, 10, 9, 8…."
Roger places his hand near the control stick again. Alan continues his countdown;
"5…4…3…2…1!"

Chapter 35 – *Showdown at Batagay*

Spirit abruptly raises its nose in dramatic fashion…and continues without hesitation to a near vertical position. The high G maneuver slams them both into their seats. Alan almost blacks out. For a brief second the side of the mountain is seen through the front windscreen before disappearing into the grey soup of the cloud cover.

Within seconds a loud but distant sound of an explosion is heard above the noise of *Spirit's* afterburners.

Alan looks up from the radar scope…looks at Roger and reports; "The MiG is gone…

He's off our scope. We lost him Rog!"

Roger remains silent…He looks down at his hands. They're both shaking. He tries to make them stop. His mouth is suddenly dry. There was an immediate elation of victory but now there's a slow disquieting realization of his "first kill".

He can't forget seeing the Russian pilot raising his visor and looking straight at him…there was no hatred there. Somehow a personal loss is felt. The Russian aircraft had a red star…*Spirit* has a white star painted on its side…that may have been the only difference between us.

We both had the same type of training and share a love of the sky that brought us together to this place and time…to do battle.

Roger suddenly realizes…no matter what language spoken; *fighter pilots* are *brothers* of a unique culture…all cut from the same cloth. Probably if they had met each other under different circumstances they would have been friends and been able to laugh, share stories and experiences together.

Alan interrupts Roger's thoughts and asks;

"Are you okay brother?"

Roger replies;

"Yea…I'm alright…it was a rush with the MiG…relaxing and coming down a little I guess…Let's catch up with the *Coronado! And go home.* What do you say Alan?"

"…'Let's do it!'"

Spirit is 150 miles and closing when a radio call is received from *Coronado* pilot Tom Winworth;

"This is *Coronado*…Alan and Roger…I'm afraid we have some bad news here…Let me turn you over to Gretchen."

Gretchen's voice is hesitant, serious and not forthcoming;

"Alan and Roger…Your father just passed away ten minutes ago. He never regained consciousness. We did everything we could to resuscitate him. The phenomena and lack of proper medication…I'm very sorry…so sorry to give you this news. "

For a moment, there is no response from *Spirit*…then Alan breaks the radio silence;

"Gretchen, I don't understand. Why did you…you and your God let this happen? We came all this way, sacrificed everything to follow His command, His mission and then He allows this?…Your God shows no justice Gretchen!…why are we being punished?"

Roger interrupts;

"Gretchen….Tom…We've been through a lot today and appreciate your efforts to save dad. I wish the mission ended differently. Our hope was running so high with the thought of having a father again after so many years…it hurts. We'll contact you in another 15 minutes…*Spirit* out.

Alan turns to Roger;

"Rog…You're always saying the prayers. We need one now. We need a prayer for a miracle…a major miracle!." Roger doesn't reply. He looks out the front windscreen. Almost as if on cue…a magnificent display of *Northern Lights* appears directly ahead. The cockpit becomes lit in a mirage like collection of shimmering color…an entire spectrum of greens, reds and yellows are alive and splash and dance across the sky as if painted by the strokes of a celestial artist. Alan exclaims; "Unbelievable!…I've never seen anything like this!"

The display is painted over a canvas of a million stars….a heavenly light show seeming to communicate that Heaven is awake, alive…. and listening.

No words are uttered, the only sound heard is the low whisper of the engines and wind noise passing over the cockpit. The response was natural and immediate. Each brother looks at the display out the front windscreen and offer their own silent prayer. The northern lights continue for only a short time, then end as abruptly as they appeared.

Alan looks to Roger;

"Something happened Rog…I felt it….Did you get it?"

Roger, nods; "Oh yea, I can't describe it either…there was a

Chapter 35 – *Showdown at Batagay*

strong presence."
The radio comes alive…it's Gretchen;
"The *Aurora Borealis* display..did you see it?…We flew
directly through its center. I was sitting next to your *father. He
was awakened at exactly that moment. He's alive Alan!…
something extraordinary happened when we passed through the
celestial light…Alan, this was a miracle!"*

Meanwhile, back at Batagay Airport

Russian Army Master Sergeant Devlin Poplavski is in the
airport office on the telephone calling Moscow and trying to
reach Soviet Airchief Marshal, General Viktor Orlov, *The Wolf.*
General Orlov is being served lunch in his office with Premier
Khrushchev. Orlov is telling Khrushchev;
"Yes Premier, the closing of the Siberian Gulags is going
extremely well in a very efficient manner…of this you can be
assured. In fact, we have just completed the closure of the
Verkhoyansk facility today. Regretfully, some of the methods I
have used have been somewhat distasteful but expedient."
Khrushchev answers;
"If you live among wolves you have to act like a wolf."
General Orlov smiles in agreement and adds;
"Yes, my sentiments exactly."
General Orlov's phone rings…
"Excuse me Premier I must answer this."
General Orlov picks up the phone and with some displeasure for
the interruption asks;

Renegades

"Who is this?"

There is some delay in the answer;

" I am Master Sergeant Devlin Poplavski. I am in charge of the detail closing the Verkhoyansk gulag."

Orlov curtly replies;

"Yes Sergeant...report!...I am in a very important meeting at the moment with the Premier."

Sergeant Poplavski reluctantly replies;

"You need to send an aircraft to Batagay to pick me up and my men as well."

The General asks;

"Pick you up? I do not understand. What happened to your Antonov-24?"

There is a long silence...Sergeant Poplavski finally answers;

"It was blown up sir...by Americans."

General Orlov replies

"Sergeant, I need to talk with the pilot; flight leader Petrov!"

Khrushchev is listening and asks;

"Is there a problem General?"

General Orlov puts the phone aside and is quick to reply;

"Oh no Premier...everything is fine."

Khrushchev stands up and says;

"An excellent lunch General but I must attend to several afternoon commitments. Please excuse me."

Khrushchev leaves the office and General Orlov returns to the phone and again asks;

"Sergeant, let me speak with the mission flight leader... Captain Petrov!"

Sergeant Poplavski realizes he has called the wrong person for assistance and answers;

"Sir, flight leader Captain Petrov and his brother Lieutenant Mikhail Petrov defected to the United Sates as well as several soldiers from my detail...and...."

General Orlov interrupts;

And?....And what?...you mean there's more?"

There is detectable pain in the Sergeant's voice as he reports;

"The gulag director, Andrey Ivanov, all the guards and over 100 prisoners with families have also defected. The Batagay airport manager has left also."

Chapter 35 – *Showdown at Batagay*

General Orlov loses control;

"You are a *durak* Sergeant! a lack-brain, a pinhead, a foozie! A constant stream of condemnations and threats continue for some time ....then, a long silence followed by calmer voice and exacting instructions;

"You and the members of your remaining detail must not speak of this incident to anyone.

Instead, this is what happened; the Verkhoyansk facility was successfully closed...The prisoners and several soldiers were killed in the AN-24 when taking off from Batagay airfield during a Siberian snow storm. You and a handful of your detail are the only survivors.

There is nothing more to discuss..understood? I will send a plane for you and your men. Upon arrival report directly to me without delay. Is that understood Sergeant Poplavski?"

"Yes General...It is most certainly... *understood*."

Chapter 36
A Call to the President
Tactical Air Command
General Walter A. Swenson
Langley AFB, Virginia

Mr. President I have good news. The crew of the Convair 990 *Coronado* radioed Cold Bay flight operations. They are on final approach returning from Siberia with 160 Russian passengers , the two young Americans and Captain McConnell. However, The F-111 encountered resistance and was forced to take down a MiG 19 and eliminate an AN-24 transport at Batagay.

The President answers;

"Yes, I just received word before you called. The CIA and State Department informed me of the successful rescue mission and is monitoring Soviet communications and media for the fallout from the loss of aircraft.

So far General, there have been no reports. It's as though nothing happened out of the ordinary. We're continuing to monitor the situation but I feel a coordinated effort is underway by Moscow to fabricate a cover story on the whole incident...and General?"

"Yes, sir"

"I want a 'lid' on this story as well...a complete media and interservice blackout of all activity related to and supporting the rescue. I ordered the State Department...no news releases or confirmation of any rescue attempt. Do you understand?"

"Yes, sir...very good sir."

The President concludes;

"One last and final item...dispatch our finest medical team to Cold Bay for Captain McConnell. He is a hero and patriot who was lost for many years. He deserves our full support and commendation. "

Cold Bay, Alaska

The *Coronado 990* lands on Runway 23... following close

behind is the F-111, *Spirit of San Jon*. The two aircraft taxi to the parking area in front of the Base Operations Office. A large handmade sign is attached to the fence at the parking area

"Welcome To The United States *Spirit* and *Coronado*"

A light snow is falling. The 20 degree air feels warm compared to the Siberian freeze left behind. A small gathering of about 50 airmen are present. A medical transport vehicle is on hand. Roger and Alan McConnell shut down *Spirit's* engines, open the canopy, climb down from the cockpit and break into a run towards *Coronado*.

The ground crew moves a stairway into place at *Coronado's* forward passenger door. Gretchen is standing at the open door. Roger and Alan arrive. Gretchen shouts down to Alan…she is animated and enthusiastic;
"Alan, this is a good day. A victory and battle has been won!"
The medical team arrives, climbs the stairs and enters the cabin. Captain McConnell, on a stretcher… is conscious and carried down the stairs to the waiting ambulance.

Father and Sons Reunited

Roger and Alan climb into the ambulance and accompany their father to the base infirmary. They sit on each side of the stretcher as the ambulance pulls away.
Alan places his hand on his father's shoulder;

"Dad….Dad can you hear us? Roger and I are both here…you'll be alright now. You're going home…We're all going home now. The war is over!"

McConnell slowly opens his eyes and looks up and closely stares at Alan and Roger. He is still very weak but whispers;
"Alan…and Roger…
 I see you clearly…
 I know you…so many years…
 I have not forgotten you."

Renegades

The brothers are unaware of the presence of two angels also accompanying them. Archangels Michael and Gabriel in spiritual form look on in reverent silence pleased with the outcome of God's miracle and seeing a family reunited.

One Week Later

Temporary on-base living quarters have been secured for the Russian refugees. A specially formed relocation team arrives composed of representatives from the State Department, Red Cross and other service organizations. A transition program for the refugees is offered to prepare them for placement and life in the United States.

State Department representatives **Jeremy Standvok** and **Lloyd Jennings** are members of the transition team; interviewing the refugees.

Batagay Airport Manager **Victor Kologrigov** and cargo pilot **Sergey Ramzin** are headed to Key Largo, Florida. A charter fishing boat company needs additional help for maintenance of their large fishing fleet. **Sergey's son, Yuri** is registered as a student at Embry-Riddle Aeronautical University, Daytona Beach, Florida; enrolled in the Airframe and Power Plant studies program.

Former Verkhoyansk District Manager, **Andrey Ivanov** is offered an administrative position in developing a security program for a new concept shopping center, the Chris-Town Mall in Phoenix, Arizona.

Soviet Air Force Captain and AN-24 pilots **Alexi Petrov** and his brother Lieutenant **Mikhail Petrov** are being interviewed by a Canadian Aircraft Charter company.

Coronado 990 pilots, **Tom Winworth** and **David Dolan** will complete flight testing of the 990 and retire but continue flying support missions for *Mission Aviation Fellowship* in the Congo **John Paul Boyer** returns to Africa and continues his agricultural research program along the Sahel.

David Richardsen returns home to the United States and is planning his political future and a run for Congress

Captain McConnell's stay at the base infirmary results in a rapid recovery. Full consciousness is regained within three days.

Chapter 36 – *A Call to the President*

Roger and Alan remain at his side.

As he regained his strength; time is needed to begin a process of reintegration into daily life. The announcement and emotional acceptance of the unsolved tragic accident and death of his wife. Time is needed for the sons and father to "get to know each other."

Captain David McConnell is unable to recall the details of his aircraft when it was hit by enemy fire over Germany. The years and details of life as a prisoner in the Soviet Union remain disconnected. Much of his time in the Siberian gulag, as a prisoner, was spent in a mental fog. It was only during the last year his mental condition improved but at the cost of his physical well-being.

Another day passes at the Cold Bay infirmary.

It's early morning. Roger and Alan walk down the infirmary's main corridor to the corner room where there father is resting. They expect to find him sleeping; but when they enter the room are surprised to find him fully awake and sitting in a chair next to a small end table holding several large stacks of *Time* and *Newsweek* magazines. He's totally absorbed in reading and at first doesn't notice the two sons arrival.

Alan knocks lightly on the door. McConnell looks up and is surprised;

"Oh, good morning boys...good to see you. As you can see I'm trying to catch up. I feel like a *Rip Van Winkle* who has just awakened to a whole new world. So much has happened and changed...you know there's been about 20 years of history that's flown by...completely unseen and unnoticed by me.

I remember the first time I looked out the window of the Convair plane I flew in on...Two engines were attached beneath the wings...but no propellers! Single engine jet fighters were only on the drawing boards in 1944. The Air Force is a separate branch of service now...and the animated screen in my room; the television! There are now space pilots...they call them astronauts; John Glenn orbited the earth in less than 5 hours and I read there's a program to land an American on the moon before the decade ends.

But there's also a lot of bad news; The assassination of our President...an increase in the number of violent crimes taking place in our cities…and I couldn't believe reading about the Soviet missiles in Cuba and what about Vietnam! It's too much to swallow all at once boys. I need a break.

What about our ranch and San Jon?"
Roger is hesitant to reply immediately;
"I'm afraid there's more change there too dad. When we lost mom we sold the ranch. It was not an easy decision but our lives took us away from San Jon. There was another consideration as well.

I was concerned about the future of the town…and property values there. Remember how Route 66 went through the center of town…there's a new interstate highway system being built…it roughly follows Route 66 but it's supposed to be rerouted and bypass San Jon completely. We sold the property and bought 50 acres of land near Taos…a lot of activity and growth starting to take place there…Don't worry dad…Alan and I will get you up to speed. We're family!

McConnell looks at Roger and Alan; puts the magazines aside, slowly stands up and put his arms around both his sons;
"God bless you…God bless you both… thank you for saving me. It's good to be home."

The Chapel of Upper Heaven

Archangels Michael and Gabriel enter *the Chapel of Upper Heaven.* The Lord is present and studying the huge *Globe Of The Universe* which dominates the Chapel.

He looks down and see's Michael and Gabriel approaching;
"Greetings faithful servants…I am very pleased with your mission on Earth. You have done well. The order of future events will take place as planned and prepare the way for a transforming miraculous event that will place all humankind on a new path."

Chapter 36 – *A Call to the President*

Santa Fe, New Mexico

Gabriel sits alone on a wooden park bench located in the courtyard of the *Cathedral of St. Francis* in Santa Fe, New Mexico. He waits patiently for Michael to arrive. The entire afternoon will be spent over a chess board that's been reset to an earlier game and is ready to play.

A middle-aged Hispanic gentleman with dark hair, wearing tan trousers, a red turtleneck sweater and tan leather jacket looking stylish in its slightly worn but fashionable condition sits down at the bench across from Gabriel. He smiles upon seeing the chess board and studies its precisely positioned pieces. He looks at Gabriel, politely smiles and initiates a move which attacks Gabriel's opposing king and announces;

"Checkmate"

Michael has arrived.

Epilogue
Leaving On A Jet Plane
Honolulu, Hawaii

Trans West Airlines, Gate 34
Time: Many Years Later – 21st Century

Scott Shepard's aviation career continues after the Vietnam war ends. He leaves the Airforce and is employed two years with North American Aviation as a test pilot on the XB-70 Valkyrie program. The flight program ends and Shepard begins a new career as a commercial pilot with Trans West Airlines...he continues flying with Trans West completing 23years service.

It's late evening. The weather is clear, calm with a 76 degree temperature. Captain Scott Shepard is on the flight line performing the ritualistic walk around inspection of a *Trans West* Boeing 777. The aircraft is being readied for final boarding at Honolulu International Airport on the island of Oahu. Flight 144 is a direct flight to Albuquerque, New Mexico.

Most airline captains overlook or don't find it necessary for a *walkaround* inspection. Shepard still prefers to get to "personally" know the aircraft that will carry him and several hundred passengers across the Pacific tonight. He's joined by his First Officer, Bill Donahue;

"Good evening Captain...Everything looking okay? You know these planes have onboard computers that run an aggressive preflight check of all the systems. You really don't have to be out here. You know that...right? "

Shepard doesn't answer. He continues the inspection and turns on his flashlight...focusing its beam on the hydraulic lines; tracing their path up from the wheel brakes to the innards of the landing gear well. He finally replies;

"Bill...I know what you're saying. I know about all those computer monitoring systems...I just feel like I know the plane better; 'up close and personal' you might say. You can tell a lot about a plane's history...How it's been flown and maintained just by looking at certain parts of its exterior."

Shepard is about to continue but is interrupted by a familiar voice...the lead flight attendant; Denise Donaldson;
"I saw you all out here on this wonderful evening and it was 'air

conditioning cold' in the terminal…so I thought I'd come out here and get warm again!"

Shepard smiles;

"Glad to have you onboard tonight Denise. Anything we need to know?"

Denise answers;

"A couple items. For some reason there are no sky marshals assigned on tonight's flight. Oh, and there was one passenger cancellation made six hours ago….but was rather unusual…he has been calling every hour to our ticket agent wanting to confirm that flight 144 was still on schedule for departure. He sounded out of sorts according to the agent. His name is kind of unusual too; Devlin Windstedt."

Shepard replies;

"I'll call security and tell them to get in touch with the agent. It's probably nothing…

Denise quietly smiles to herself but finally says;

"Congratulations Captain…I understand this is your 'retirement flight'"…23 years with *Trans West!*

Shepard is quick to reply;

"Now Denise, I don't want you spreading the "retirement" word to any other members of the crew….that's an order…and this goes for my first officer too! I'm looking forward to an uneventful evening above a wonderful calm and storm free Pacific!"

The story continues with the 2rd novel of the trilogy;

A Time For Miracles
BREAKAWAY

and
The final 3rd instalment;

A Time To Explore
DESTINY
(Available 2018)

Renegades

The Author's Notes

Selected nuggets of information, notes of interest and facts I've "flown over" and collected in writing this novel.

T.H.

Photo:
On The F-111 flight line - 1971, Cannon Air Force Base - Clovis, New Mexico

"I pray that you all put your shoes way under the bed at night so that you gotta get on your knees in the morning to find them, and while you're down there thank God for grace and mercy and understanding."

Denzil Washington

Trinity –The Christian doctrine of God as Father, Son, and Holy Spirit.

The Holy Spirit – The third person of the Holy Trinity; known also as the *Counselor* who is active in the lives of believers

---

"Angels"

From Bible.Org
A Simple Definition

Angels are spiritual beings created by God to serve Him, though created higher than man. Some, the good angels, have remained obedient to Him and carry out His will, while others, fallen angels, disobeyed, fell from their holy position, and now stand in active opposition to the work and plan of God.

Billy Graham;

"They are God's messengers whose chief business is to carry out His orders in the world. He has given them ambassadorial charge. He has designated and empowered them as holy deputies to perform works of righteousness. In this way they assist Him as their creator while He sovereignly controls the universe. So he has given them the capacity to bring His holy enterprises to a successful conclusion."

"The attributes of angels include invisibility. They are spirits. But angels have the ability to change their appearance and are able to travel instantly between Heaven and earth. They sometimes take on human form when God assigns them a special task."

Angels Are Created Beings

Though the exact time of their creation is never stated, we know they were created before the creation of the world. From the book of Job we are told that they were present when the earth was created (Job 38:4-7) so their creation was prior to the creation of the earth as described in Genesis one.

That angels are created beings and not the spirits of departed or glorified human beings is brought out in Psalm 148. There the Psalmist calls on all in the celestial heavens, including the angels, to praise God. The reason given is, "For He commanded and they were created" (Ps. 148:1-5). The angels as well as the celestial heavens are declared to be created by God.

Though at times they have revealed themselves in the form of human bodies (angelophanies) as in Genesis 18:3, they are described as "spirits" in Hebrews 1:14. This suggests they do not have material bodies as humans do. This is further supported by the fact they do not function as human beings in terms of marriage and procreation (Mark 12:25) nor are they subject to death (Luke 20:36).

Mankind, including our incarnate Lord, is "lower than the angels" (Heb. 2:7). Angels are not subject to the limitations of man, especially since they are incapable of death (Luke 20:36). Angels have greater wisdom than man (2 Sam. 14:20), yet it is limited (Matt. 24:36). Angels have greater power than man (Matt. 28:2; Acts 5:19; 2 Pet. 2:11), yet they are limited in power (Dan. 10:13).

Angels, however, have limitations compared to man, particularly in future relationships. Angels are not created in the image of God, therefore, they do not share man's glorious destiny of redemption in Christ. At the consummation of the age, redeemed man will be exalted above angels (1 Cor. 6:3).14

Biblical Notations

Angels are mentioned directly or indirectly in both the Old and New Testaments of the Bible nearly 300 times.

Historic

John Calvin

"Angels are dispenser and administrators of the divine benefice toward us. They regard our safety, undertake our defense, direct our way, and exercise a constant solicitude that no evil befall us."

Since they are spirit beings, they are usually not seen, unless God gives the ability to see them or unless they manifest themselves. Balaam could not see the angel standing in his way until the Lord opened his eyes (Num. 22:31) and Elisha's servant could not see the host of angels surrounding him until Elisha prayed for his eyes to be opened (2 Kings 6:17). When angels have been seen as recorded in Scripture, they were often mistaken as men because they were manifested in a man-like appearance (Gen. 18:2, 16, 22; 19:1, 5, 10, 12, 15, 16; Judg. 13:6; Mark 16:5; Luke 24:4). Sometimes, they appear in a way that either manifests God's glory (Luke 2:9; 9:26) or in some form of brilliant apparel (cf. Matt. 28:3; John 20:12; Acts 1:10 with Ezek. 1:13; Dan. 10:6). Consistently, they have appeared as real men, never as ghosts, or as winged animals (cf. Gen. 18:2; 19:1; Mark 16:3; Luke 24:4).

All angels were created holy, without sin, and in a state of perfect holiness. Originally all angelic creatures were created holy. God pronounced His creation good (Gen. 1:31), and, of course, He could not create sin. Even after sin entered the world, God's good angels, who did not rebel against Him, are called holy (Mark 8:38). These are the elect angels (1 Tim. 5:21) in contrast to the evil angels who followed Satan in his rebellion against God (Matt. 25:41).17

Martin Luther: "An Angel is a spiritual creature without a body created by God for the service of Christendom and the church."

The Division of Angels—Good and Evil

While all the angels were originally created holy and without sin, there was a rebellion by Satan, who, being lifted up by his own beauty, rebelled and sought to exalt himself above God. In his rebellion, he took with him one-third of the angels (Rev. 12:4). This rebellion and fall is probably described for us in Isaiah 14:12-15 and Ezekiel 28:15 embodied in the kings of Babylon and Tyre.22 Prophesying of a future angelic conflict that will occur in the middle of the Tribulation, John wrote, "And there was war in heaven, Michael and his angels waging war with the dragon. And the dragon and his angels waged war" (Rev. 12:7). In other words, there are good angels and there are evil angels. Regarding their fall, Bushwell writes: "We infer that the angels which sinned did so in full knowledge of all the issues involved. They chose self-corruption, knowing exactly what they were doing.

A Time to Build - thedlin

"I once traveled to Haiti on a mission
trip with a team of college students. Our
project was to build a fish pond in support
of a small mountain village. On that trip I
remember one particular day walking down
a side street in the capital city of Port- au-Prince.
A song written by Paul Simon reminds me of that day."

"You Can Call Me Al"
Paul Simon

A man walks down the street
It's a street in a strange world
Maybe it's the Third World
Maybe it's his first time around
He doesn't speak the language
He holds no currency
He is a foreign man
He is surrounded by the sound
The sound
Cattle in the marketplace
Scatterlings and orphanages
He looks around, around
He sees angels in the architecture
Spinning in infinity
He says Amen! and Hallelujah!

Definition: *Renegade*
Having rejected tradition or orders, unconventional, stepping
apart, non-participant, rejecting, to leave one group and join
another.

Music:
The Byrds – Turn! Turn! Turn! Lyrics

To everything, turn, turn, turn.
There is a season, turn, turn, turn.
And a time to every purpose under heaven.
A time to be born, a time to die.
A time to plant, a time to reap.
A time to kill, a time to heal.
A time to laugh, a time to weep.

To everything, turn, turn, turn.
There is a season, turn, turn, turn.
And a time to every purpose under heaven.
A time to build up, a time to break down.
A time to dance, a time to mourn.
A time to cast away stones.
A time to gather stones together.

To everything, turn, turn, turn.
There is a season, turn, turn, turn.
And a time to every purpose under heaven.
A time of love, a time of hate.
A time of war, a time of peace.
A time you may embrace.
A time to refrain from embracing.

To everything, turn, turn, turn.
There is a season, turn, turn, turn.
And a time to every purpose under heaven.
A time to gain, a time to lose.
A time to rend, a time to sew.
A time for love, a time for hate.
A time for peace, I swear it's not too late.

Songwriters: Words from the book of Ecclesiastes;
French, George Aber Adaptation and Pete Seeger

Africa 1960: The Year of Independence

Between January and December of 1960, 17 sub-Saharan African nations, including 14 former French colonies, gained independence from their former European colonists

The rise to independence of 17 sub-Saharan African countries in 1960 is in part the result of a long process that began fifteen years earlier in the tumult of World War II.

At the end of the war, Africans involved in pro-independence movements put pressure on colonial powers, reminding them of promises made to secure their support in the war effort. The colonizing countries, chaperoned by the United States, were thus obliged to let their colonies go.

In 1944 in Brazzaville, General de Gaulle suggested that it was time for France to take "the road of a new era". Two years later, the French colonial empire was replaced by the French Union, which in turn became the French Community in 1958.

At the same time on the African continent, Morocco, Tunisia, Sudan, Ghana, and Guinea won their independence, while the unrest in Algeria continued to exhaust and damage France's reputation.

CAMEROON – January 1. A former German colony divided between France and the United Kingdom in 1918, Cameroon acquired its independence thanks to armed movements. Less than a year after the United Nations announced the end of French control, French Cameroon proclaimed its independence. The following year, the southern part of the country, under British control, merged with the north. On May 5, 1960, Ahmadou Ahidjo was elected as the country's first president.

TOGO – April 27. A former German colony subsequently under French and British mandates following World War I. The part of the country administered by the French had a status of "associated territory" in the French Union established in 1946. The country became an autonomous republic (within the French Union) by referendum in 1956. In February 1958, victory for the Togolese Unity Committee, a nationalist movement, in legislative elections opened the way to independence. Elected first president of the republic, Sylvanus Olympio was later killed in January 1963 during a coup d'état.

MADAGASCAR – June 26. A French overseas territory as of 1946, this island was proclaimed an autonomous state within the French Community in 1958. In 1960, President Philibert Tsiranana succeeded in convincing General de Gaulle to grant Madagascar total sovereignty and, in doing so, became the first president of the republic.

DEMOCRATIC REPUBLIC OF THE CONGO – June 30. In January 1959, under the leadership of Patrice Lumumba, riots broke out in Léopoldville (now Kinshasa) in what was then known as the Belgian Congo. Belgian authorities called the main Congolese leaders to Brussels and decided to withdraw from the country, fearing a war of independence similar to the one that was ravaging Algeria at the time. Belgian Congo thus became the Democratic Republic of the Congo, and would later temporarily be called Zaire under the rule of Mobutu Sese Seko.

SOMALIA – July 1. A former Italian colony, Somalia merged on the day it became independent with the former British protectorate of Somaliland in 1960 to form the Somali Republic. Somaliland had itself gained its full sovereignty five days earlier. The objective was to reconstitute the "Greater Somalia" of the pre-colonial era, which had included Kenya, Ethiopia, and the future Djibouti, which was at that time under French control.

BENIN – August 1. A referendum on September 28, 1958, proposing a plan for a French-African Community, paved the way for the independence of Dahomey two years later, when power was transferred to President Hubert Maga. The country, renamed Benin in 1975, has had a tumultuous political history since independence.

NIGER – August 3. A referendum in 1958 propelled Diori Hamana to power. The republic is proclaimed on December 18, 1958, but independence is solemnly declared on August 3, 1960.

Hamani, the country's first president, is overthrown by a coup d'état in 1974.

BURKINA FASO – August 5. A French protectorate, the Republic of Upper Volta is proclaimed on December 11, 1958, but remains part of the French community, before gaining full independence on August 5, 1960. In 1984, the country takes the name of Burkina Faso under the presidency of Thomas Sankara, who was assassinated in 1987.

IVORY COAST – August 7. A referendum in 1958 resulted in the Ivory Coast becoming an autonomous republic. In June of 1960, the pro-French Félix Houphouët-Boigny proclaimed the country's independence, but maintaining close ties between Abidjan and Paris. The Ivory Coast became one of the most prosperous West African nations.

CHAD – August 11. Two years after becoming a republic, Chad achieved independence on August 11, 1960. The prime minister at the time, François Tombalbaye, thus became the first president of a country that deteriorated rapidly into civil war between the Muslim north and the Christian-majority south.

CENTRAL AFRICAN REPUBLIC – August 13. Under French control as of 1905, Ubangi-Chari became the Central African Republic on December 1, 1958. When independence was proclaimed on August 13, 1960, David Dacko, cousin of national hero Barthélémy Boganda, was propelled to the head of the country. A committed pan-Africanist, Boganda presided over French Equatorial Africa (the federation of French colonial territories in Central Africa) for two years, working for the emancipation of Africans. He died on March 29, 1959, in an airplane accident.

THE REPUBLIC OF THE CONGO – August 15. Ninety nine percent of the Congolese people voted to join the French Community in a 1958 referendum, making the country an autonomous republic. The following year, violence broke out in Brazzaville, triggering a French military intervention. On August

15, 1960, Congo gained independence.

GABON – August 17. Criticized by several opposition parties for being anti-independence, Prime Minister Léon M'Ba was nevertheless resigned to proclaim it on August 17. He would have preferred that Gabon become a French department, but had to back down when General de Gaulle refused.

SENEGAL, MALI – August 20, September 22. The independent republics of Senegal and Mali were born from the ashes of the short-lived Federation of Mali – established on January 17, 1959 – made up of Senegal and former French Sudan. The two countries had initially intended to form one, but after significant differences between Léopold Sédar Senghor, the Senegalese president of the Federal Assembly, and Modibo Keita, his Sudanese prime minister, the authorities in Dakar withdrew from the federation and declared independence on August 20. Authorities in Bamako followed suit a month later.

NIGERIA – October 1. Divided into a federation of three regions – North, East, and West – by the Lyttelton Constitution in 1954, Nigeria, with its population of 34 million, was already considered the giant of the African continent. As soon as independence was declared on October 1, the former British colony was confronted with its deep ethnic and religious divisions, which quickly became the cause of severe political instability.

MAURITANIA – November 28. Mauritania proclaimed its independence on November 28, despite opposition from Morocco and the Arab League. The country's constitution, established in 1964, set up a presidential regime, with Prime Minister Ould Daddah becoming president. He remained in power until 1970.

By FRANCE24.com

Doctrine of Demons
From "A Synopsis of Bible Doctrine by Charles C. Ryrie*

I. **Origin of Demons**
   A. **Souls of Departed Evil People.** A heathen Greek view.
   B. **Disembodied Spirits of a Pre-Adamic Race.** The Bible nowhere speaks of such a race.
   C. **The Offspring of Angels and Antediluvian Women** (gen. 6: 1-4).
   D. **Fallen Angels.** Satan is an angel and is called prince of the demons (Matt. 12:24), indicating that the demons are angels, not a pre-Adamic race. Furthermore, Satan has well-organized ranks of angels (Eph. M6:11-12), and it is reasonable to suppose that these are the demons. Some demons are confines already (2Peter 2:4; Jude 6) and some are loose to do Satan's work. It is thought by some that the reason certain demons are presently confined is that they participated in the sin of Gen.6: 1-4.

II. **Characteristics of Demons**
   A. **Their Nature.** They are spirit beings. Note that the demon in Matt17:18 is called an unclean spirit in the parallel account in Mark 9:25. See also Ephesians 6:12.
   B. **Their Intellect.** They know Jesus (Mark1:24), their own doom (Matt. 8:29), the plan of salvation (James 2:19). They have a well-developed system of doctrine of their own (1 Tim. 4:1-13).
   C. Their Morality. They are call unclean spirits and their doctrine leads to immoral conduct (1 Tim. 4:1-2

III. **Activity of Demons**
   A. **In General**
      1. Demons attempt to thwart the purpose of God (Dan. 10: 10-14; Rev. 16: 13-16).
      2. Demons extend the authority of Satan by doing his bidding (Eph. 6: 11-12).
      3. Demons may be used by God in the carrying out of his purposes (1 Sam. 16:14; 2Cor. 12:7).
   1. **In Particular**Demons can inflict diseases (Matt. 9:33; Luke 13:11, 16).
   2. Demons can possess men (Matt: 4:24).
   3. Demons can possess animals (Mark 5:13).
   4. Demons oppose the spiritual growth of God's children (Eph. 6:12).
   5. Demons disseminate false doctrine (1 Tim. 4:1).
   IV. **Destination of Demons**
      Temporary Destiny.
      1. Some free ones were cast into the abyss (Luke 8:3; Rev. 9:11).
      2. Some confined ones will be loosed in the Tribulation (Rev. 9: 1-

11; 16:13-14).
B. Permanent Destiny. Eventually all demons will be cast with Satan into the lake of fire (Matt. 25:41).

Ryrie Study Bible, New American Standard Bible
Charles Caldwell Ryrie, Th.D., Ph.D.
Moody Publishers, Chicago - c.1986, 1995, 20

Selected Bibliography

Charles Caldwell Ryrie, Th.D.,Ph.D. , *Ryrie Study Bible-New American Standard Bible*, Moody Publishers, Chicago - ©1986,1995,2012.

Billy Graham, *Angels: God's Secret Agents*, Guideposts Associates,Inc., Carmel, New York - ©1975

Johnathan C. Dowty, *"Christian Fighter Pilot" is not an oxymoron*, Amazon -©2007.

Ken March, *A Fighter Pilot's Guide To Spiritual Warfare*, Pleasant Word (a division of Wine Press Publishing, Enumclaw, Washington, ©2008.

Hugh Vest, *Pulling Gs: Fighter Pilot Perspectives On Faith*, Cross Link Publishing, Castle Rock, Colorado ©2014.

Brig. Gen. Jerry W. Cook, USAFR, Retired, *Once A Fighter Pilot...*, McGraw-Hill, ©2002.

Col. Robert E. Venkus, *Raid on Qaddafi*, St. Martin's Paperbacks, ©1993.

Peter E. Davies, *F-111 & EF-111 Units In Combat*, Osprey Publishing Limited, New York, NY, © 2014.

F-111 Aardvark Pilot's Flight Operating Instructions, Periscope Film, ©2007.

Steven Hyre and Lou Benoit, *One-Eleven Down - F-111 Crashes* and Combat Losses, Schiffer Publishing Ltd., Atglen, PA ©2012.

Jon Proctor, *Convair 880 &990*, World Transport Press, Inc., Miami, Fla., ©1996.

About The Author

Tim Hedlin is an Air Force veteran, Mission Aviation Fellowship Advocate (MAF), served on executive committees of UNICEF-Chicago and Covenant World Relief.

Your Notes

Made in the USA
San Bernardino, CA
29 April 2017